HIDDEN POWER

THE GATEKEEPER'S TRIALS: BOOK THREE

EMMA L. ADAMS

This book was written, produced and edited in the UK, where some spelling, grammar and word usage will vary from US English.

Copyright © 2019 Emma L. Adams
All rights reserved.

To be notified when Emma L. Adams's next novel is released, sign up to her author newsletter.

PREFACE

And pleasant is the fairy land
  But, an eerie tale to tell
  Ay, at the end of seven years
  We pay a tithe to hell.

Tam Lin

PREFACE

And pleasant is the fairy land
  But, an eerie tale to tell
  Ay, at the end of seven years
  We pay a tithe to hell.

Tam Lin

1

If there was one activity faeries loved more than they loved creating a spectacle, it was playing practical jokes on humans.

And yet, the Erlking's sprite appearing in a box on my cousin's doorstep after being declared dead was no joke, however impossible it seemed. I let the engraved box fall from my hands, where it vanished before it hit the floor. My circlet's light dimmed, but the sprite remained perched on my shoulder, his shiny wings tickling my chin, his small semi-transparent form clothed in a miniature version of a noble's uniform.

Sprites—small fae often employed as servants or messengers—couldn't come back from the dead. Even the mighty Sidhe couldn't. Yet somehow, he'd escaped the cage the merciless nobles had caught him in and found his way to me.

My sister, Ilsa, wore a mirror of my own surprise on her face. "He was alive all along?"

"I guess so," I said. "I don't know how Lord Daival got away with lying to all of us, but he did."

"Holly's still outside," Ilsa added. "Should I tell her to leave?"

"I'll talk to her." Mum exited the living room and made her way across the hall to the front door. She was the only one of us who didn't look totally stunned by the sprite's appearance, but very little fazed the former Summer Gatekeeper. She and I had once shared the same vibrant green eyes, but now hers were the same dark brown colour as Ilsa's. Her hair, tinted with blond streaks from long years in the sunlight, was tied in a topknot, while her strong, tanned arms spoke of experience dealing with everything Faerie could throw at her.

"Thanks." I glanced at the sprite on my shoulder. "Please tell me you can speak English."

"I can," he said, his voice a quieter version of a Sidhe's, melodic and resonant. "I am Swift, the Erlking's advisor. I dared not speak to you before, for fear my master's killers would find you."

"Speaking of killers, Lord Daival told me he killed you," I said. "I don't know how he was able to lie, but I'm very glad you survived, and I think the Sidhe will be, too."

"Did Lord Daival use those exact words?" Swift asked.

I thought back. "You know, I'm not sure he did. He said you told him you'd rather die than reveal the truth, but you ran away, didn't you? *That's* why he was mad at you."

Lord Daival had lied by omission to take away the Summer Court's hope of electing a leader chosen by the Erlking himself, as the sprite was the sole person in the Court who'd known the Erlking's intentions.

The slight issue? I'd been exiled from Faerie a week ago for conspiring behind the Sidhe's backs and claiming the deceased Erlking's talisman. By accident, I should add. Gaining possession of a staff with the power to destroy any living thing it touched would be bad enough on its own, but in the Sidhe's eyes, taking their former king's property was a grave offence of the highest order. Never mind that the talisman had an agenda of its own.

The sprite must know what I'd done, but he seemed comfortable enough sitting on my shoulder. "I apologise for deceiving you, my Queen."

"I'm not your queen," I said. "I'm a human and an exile."

"You wield my master's talisman," he responded.

"That doesn't make me a noble Sidhe," I said firmly. "The opposite, in fact. I got kicked out of Faerie for being the first Gatekeeper to lie to the entire Court. I'm not allowed back into Summer at all."

"But you must go back," the sprite insisted. "The Erlking needs a successor."

"You *do* know who the Erlking's heir is." My heart lifted. "That's why Lord Daival captured you, but you escaped without giving away the heir's identity. Can you tell me who it is?"

Swift remained silent for a moment. "He did not name an heir."

My hopes, risen from the ashes, returned to dust once more. "He didn't? But I thought—"

"The Erlking intended for the heir to be given the chance to prove their worth," he went on. "Therefore, he selected a number of potential successors who will be required to compete to take the throne."

"Like the Gatekeeper's Trials," said Ilsa. "Right?"

"Yes, like your Trials." Swift bowed his head. "The chosen few will compete for the crown and the winner will be crowned as the next monarch of the Summer Court."

Well, shit. Given the chaos Summer had faced since the Erlking's death, the sooner they nominated someone, the better—but the recent drama might not be so easily laid to rest. While the majority of the Sidhe supported following the Erlking's last wishes, others wanted to nominate themselves for the position, while still others believed the Erlking wasn't dead and would soon return to reclaim his throne. A contest would choose a leader in a decisive way, though, and everyone would have to honour the choice.

I nodded. "Okay. I'll take you to the Summer gate and let you into the Court so you can tell the other Sidhe."

Swift shook his head. "You must take me there yourself, Gatekeeper."

"They don't trust me at all." A hard lump settled in my throat. "They want me dead because I stole the Erlking's talisman."

"The talisman chose you," corrected the sprite. "That makes you a contender for the throne, my Queen."

"Oh no." I raised my palms. "A human can't rule Faerie. The Sidhe might not be immortal any longer, but my lifespan is a fraction of theirs. I won't bring peace to the realms even if I wanted to rule, which I don't."

"It was the Erlking's wish that his successor wielded the talisman, my Queen," he said.

"He of all people should know the talisman does whatever the hell it wants." I lowered my hands. "Look, I can take you to Summer, but I can't promise they won't throw me in jail before they listen to you. The only reason I'm allowed to stay in the Gatekeeper's house is because everyone in the Court is scared that I'll turn them to dust if they piss me off."

On the other hand, if I told the Sidhe the Erlking himself had asked me to accompany the sprite back into the Court, even they would have to let me back in. He might be dead, but he retained the highest authority in Summer.

Ilsa cleared her throat. "I think the sprite is right. You should go with him to make sure he's not attacked on the way to the palace."

"Agreed." Mum was back, and from her expression, she'd heard every word. "Hazel, if you carry the staff, none would dare to harm you. You might be able to repair your standing in the eyes of the Sidhe if you bring them proof that not all hope is lost after all."

My hands twisted together. "I don't know. Taking the talisman with me seems like I'm rubbing it in their face."

"You found the Erlking's sprite," said Ilsa. "They have to acknowledge that, at least."

"He found me, technically." There was nothing I wanted *less* than to see Lady Aiten or Lord Raivan again, but the sprite had nearly died at the enemy's hands and sending him into Faerie alone would put his life at risk once again. *All right.* "Better throw on a glamour first."

Since my exile, I'd been dressing casually for the first time in my life. For years, I'd secretly envied Ilsa her freedom to lounge around in a hoody and jeans while I had to apply several layers of glamour so the faeries wouldn't kick me out for not looking adequately pristine.

The Sidhe already thought me an imperfect human who would never match their majesty. My long blond-tinted hair tangled too easily, while my figure was strong and curvy rather than tall and willowy like the Sidhe. I'd spent years learning to walk like one of them, but I'd never be able to move with their level of otherworldly grace. Still, I put on my best glamour, a knee-length armoured coat with gold cuffs in the style of the ruling Sidhe.

The circlet sitting on my head glowed with the green shimmer of Summer magic, while the symbol beneath gleamed silver. The symbol meant *Gatekeeper* in a language older than the Courts, belonging to the Sidhe's ancient and feared predecessors, of whom nothing remained but fragments of their magic encased in objects of power. Like the staff in my hand, for instance.

Cool to the touch and engraved with intricate, softly moving runes, the staff touched the ground at my feet. Shadows curled around its edges as though it sensed my nervousness, which it probably did. Some might find that creepy, but I wore my heart on my sleeve anyway. A smile came to my lips at the memory of Darrow taking the phrase in a literal sense. Like many faeries, he didn't always grasp double meanings. I wished I'd asked him to stay here. I could use the moral support for when I faced Summer's soldiers.

Ilsa prodded me in the shoulder. "Are you going to stand there staring into the mirror all day?"

I blinked and looked away. "I'd have expected you to be advising me to stay the hell away from Summer, especially with the talisman. You aren't just worried about the Erlking's replacement, are you? There's another reason."

"There is," Ilsa admitted. "If a new monarch of

Summer takes the Erlking's place, it might be an opportunity for you to undo the Gatekeeper's curse."

It was a nice thought, but the faeries rarely left loopholes in their bindings. None of us knew which Sidhe had cursed our family to be bound to the Courts, but even the Erlking's death hadn't set us free.

"Don't worry about that now," said Mum. "Call me if you need me."

Mobile phones didn't work in Faerie, but I appreciated the sentiment. "See you soon. You too, Ilsa. With any luck, they won't throw me out on my arse."

I left the house via the back door in the kitchen, crossing the bright lawn towards the gate at the rear of the grounds. Fuelled by Summer magic, our garden boasted vibrant flowerbeds overflowing with wildflowers, ponds fringed with weeds, and thick hedges surrounding a pool of water which could heal almost any injury. Without the talisman's poison, the waters of the Inner Garden had turned back to their clear blue colour, while every strand of grass was vibrant and alive.

The talisman was anathema to Summer's natural state, but now I'd gained control over it, the creeping shadows in my hand didn't so much as disturb a single leaf as I approached the doorway into the Summer Court.

Carved hawthorn spikes formed a set of gates topped with a swirling symbol that matched the one on my forehead. The Gatekeeper's magic, which could somehow even resist the dark power of the talisman, didn't twinge with a warning alarm when I pushed open the gates, so I assumed there wasn't an ambush waiting on the other side. I was lucky the Sidhe hadn't locked the gate against me, really, though my talisman's power could counter any magic it came into contact with. One reason all the Sidhe feared it—and me by extension.

The moss-covered gates led me onto a sun-dappled path. I gagged on the smell of rot, my eyes widening at the sight of the trees stripped of their leaves and covered in clouds of rotting fungus. Piles of desiccated leaves blanketed the ground, while the once-evergreen foliage hung like moth-eaten curtains.

This is wrong. In Summer, death fuelled life, and nature was supposed to reclaim the dead, not leave it to fester. Though in Faerie's time, little more than a day would have passed since I'd been gone, the forest's decay had grown worse already and would continue to eat away at the magic of the Court until a new heir took the throne.

Beyond the decay, unfamiliar forests surrounded the gate. The Sidhe had probably shoved it into some dark forgotten corner in the hope that it'd vanish along with me, so it would be a long, annoying trek to find my way to the ambassadors' palace. Swift clung to my shoulder, pointing to the right. "That way, my Queen."

"I'm not your—" My boot crunched on the skull of some dead creature, and a shudder of revulsion seized me.

The first time I'd entered the gates to begin my Gatekeeper's Trials, a committee had been waiting on the other side to accuse me of murdering the Erlking—including Darrow, a hybrid half-blood who belonged to the underground Court of the Aes Sidhe. With his own Court assumed extinct by both Summer and Winter, Darrow had talked his way into Summer in order to get hold of the Erlking's talisman for his own leader.

He'd taken a major risk going back to her after he'd let me keep the talisman without challenging me, but it wasn't much safer for him in the Courts, considering my exiled status. Which gave us one major thing in common, at least. Having to weave between magical powerhouses who cared little for who they hurt had been an exercise in extreme caution, not something I possessed much of. I preferred the direct approach, and hesitation wasn't my style.

I rounded the corner and found myself with several weapons pointed at my throat. *Just like old times.*

"Hi, Lady Aiten," I said. "Look who I found?"

Lady Aiten, a tall Sidhe with olive skin and dark hair, stood flanked by two armoured soldiers. One, a female with fox ears and auburn hair, narrowed her eyes at me, but the wolf-faced Sidhe on Lady Aiten's other side gasped aloud as the Erlking's sprite flew in front of their group.

The sprite bowed to the three Sidhe. "I have come to pass on word of the Erlking's successor to those in charge of his estate. I came here with my Queen, and I would not see her come to harm."

I winced inwardly. Referring to me as his 'Queen' in front of the other Sidhe wouldn't make them hate me any less.

The Sidhe, however, didn't seem to have heard that part. They all gaped openly at him, their features shining with wonder and hope.

"He knows the heir," said Lady Aiten. "Why—we must inform them at once."

"Not quite," I said hastily. "That is—he mentioned the Erlking intended there to be a contest to choose a worthy heir, based on a list of those chosen by the Erlking himself."

Lady Aiten ignored my words. "Who is the heir?"

"As my Queen says," said the sprite, "the Erlking hand-picked a selection of those who he decided had the potential to be his successor. Since it has been such a long time since a new heir of Summer ascended to the throne, he believed it would be fairest if all the potential contenders were allowed to prove their worth."

"What manner of test would this be?" asked Lady Aiten. "Claiming a talisman?"

Her gaze went to the staff in my hands, and the merest hint of shadows flickering around the edges.

"No," said the sprite, his wings beating quickly. "The Erlking believed talismans such as this one are not objective entities. They have their own agendas, and the heir needs to be chosen by Summer itself. He laid out a number of tests, but I am only allowed to speak of the details to the potential heirs."

"We will discuss this further," added Lady Aiten. "Gatekeeper, you may leave."

She was still calling me 'Gatekeeper'? That was reason enough to believe she wasn't going to sentence me to death, at least.

Swift flew to my shoulder. "I require the assistance of my Qu—"

"Please, just call me Hazel," I said. "I'll be fine if you stay here. If you need me, you know where to find me."

"Assemble a list," Lady Aiten ordered Swift, "and we will send out invitations to those selected by the Erlking. If they accept, the event will start tomorrow."

"I will." The sprite fluttered his wings. "As the Erlking wished."

I turned to face Lady Aiten once again. "I know you

and I don't see eye to eye, but the Erlking's sprite wishes to stay with my family at the moment. If you allow us to move our gate back to the ambassadors' palace, it would enable Swift to travel back and forth without risking encountering dangers elsewhere in the Court."

Lady Aiten's eyes blazed with magic. "We will consider granting your request, Gatekeeper. Leave, now."

2
―――――

I woke the following morning feeling more optimistic than I had the right to, considering the Sidhe hadn't outright *said* they forgave me for claiming the Erlking's talisman. Nor talked to me at all, except to order me to leave. Still, I was lucky they hadn't just skewered me there and then and let the consequences work themselves out.

A pair of bright eyes blinked at me, and I jumped at the sight of the Erlking's sprite perched on my bedside table. "Whoa. Don't startle me like that."

"Apologies, my Queen."

I groaned. "Please, don't call me that. If the Sidhe hear, they'll think you're claiming I have a higher authority than them, and they'll punish me for it."

"They should not!" Swift flapped his wings in an agitated manner. "You are the Summer Gatekeeper, wielder of my master's talisman."

"Then you can call me Gatekeeper if you really don't want to call me Hazel," I said. "Please."

"As you wish, Gatekeeper." He bowed, flitting back to where I'd propped the staff against the wall.

"You don't fear it, do you?" I observed. "Did the talisman's magic not affect you?"

"My master would never have harmed me," he said.

"He did have control over its magic?" From the look of his territory, he hadn't, unless he'd left the clearing in its rotting state to discourage anyone from trespassing and challenging him. That was actually a smart idea, and it'd worked for a few centuries, too.

"Yes." The sprite fluttered down over the staff's hilt. "As do you, which proves your worthiness."

"I'm not its long-term owner." No way in hell. I pushed back the covers. "Can you go outside while I get dressed, please?"

I ran a hand through my dishevelled hair and replaced the circlet on my brow. I wore it every day out of habit, but as an exile, it seemed absurd for me to be forced to take part in every step of the process of electing a new monarch. The Sidhe shouldn't be my responsibility. Yet I'd been focused on survival—not just my own, but my entire family's—for so long that it made it difficult to plan for the future, and right now, I couldn't think of anything better to do but see to it that the Sidhe didn't screw up the process of replacing the Erlking.

And ensure the Seelie Queen didn't ruin everything again.

After I'd showered and dressed, I went downstairs. The sound of chattering from the living room told me the sprite had waylaid Ilsa, and sure enough, I found my sister sprawled on the sofa with Swift perched on the arm. The half-formed family tree spread across the coffee table had become a permanent fixture here, more or less. I rolled my eyes at Ilsa's dishevelled hair and the pile of blankets indicating she'd slept here. "Really, Ilsa? You're still working on the family tree?"

"It looks like the Erlking picked some of his descendants as his nominees." Ilsa waved a long curling roll of parchment in the air.

"Whoa, you have the list?" I took the parchment from my sister and gave it a scan, recognising some of the names. "Do the Sidhe listed here all know they might be the next monarch?"

"Lady Aiten has informed the heirs of the impending trials," said Swift. "They will begin as soon as dawn breaks in Faerie."

"And you'll be supervising?" I handed the list back to Ilsa and grabbed an apple from the fruit bowl on the coffee table. 'As soon as dawn breaks' didn't tell me much, since the Sidhe's magical influence over time in their realm meant they could have a month of perpetual midnight if the mood took them.

"I will inform the heirs of the requirements of the trials, and they will swear a vow to take part if they wish," the sprite said solemnly.

Vows. Of course vows would be involved. "You can go and do that. You don't have to ask my permission."

The sprite fluttered over the fruit bowl. "You must be present for the ceremony, Gatekeeper."

I sank my teeth into the apple and chewed. "Didn't you see how the Sidhe reacted to me yesterday? I betrayed them when I claimed the Erlking's talisman and then lied to them about it. They will never forgive me."

"You must be present," he repeated. "The Erlking

requested the Gatekeeper participate in the process of selecting his successor."

Of course he bloody well did. But he didn't predict that I'd claim his talisman, did he?

"Tell you what," I said. "You wait for me there. Tell the Sidhe I'm coming, so they don't set up an ambush, okay?"

"I will do as you wish, Gatekeeper." The sprite flew from the room, while I finished my apple and grabbed a slice of toast from the plate which had materialised on the coffee table.

"I'm guessing the Erlking didn't know you'd be in disgrace when he gave the sprite orders," said Ilsa.

"There were a lot of things he didn't know." I kept my voice low in case Swift could hear me from outside the room. "He overestimated how much the other Sidhe liked me, too."

"You're not wrong." Ilsa yawned, helping herself to a piece of toast. "Dad texted you earlier, by the way."

I picked my phone up from the coffee table. I never bothered to take it to Faerie, for obvious reasons, and often went without a signal for days even at home.

Dad's message said, *how's life?*

"He doesn't expect me to *actually* tell him what's going on in Faerie, does he?" I composed a generic reply, wishing I could have a normal human's level of blissful ignorance of the drama in the Courts.

"Not if you don't want to traumatise him for life." Ilsa stood. "I'm going to shower."

"I'm going to purgatory." I finished my toast and swiped the remains of Ilsa's, then consulted the sprite's list of the next potential rulers of Summer. Lady Aiten wasn't on the list, and nor was Lord Raivan. Nor, to my relief, was Lord Niall. I'd probably met most of the contenders at some point or other, but I was in no way qualified to help judge who would succeed the Erlking.

In fairness, the Erlking himself hadn't done much actual ruling. That had been up to his council—and at one point, the Seelie Queen—while he'd hidden away in his clearing, pretending to be on his deathbed.

As I walked out the front door, I nearly collided with Swift coming the other way. "Gatekeeper, you must come! There's trouble!"

Oh, boy. I gripped the staff and walked towards the gate, wrenching it open to the sound of guttural screaming. Beside the gate lay the entrance to the ambassadors' palace—the Sidhe had at least moved it as I'd requested—and dark shapes flitted behind the hedges surrounding the palace. *Sluagh.*

Partly spirit and partly corporeal, sluagh could give even the Sidhe a run for their money, but my talisman made their shadowy forms look dim and wispy. As I walked between the twin leafy plants flanking the entrance, shadows extended from the staff's base, eagerly seeking their prey.

The air rippled overhead as a sluagh descended on me, morphing into a humanoid creature wearing a tattered cloak. Tendrils of shadow lashed out from my hands, and the sluagh evaporated into grey mist.

A second sluagh blasted me with icy energy from behind. The attack bounced off my magic-proofed shield, and I spun on the spot, talisman in hand. Shadows curled around the sluagh's insubstantial form, eating away at the remnants of magic holding it together.

As the last sluagh evaporated into wisps, the Sidhe

watched me from inside the entrance hall, their expressions varying from hostility to anger. The talisman hummed in my hand as though sensing their fear and revelling in it, but I'd quietened the Devourer's voice when I'd mastered the talisman's magic for my own and I wasn't about to get swept up in its lingering satisfaction at making the almighty Sidhe fear a pitiful human. It was the talisman they feared, not me, and for good reason.

The Devourer might be gone along with its Ancient brethren, but the conscious remains of its magic sought only to unleash as much destruction as possible. Let's just say we were motivationally at odds, to say the least, but we were also stuck with one another. Damn if that didn't sum up my relationship with Faerie as a whole.

"The sluagh are dead," said Lady Aiten, striding into view. A glittering blade hung from her hand, while she wore armoured clothing like mine, as though she was going into the trials as a participant, not a spectator.

"Where did they come from?" I asked. "Did someone try to sabotage the trials before they even started?"

Lady Aiten's gaze panned across the entrance hall, from its flower-encrusted ceiling to the intricate tapestries hanging from the walls. "Someone opened a doorway into the Vale here in the palace."

"Don't look at me. I was at home." I took in her suspicious expression, the way her gaze darted to the talisman in my hand. "Oh no, I am *not* doing this again."

What would it take for the Sidhe to believe I had no intention of using the talisman against them? My gaze caught on the Erlking's sprite, who flew into the centre of the hall.

"It is I who brought the Gatekeeper here," Swift said.

"She knew nothing of the attack until I told her. It is the truth. I swear it on my master's name."

"The sluagh were sent to intercept the Erlking's potential successors," said a Sidhe male with warm brown skin and a waterfall of gleaming dark hair. "This is the Seelie Queen's work."

"Exactly." I nodded to Lady Aiten. "She was counting on nobody knowing who the heir is, and these trials have the potential to seriously mess up her plans to take the Erlking's throne."

If she knew the testing would begin today, either she'd been in the Court herself or a spy had taken the news to her hideout in the Vale. Neither of those things boded well for the safe ascension of a new monarch.

Lady Aiten's mouth thinned. "We will proceed with the preparations for the arrival of the contestants. Gatekeeper, kindly stand beside the doors and keep watch for any more intruders."

I'm a security guard now? It beat being accused of crimes and thrown out of the Court, and besides, if the Seelie Queen showed her face, it'd be my pleasure to kick her headfirst out of the palace.

I took up my position by the oak doors and peered outside. Judging by the grey light seeping across the lawn, the promised dawn had arrived, though it was anyone's guess as to whether a night had preceded it. Within a few minutes, the doors opened, and a group of half-Sidhe entered. Among them, I caught sight of a familiar figure wearing a mottled cape around her shoulders.

"Coral?" I said. "What're you doing here?"

"Looks like someone's in need of a bodyguard again."

She eyed the talisman. "Though you weren't doing a terrible job on your own."

"I didn't volunteer for security duty, but here I am." I rolled my eyes in Lady Aiten's general direction. "Have you heard—"

"There's going to be a trial for the Erlking's successor?" she said. "Of course I have. The Sidhe sent out invitations to every corner of the Court in search of the chosen few, then asked for volunteers to guard the palace."

"No wonder the Seelie Queen found out so fast." I watched the half-Sidhe disperse throughout the room. "I was beginning to worry we had a spy in here again."

"I wouldn't rule it out." She took up a position on the other side of the oak doors. "Things are quiet on Half-Blood Territory. It's always more exciting when you're around."

"Probably because trouble tends to stalk my every move."

Coral had moved to live on Half-Blood Territory when I'd been booted out of Summer. The borderlands, which had previously been split between warring monarchs who distanced themselves from the main Courts, had faced some major changes during the months I'd been waiting to start my Gatekeeper's trials, and were now one of the few places half-faeries could freely live without the Sidhe breathing down their necks. This very palace was supposed to be another such location, but it seemed the Sidhe had opted to borrow it for their trials.

Swift flew over to me, his wings beating. "We must be careful. The Vale folk are cunning, and the sluagh will be the least of the intrusions we might expect."

"I figured," I said. "Ah—this is Coral, the heir to the Sea Court. Coral, this is Swift, the Erlking's sprite."

Her eyes widened. "Oh, so *that's* how all this started. I was picturing the Sidhe finding a random document of the Erlking's buried somewhere in his territory."

"Not quite," I said. "Swift is the only person who had access to the list of nominees. Though it sounds like the whole Court knows now, and probably Winter, too."

"Wouldn't surprise me," said Coral. "It's hard to keep this type of thing quiet."

"Gatekeeper." Lady Aiten strode over to me. "Come this way."

With an apologetic look at Coral, I walked with Lady Aiten to an alcove between two carved statues of a unicorn and a gryphon. Lord Raivan waited there, an antlered hat atop his silvery blond hair. Like Lady Aiten, he wore a green armoured outfit edged in gold, as though he'd come to declare war, not witness the choosing of the next monarch.

"Gatekeeper," he said, his lip curling on the word as though pronouncing the name of an unpleasant creature.

"What is it?" I asked.

Lady Aiten's gaze lingered on the staff resting on the ground at my feet. "It is my expectation that the Seelie Queen will attempt to undermine the trials again, and she will not be deterred by any weapon that we possess."

"So you want me to use the talisman to make sure nobody interferes with the trials," I concluded. "Really?"

"It is… unfortunate." Lady Aiten wore an expression as though she was sucking on a lemon. "The Erlking's talisman is better equipped to deal with the Vale's threats than most, and if the trials are to proceed without further interference, we will need it."

Damn. They *wanted* me to use the talisman? They must be desperate. Lord Raivan didn't look too thrilled at the prospect, but then again, he never did.

"I will," I said, "if you reinstate my position as Gatekeeper and swear that neither I nor any of my family members will be punished as a result of me wielding the talisman. I told the truth when I said I didn't want to claim it, but you must know the cost of giving up one's magic."

The green glow in her eyes brightened, a reminder of the restrained danger hidden behind her polite words. "Until the trials are finished and a new monarch is chosen, you may continue to wield the talisman in defence of our Court. Afterwards, you will surrender it to the Sidhe of Summer. Those are my terms, and you will agree to them if you wish for us to honour our word."

Annoyance gripped me. "You must know the talisman might not choose the next heir as its wielder. It has as much of a will of its own as anyone else does."

"The talisman is not a living being," she said. "You will agree to these terms or your family will not be protected from harm. I might remind you that a large number of the other Sidhe believe you should be executed or imprisoned for the crime of betraying the Summer Court."

Damn her. She might have lived for a few centuries, but neither she nor Lord Raivan belonged to the generation of Sidhe who'd seen the gods walk among them and knew the precise origin of the talisman's power. Lord Kerien had been the oldest Sidhe in the Court I'd known, aside from the Erlking, and both were dead now.

In fact, the only Sidhe I knew of who'd lived as long as the Erlking had were the Seelie Queen and Etaina, leader of the Aes Sidhe. I would prefer not to have to appeal to either of them to help me out if the Sidhe tried to take the talisman away, but it'd be nice if someone reliable showed up to take it off my hands. Maybe the next leader of Summer would be like the Erlking, able to tame and control its power without succumbing to temptation.

Or maybe the talisman would refuse to give up its current wielder without a fight.

Chills raced down my spine. I couldn't risk pissing off the Sidhe *again*, but Lady Aiten wasn't kidding when she said my family and I were all at risk as long as I remained an outsider. Some of the Sidhe already believed the Gatekeeper's position was obsolete, and if the next monarch agreed, we'd be unceremoniously kicked out for good this time. Others might support my position as Gatekeeper, but the idea of a human wielding a Sidhe's talisman was more than most could bear. Humans weren't supposed to be able to use faerie magic at all, let alone a staff which had once been wielded by their beloved king.

You never know. They might have a change of heart when there's a new monarch on the throne.

I drew in a breath. "Very well. I accept the terms, with the caveat that I have no control over who the talisman selects as its wielder. If I had, I would not have claimed it myself."

"And do you swear you will not go back on your word?"

My throat went dry. I wasn't technically going back on my word if the talisman decided not to listen to me, right?

"I swear."

An invisible force tugged at something deep inside me, the power of the binding spell connecting me to Lady Aiten. Faerie vows backfired if disobeyed, often with fatal consequences. If I didn't at least try to surrender the talisman, the vow would rip me to pieces, but there was always a way around a binding if you found a loophole. And if the talisman itself was set on keeping me alive, Lady Aiten wouldn't be able to prise it from my hands without risking the backlash hitting her.

"There." I clenched my hand over the talisman's hilt to distract myself from the unpleasant tugging sensation in my chest. "That's done. Should I resume my place by the doors, or is there somewhere else you want me to stand?"

"The doors will do." Her gaze fixed on a point over my shoulder. "The heirs have arrived."

She swept across the hall and through the oak doors, descending the steps outside the entrance. I, meanwhile, retook my position opposite Coral on the inside and waited for the heirs to enter.

"Have the Sidhe ever considered that the reason they have so many so-called traitors is because of the impossible promises they make everyone swear?" Coral murmured.

"That would require having any sense of self-awareness whatsoever." I watched the procession of new arrivals enter the palace. All were Sidhe nobles, a mixture of genders and ages, though it was hard to tell a Sidhe's age from outside appearances. The only features they all had in common were their towering height and bright Summer eyes. A female warrior wearing armour textured like overlapping scales walked beside a tall male Sidhe with crow feathers patterning his armoured coat. They were all dressed for war, some carrying swords, others knives or staffs or crossbows, and all were sharp-edged and deadly as their weapons.

One of these people would be the next ruler of the Summer Court.

The Erlking's sprite fluttered into the centre of the hall. His voice echoed from the high ceilings as he addressed the assembled Sidhe. "You have been invited here by the Erlking himself to compete for the honour of sitting on the throne of the Summer Court. The winner of these trials will wear the Erlking's crown."

"And the losers?" asked the female Sidhe with the scaled armour.

"One alone will stand victorious," Swift proclaimed. "There will be three rounds of trials. Half of the competitors will be eliminated in the first round. In the second, the remaining contestants will be whittled down to the sixteen best, while the final round will end with only one victor."

"Damn, he's pretty good at this," I said to Coral in an undertone.

"He worked for the Erlking," she said. "Probably saw him making dramatic speeches for years."

"Not sure he did much of that," I reminded her. "World-destroying talisman, remember?"

"Good point."

Though given the sprite's words yesterday, I was starting to suspect that the Erlking had played on the talisman's fearsome reputation both to keep himself safe from being challenged and to ensure nobody disturbed him. Which was fair enough. Ilsa had remarked that she'd often been tempted to do the same if she wanted to finish a good book without being interrupted. Being alone for a few hundred years was a bit excessive, but who was I to judge?

"The first test will begin momentarily," Swift said. "It is intended to eliminate those whose temperaments aren't becoming of a ruler."

"Temperaments?" I whispered. "Does he mean people who won't throw tantrums when they don't get their way?"

Almost all the Sidhe I'd met had been volatile by nature, but I would feel much easier about handing over the talisman if I knew the person wouldn't use it to slaughter anyone who didn't agree with them. The monarch's main goal was to ensure peace and prosperity. Thank the gods the Erlking had understood that, at least.

Murmurs travelled through the group of gathering Sidhe. Then Lady Aiten spoke. "The palace is already set up for the first trial, which will take place here and now. Your goal is to reach the doors behind me."

My body tensed in anticipation as a wave of magic swept through the hall. Coral and I grabbed the handles of the oak doors for balance when the floor slid backwards, the statues and fountains folding back as though the whole room was nothing more than a cardboard model.

When the palace ground to a halt, I let go of the door handle and stared down into an enormous pit dominating the space where the floor had once been. The contestants stood within the arena below, while Lady Aiten and the other non-participants gathered around the edges.

A rumbling sensation beneath my feet prompted me to grab the door handle again. Rows of stone seats appeared in tiers, coliseum-style, surrounding the pit. Coral exclaimed as the doors flew from our grip, opening to allow a swarm of Sidhe to enter. Head swimming, I held onto the staff for balance, while a tide of finely dressed courtiers filled the stands around the arena, accompanied by attendant hobgoblins and piskies and sprites. Lord Niall swaggered in, taking a seat in a central row, and cups of elf wine appeared in the hands of everyone around him. Luckily, they were too interested in the arena to notice me standing by the doors.

Speaking of which, the world outside the doors looked the same as ever. Only the inside of the palace had changed. The steady flow of guests petered out, and the doors closed behind me, prompting me to turn back to the arena. The Erlking's sprite flitted above a podium on the highest tier, where Lady Aiten stood overlooking the curving seats surrounding the pit.

Below, hedges had sprouted from the floor in zigzagging patterns around the contestants, turning the arena into a vast maze, while the doors that had once led onto the back lawn of the palace had dropped to ground level along with the contestants.

"Let the test begin," said Lady Aiten.

May the best Sidhe win.

3

The Sidhe in the arena below remained still for a moment, as though adjusting to the sudden change of surroundings. The hedges were tall enough to tower above their heads, and within, dark shapes moved among the leaves. I tensed, my hand on the talisman. If an outside force attacked them within the maze, I wasn't convinced I'd reach them in time, unless the sudden distance between us was an illusion. And how was I supposed to tell if the threat was part of the test or not?

"There will be no outside threats within the maze," Lady Aiten said, as though sensing my thoughts. "The contestants will face various obstacles, but your job is to watch for threats on the outside. There's no way into the palace aside from the doors behind you."

"Uh-huh." I looked around, marvelling at the utter transformation of the entrance hall. If the arena was just an illusion, it was almost worthy of the Aes Sidhe. "Why hold the contest in the palace? It's an obvious target."

"The tests must take place on neutral territory that doesn't belong to any individual Sidhe," she explained. "This is the only way to ensure nobody interferes."

Ah. Some of the Sidhe might well have tried to manipulate the tests if they'd been held elsewhere. There was a good reason the Erlking hadn't opted to have a vote based on popularity, considering the racket coming from the row where Lord Niall sat with his group of cronies.

Swift landed on my shoulder. "The task is beginning."

I followed his line of sight to the maze. Rippling hedges formed dark walls between winding paths, and only one route led to the doors at the back. From ground level, the way out wouldn't be obvious at all.

"What's the test?" I asked. "Reach the doors and don't get killed on the way?"

"Before the test began," said the sprite, "half the Sidhe in the maze were given keys to the door. The other half were not."

"Really?" I frowned. "Doesn't that give half the Sidhe an advantage over the others?"

"The choice was random," the sprite went on. "Only one who holds the key is able to get out of the maze."

Still not getting it. I glanced down again. Some of the Sidhe had begun to advance through the maze, but others remained oddly still. "Are they under a spell?"

"They are," Coral said, pointing at the male Sidhe immediately below us. His body had frozen to the spot as though caught in a Winter Sidhe's magic. "What caused that? I didn't see."

He wasn't the only one. All over the maze, the Sidhe stilled, their bodies locking in place, as though an unseen spell pinned them to the spot. Within a minute or two, it became clear about half the Sidhe in the maze were stuck under the spell, while the others were free to find their way through the labyrinth unhindered.

I looked down at the sprite. "It's the keys, isn't it? Half the Sidhe have the keys, but they can't move. The other half can move but they can't get out."

Coral pointed. "That guy's already at the door, look."

A male Sidhe with pale skin and long silky dark hair had reached the pair of oak doors at the back. As he touched the door handle, a flare of vibrant green light blasted him off his feet, sending him flying into the hedge. He sprang upright and tried again, with the same result.

"Yeah, he's not cut out to be a ruler," I said. "Let me guess… he doesn't have a key."

The Sidhe had finally figured out the door wasn't going to open for him. He turned down the left-hand path, towards the spot where one of the other Sidhe stood frozen on the spot. For a moment, he stood still, examining his fellow Sidhe. Then he reached for something gleaming in the statue-like Sidhe's hand. *The key.*

In one decisive move, the Sidhe took the key from the other man's hand. At once, his own body locked into position, freezing mid-motion. The Sidhe he'd stolen from, meanwhile, stirred, his hand dropping to his side. Shaking off the spell's remnants, he edged around the newly trapped Sidhe.

"Oh." I nodded in understanding. "The Sidhe have to cooperate to get out of the maze. The half who are carrying the keys can't move, and can't give up the keys, either. If someone tries to steal it, they end up frozen themselves."

"So the non-frozen Sidhe have to take a frozen

companion with them to get out of the maze?" asked Coral. "There's got to be another catch there. How are you going to eliminate exactly half the competitors?"

"Wait and see," said the sprite.

"I get where the Erlking was coming from," I said. "A ruler who acts rashly and thoughtlessly isn't going to last long. Nor is one who tries to steal from others rather than winning fairly."

"Or who throws parties while there's a war on," added Coral, with a meaningful look at Lord Niall. He and his friends weren't even paying attention to the task, too intent on swapping outrageous stories.

"Bet he organises the after-party," I muttered. "Does the task have a time limit?"

"The maze is enchanted to vanish in one hour," said Lady Aiten. "Those who are left behind will be disqualified. If nobody makes it outside, then a second test will be devised to lower the numbers."

One of the Sidhe had figured it out. He waved a hand, levitating his frozen companion into the air, and carrying him along through the maze's winding paths. As they rounded a corner, the maze's walls *moved*, leaves rustling together and swallowing both Sidhe whole.

"Oh, come on," I said. "That's not fair. What did he do wrong?"

"He didn't watch his step," said Lady Aiten.

And you could do better, could you?

The hedges had claimed a few more victims, forming barriers to halt the Sidhe in their tracks. Some tried to cut the bushes down, only to end up ensnared twice as fast. Others tried to use their Summer magic to force the hedges to bend to their will and let them through, but the hedges always moved back into place, taking their prey along with them.

Other Sidhe were out to make trouble. Two of them attempted to use their bare hands to break down the doors rather than finding a Sidhe with a key to aid them, but the resulting blast sent them flying back into the hedges. Only the keys planted on the frozen Sidhe would allow anyone to leave the maze at all, and if anyone tried to cheat, they found themselves unceremoniously thrown into a hedge or frozen into an unmoving statue.

After ten minutes or so had passed, Lady Aiten stiffened. "That is not part of the task."

Her sharp eyes fixed on a point where a dark shape hovered above the maze. *Wraith.*

I took a step forward. "I can't reach it from here. Not without causing a scene, anyway."

The audience's attention was fixed on the maze and none of them seemed to have noticed the intruder yet. Inside the maze, meanwhile, the Sidhe carried on making their way to the exits, oblivious to the dark form hovering above their heads. When Lady Aiten had claimed there were no ways in or out of the palace aside from the doors, she hadn't accounted for ghostly forms which could pass through walls.

Coral drew her knife. "That's a wraith, right? Can it hurt the contenders?"

"Depends what its magic was like when it was still alive."

Wraiths were rarely as powerful as the Sidhe they'd once been, but nobody in the arena would see the threat until it descended on them. Those who were frozen were completely undefended, and if the wraith caused them to lose the challenge, it wouldn't be a fair way to get eliminated.

"Someone must stop that creature!" Swift insisted. "If they don't, it will disrupt the task and invalidate the results."

"This is unacceptable," said Lady Aiten. "If the task is ruined, there will be no second chances, and I will *not* allow the outcasts to have a say in who we elect as our new ruler."

Yeah, but I can't stop it without the talisman. Problem was, the shadows might well devour the maze as well as the wraith if I wasn't careful. And just where had it come from? "Did it get in from outside? Because I can't watch the doors at the same time."

"No." Lady Aiten's eyes narrowed to angry slits. "The palace is guarded on the outside. The doorway to the Vale must lie within the maze itself."

One of the contestants did it. The thought banished any notions of avoiding using the talisman inside the maze. If the doorway remained open, much worse than a single wraith might infiltrate the challenge. The Seelie Queen herself, for instance.

"I might not be able to reach it without the talisman interfering with the magic of the maze itself," I warned her. "Do you want to risk it?"

"Do it," she ordered. "If the task is disrupted by this wraith, the results will become irrelevant, and we cannot reset the spell now it's already in motion. The trial must go ahead as planned."

So be it. I climbed into the row of seats below, landing between two finely dressed Sidhe. They recoiled from my staff with outraged expressions.

"Don't panic!" I moved to the edge of the tier. "I just have a little security issue to take care of."

The wraith hovered above the arena, a cloud of darkness wreathed in icy magic. The talisman hummed in my hand, reacting to the presence of the magic sustaining the arena. I mentally pleaded with it to stay calm and not react until I got to the wraith.

Keeping one eye on the intruder, I climbed down to another row of seats. One of Lord Niall's buddies damn near elbowed me in the face and I gave him a firm shove as I passed by, unwittingly causing him to tumble head-first into the row below. The resulting chaos distracted everyone from the human awkwardly climbing through the stands, and as a bonus, stopped them from noticing the wraith's hovering form. When I reached the ground, however, the wraith was no longer visible to me. I'd need to enter the maze to stand a chance of banishing it, let alone closing the doorway.

The shadows from my staff licked eagerly at the magic fuelling the hedges, and I gave a sharp tug, demanding they stay put. *Not the time, talisman.*

Finding a gap leading into the maze, I ducked between the hedges. At once, magic blasted into me, sending me sprawling onto my back. The world spun like a merry-go-round, and the shadowy magic in my hands threatened to pull the threads of the illusion undone.

"Don't you even think about it," I growled. "I don't like this either, but it's my job, and that makes it your job, too."

I walked around the maze's edge, gripping the staff with both hands to restrain its shadows. An angry shout from the stands behind me told me that the Sidhe had noticed my intrusion and weren't pleased about it. *Tough shit*. I was here to get rid of that wraith and I was damned if I let it get away with wrecking the trial.

Finding an undisturbed stretch of maze close to the wraith's location, I pressed my hand to the hedge and sent in a jolt of Summer magic. The hedge didn't budge, but it didn't shove me out, either. I tapped into the Gatekeeper's mark and fed more power into the hedge. "I am the Summer Gatekeeper, and I am here to ensure the task proceeds as planned. I'm not here to attack anyone. Let me in."

The hedge began to unfold, a window-sized gap growing beneath my touch. I pushed, making the hole bigger, and climbed through. Branches scraped at my arms and tangled in my hair, but the maze's magic didn't react to me this time. I'd have to avoid using any more magic on the hedges if I didn't want them to attack me, but the hard part was done. *I hope.*

Around the corner, I found a Sidhe trapped in the freezing spell, his body locked in position though someone had hit a pause switch on a remote control. Around him, threads of magic swirled from the hedge, tendrils waiting to ensnare anyone who got too close. This must be what the maze looked like to the Sidhe. But there was no sign of the wraith, and the path came to a dead end surrounded by hedges.

I turned back the way I'd come, but the path had vanished. *Of course the bloody paths move. This is Faerie, it goes with the territory.* The wraith had been on my left, so I took the nearest turn, dodging threads of hedge-magic.

Soft footfalls came from ahead of me, and a Sidhe glided around the corner, his angular face furrowed in concentration. He held no key—but he did have a weapon, a gleaming dagger which shone with the light of a talisman.

"Hey, there," I said. "Don't let me interrupt your test. I'm just here to deal with a little security issue."

His gaze went to the staff in my hands. "You're the human who stole the Erlking's talisman."

My grip tightened on the staff. "Don't you have a task to be getting on with?"

"That," said the Sidhe, "is mine."

In a blur of movement, he was in front of me, and he reached out to grab the staff. Shadows lashed at him, cloaking him from head to toe. He had no time to draw breath to scream before the magic ate through his bones, leaving nothing behind but a fine scattering of ashes.

A hushed silence fell. Only then did I remember that the entire audience would be watching me from above. They'd have seen me use the Erlking's talisman to kill another Sidhe and control its magic as though I were the king himself.

Fuck it. Nothing to do but march on through the maze. Where was that damned wraith? I'd rather not have to leave a trail of bodies behind me before I found it, if just because there'd be nobody left to take the Erlking's throne if the talisman's magic disintegrated all of them.

A frosty breeze wafted overhead, bringing the chill of the grave. *There it is.* The wraith must be Unseelie, which at least made it easier to track. I quickened my pace, stepping left and right to dodge the threads of maze-magic beneath my feet. My talisman itched to devour them, but I'd sworn not to disrupt the task, so I held the staff high to avoid tempting fate.

Around a corner, the wraith hovered above the bodies

of three frozen Sidhe—now frozen in a literal sense as the wraith's icy magic formed a rippling blue wall around their bodies. Ice slid over their faces and sealed their mouths shut. If I didn't kill that wraith, they'd suffocate where they stood.

"Hey, dickhead." I raised the staff. "Catch."

I threw a handful of shadows at the wraith, which dodged by way of throwing itself on top of the frozen Sidhe. At the last second, I ordered the shadows to move sideways, narrowly missing the captive Sidhe, and a jet of icy magic slammed into my shield, ricocheting off into the hedge. I backed up, cursing. The wraith was using the other Sidhe as a shield, knowing I wouldn't use the talisman against them. How the hell was I supposed to draw it out without harming the competitors in the process?

A blast of green-blue magic flew over my shoulder, and the ice melted, freeing the Sidhe from its grasp. The wraith rose into the air in a blanket of shadows, dark tendrils reaching for the new arrival.

"Stop right there," commanded a voice, and a tall, lean warrior ran to my side, his aquamarine eyes gleaming with magic.

Darrow.

4

Another blast of green-blue light ignited the air, sending the wraith flying backwards over the hedges. I darted over to the group of frozen Sidhe, gingerly pressing my talisman to the remaining ice encasing them. Shadows ate through the ice, releasing the Sidhe from its grasp.

Darrow stepped to my side. "Are they supposed to be frozen like that?"

"Frozen in every sense apart from the ice, yes," I said. "Did you mean to put yourself forward as a contender for the Erlking's throne?"

"Only if you did."

"I was chasing a wraith." I peered over the hedge, trying to see a way through to reach it. "I need to kill it before it disrupts the trial. What on earth are you doing in here? Who let you in?"

"Nobody."

Meaning, he glamoured his way in. "Good. Let's get this undead pest out of the maze. Also, try not to damage anything or anyone. This is a contest to determine the next ruler of Summer."

"So I hear." He walked down the nearest path on our right. "The wraith went this way, I think."

"Nice aim, by the way." I trod after him. "I'd have done the same if my magic wasn't quite as destructive. I'm surprised the maze even let me in."

A thread of magic lashed at him from the hedge, and he darted aside with effortless grace. *How* did *he get in here?* He couldn't have glamoured the entire audience, surely. Sneaky bastard.

"This labyrinth is a creation of magic," he said. "Perhaps it let us in because it sensed we were no threat to the results of the challenge."

How had he even known the trials were happening today? It felt like an age since we'd last seen one another, though it'd been less than a day. If word of the trials had reached the Aes Sidhe already, wraiths were the least of the problems we'd face.

Pursuing the chill of the wraith's magic, I followed the paths through the hedges until we came to a halt at the exit. The wraith hovered above the doors, preventing anyone from getting out.

"Hey, dickhead." I hefted the staff. "Fancy a duel?"

Magic blasted from the wraith's hands, aimed at Darrow. *It knows not to hit me.* It'd been sent here with instructions, which meant this was without a doubt the Seelie Queen's handiwork.

I threw myself in the way and the attack slammed into my shield, ricocheting away into the hedges. An exclamation of pain came from somewhere behind, and two Sidhe ran into view. Or rather, one carried the other on his shoulders, his companion's frozen hand still grasping the key.

At the sight of the wraith, the first Sidhe drew his blade, sending a wave of Summer magic rippling from the sword to the wraith. The transparent creature reeled back, then flew behind the Sidhe himself. Forced to divert his attack at the last second, Darrow sent green-and-blue magic crashing into the hedge.

At once, the hedges moved, threads of magic sweeping across the ground like vines.

"Shit, you pissed off the maze." I backed up, restraining the staff from lashing out in retaliation. Shadows crept up and around my legs, prompting the Sidhe to back away from me. The frozen Sidhe wasn't so lucky. The hedge's tendrils lashed out, dragging him into its leafy embrace.

In a flash of blue light, the wraith appeared in front of the doors once again.

"You asked for it." I held the staff over my shoulder. "Everyone stand back."

I ran directly at the doors, crashing through them and skidding out of the palace onto the lawn. Catching my balance, I whirled around and sent a wave of shadows at the wraith. Unable to hide in the brightness of the garden, it fell beneath my talisman's lethal touch, evaporating into mist. The staff's shadows sucked greedily at the pristine grass and bright flowerbeds, but I gave it a firm shake and the oozing darkness returned to the staff.

Darrow exited the palace behind me. "Is it gone?"

"Yep." I turned to him, my head spinning a little to see the vast arena contained within the palace while the back garden looked the same as ever. "Shit. I never did find the doorway it came from."

Darrow stiffened as the doors opened again, but it was only the contestants. Two Sidhe halted in the doorway, facing the lawn warily as though unsure if another invisible wraith waited to ambush them.

"I killed the wraith," I called to them. "It's safe."

The contenders left the maze in twos and threes. When they passed the threshold, the frozen Sidhe holding the keys returned to normal. Both the female Sidhe with the scaled armour and the male with the outfit decorated with crow feathers had made it out. A pale guy with a spiked hat and bark-like hair gave me a derisive look as he saw me assessing the surviving competitors.

When a large number of Sidhe filled the lawn, a ringing noise echoed from inside the palace, followed by a torrent of magic and noise which suggested the arena was returning to its former state. As the rumbling noise ground to a halt, a blast of magic shone from behind the palace doors, raising the hair on my arms and rippling across the lawns.

Time was up. The task was over, and half the competitors eliminated.

"Come back in," Lady Aiten's resonant voice called. "Your audience awaits."

I gave Darrow a grim nod. "Time to find that doorway."

The doors opened to reveal the entrance hall of the palace back to its former state, filled with carved statues, hanging tapestries, and a stage flanked by midnight-blue curtains. Lady Aiten stood on the stage with the Erlking's sprite hovering over her shoulder, while the crowd drew back to clear a wide space in the centre of the room for the winners to assemble. No signs of any opening to the

Vale remained in sight. *They must have closed it.* With the maze gone, spotting the source of the intrusion would have been a simple task.

As we entered, the crowd exploded with cheers. I knew they were cheering the Sidhe and not Darrow and me, but I couldn't resist taking his hand and dragging it into a wave. He frowned sideways at me. "What are you doing?"

"It's the closest we'll get to being congratulated for our trouble," I murmured to him. "Now that's done, I really would like to know how on earth you managed to gatecrash the Erlking's trials. How did you even get here?"

"I walked."

"Ha." His rare humour always disarmed me because his deadpan tone carried not a hint of irony. Something soft brushed my cheek, and I tilted my head back to see ruby red and bright gold petals raining down from the ceiling like confetti. Ducking around a large statue of a satyr in a suggestive pose, I found a clear spot near a tapestry to speak to him in peace. "Go on, tell me."

"There are a fair few questions I'd like to ask you, too," he said, "but your sprite is trying to get your attention."

"He's not mine. He's the Erlking's."

His brows lifted. "He lived?"

"He escaped Lord Daival unharmed," I explained. "Turns out the Erlking had a whole plan figured out to put the potential heirs through trials in order to pick the worthiest to rule. Apparently, the Seelie Queen took offence at being left off the guest list."

"I thought so," he said. "I heard the news of the trials, but only when I entered Faerie."

"So you did go back to Etaina first."

The leader of the Aes Sidhe had an iron grip on her subjects, and while Darrow had implied that he planned to walk away, everything he'd ever known lay within Etaina's domain. Like any faerie, she'd offer you everything you wanted most in the world, and only reveal the price when you were already in too deep to go back. And what *she* desired above all else was to wield the Erlking's talisman.

He drew in a breath. "Etaina is angry. She knows you claimed the talisman. I was unable to avoid telling her. For a while, I feared she'd come after you, but this morning, wraiths attacked our Court in a large number. There were causalities."

"You mean to say the Seelie Queen knows how to get into your kingdom?" The Courts might believe the Aes Sidhe were extinct, but the Seelie Queen had witnessed Darrow use their deadly glamour against her when she'd set an army of the dead upon us. I should have guessed she wouldn't hesitate to strike. The Seelie Queen was also Etaina's sister, but I didn't know if Darrow was aware of that fact.

"She knew of our survival after she saw me in the Vale," he said. "It was inevitable that she'd figure out how to track us down. Etaina was enraged. At once, she ordered her soldiers to eliminate the Seelie Queen. She sent me here—"

"To kill her?" Her own sister? With the Sidhe, nothing should surprise me, but it was more noteworthy that Etaina hadn't come in person. She'd struck me as the type who'd want the Seelie Queen's death to be personal.

"Yes," he said. "I searched for her in the Vale, but the moment I heard of this event, I knew what I'd find."

"Me, causing trouble again." I didn't quite manage a smile. It was just my luck that he'd come back into my life because of Etaina and her never-ending quest for domination. Not that his company wasn't welcome all the same. The upside was that we had the same goal this time, albeit from two vastly different places. If Etaina found out Darrow secretly supported my wielding the talisman, we'd both be royally screwed—yet my heart lifted at the knowledge that for a while, I was safe from Etaina using him to steal the talisman back for her.

"You, putting your training to use," he answered. "I thought I'd have to use glamour on the guards to get in, but luckily, your friend Coral trusted I hadn't come here to harm anyone. Given the events in the Court, it's not unrealistic to expect her to show her face here."

"Maybe not, but Etaina knows the Seelie Queen has a super-charged healing power, doesn't she? Even my talisman can't kill her. I suppose you could glamour her into walking off a cliff, but I bet she has other tricks up her sleeve."

"I know," he said, "but Etaina is confident I can overcome her."

No doubt he held one of the stones that countered the talisman's magic, so we'd be at a stalemate if we ever faced off, but the idea of Etaina sending him to eliminate *me* next made a cold fist clench around my heart. Nobody could fight a faerie vow. Not even Darrow.

"Did you know Etaina is her sister?" I asked. "The Seelie Queen's, I mean?"

Shock blanked his face. "No, but it explains why she reacted so harshly to the attack. How do you know?"

"The Erlking's family tree," I said. "Etaina is there

under the name *Lady of Light*, so it took me a while to figure out it was her. I don't know anyone else who goes by that title."

Darrow's mouth pinched, and he glanced at my talisman. "Once I've taken care of the Seelie Queen, I won't be able to stop Etaina from coming after you, Hazel. She wants that talisman."

"Next you'll tell me she also wants the Erlking's throne," I said. "Wait, she *doesn't*, does she?"

One power-crazy queen interfering in the trials was bad enough on its own, thanks. Though with them being siblings, who knew?

"If she does, she hasn't mentioned it," he said. "The talisman is her priority, as it always has been."

"But she sent you to take down the Seelie Queen first," I said. "If that's the case, you can claim her super-charged healing powers made it impossible to accomplish your goal, and stall for time. Once there's a proper monarch on Summer's throne again, they'll be more than a match for her. We only need to last until the end of the trials."

"I can try," he said, "but that won't stop her from coming after you, and I might not be able to defend you."

You mean, might not be allowed *to defend me.*

I gave myself a mental slap. Had I really expected any different? I should have seen it coming from the moment I'd learned we were from Courts with opposing goals. Everyone knew not to trust any faerie at all, for that matter, and I knew it better than most.

But I'd never fallen in love with one of them before.

"Gatekeeper," said Swift, flitting out from behind the satyr statue. "I am sorry to disturb you, but Lady Aiten wishes to speak to you."

I sighed inwardly. "Guess I'd better go and see what she wants."

Darrow remained beside the statue, a preoccupied expression on his face, while I followed the sprite back to my stony-faced supervisor. Lady Aiten stood beside the stage, one hand resting on the blade sheathed at her waist.

"We found and closed the opening to the Vale," said Lady Aiten. "It lay in the centre of the maze."

"So they really did open the doorway in the middle of the task," I said. "Someone made a deal with the Seelie Queen. Before or after being chosen as a contender."

"Precisely," she said. "There is a traitor among the contenders for the throne."

Shit. Maybe electing a new leader won't be the end of it after all.

"But did they make it out?" I said. "Half the Sidhe were eliminated, but the other half made it to the end. There's no way to tell if the person responsible is still in the running or not."

"It seems more likely than I'd prefer," she said. "However, none of the Sidhe who made it to the end of the challenge have been seen to behave in a suspicious manner."

"Can't you just ask them?" I said. "I mean, they can't lie."

Her expression turned frosty. "If that were a barrier to deceit, there would be no traitors, Gatekeeper."

Touché.

"Then spy on them," I said, undeterred. "You can order them to stay in the palace for the duration of the trials, can't you? There's more than enough rooms, and you can ask the brownies and sprites who work here to keep an eye out for trouble."

"We already have everyone under close watch," she said. "However, we cannot easily challenge the participants' actions during the trials themselves, and it may be that the culprit made their arrangements before they arrived at the palace."

I frowned. "What, you want to nominate an insider? Tell one of the participants to keep an eye out for spies? Is there anyone you absolutely trust?"

The sprite landed on my shoulder. "You made it to the end of the maze, Hazel. You and Darrow."

"What?" I twisted my head to look down at him. "What are you saying?"

He had to be kidding me. Please say he didn't mean what I thought he did.

"You both completed the trial," said Swift. "According to the rules, that means both of you are on the list of contenders."

"We weren't *on* the list to begin with," I pointed out. "This isn't going to work."

"It might," said Lady Aiten. "The magic binding the contenders would allow you to enter the next trial as a spy and track down the person responsible for summoning the wraith."

"Look, you must know that if the other Sidhe find out I'm taking part, they'll know I'm a spy," I told her. "A human can't rule a Court. Or a half-faerie, either. Have you told Darrow?"

"Bring him to me," she commanded. "We will sort this out."

The sprite flew alongside me as I walked through the

crowd, my thoughts whirling. *A contender?* The Sidhe would try to slit my throat in my sleep if they found out a human was taking part in the next challenge. Look at that guy in the maze who'd tried to take my talisman.

I can't be in line for the throne. No way.

"This is ridiculous," I said. "Darrow isn't even from this Court. And I'm human, not to mention the wielder of—"

"The Erlking's talisman," said the sprite. "You were chosen."

"I was *claimed* by the talisman," I corrected. "For its own reasons, none of which involve me being a good leader. I don't want a throne. I never have."

I'd wanted to do a decent job as Gatekeeper because I wasn't qualified to do anything else. A lifetime in training for the position had given me a decent level of advantages over most humans, but a crown and a throne had never been involved in my plans. I'd rather break the Gatekeeper's curse and get the hell out of here, thanks.

"You must join the other contenders," Swift insisted. "Regardless of your wishes, the maze's magic has recognised you as among the Sidhe. Unless I break the binding vow the Erlking placed upon me, I must treat you as one of the participants."

"You didn't tell that to Lady Aiten?" I cast a glance over my shoulder. "She'd never have agreed if she knew I was in with a real shot of winning." In theory, at least.

I spotted Darrow standing beside the statue, speaking to his sprite, Hummingbird.

"Lurking in corners again?" I hurried over to him, and his sprite vanished in a flash of light. "I have bad news. We both made it to the end of the maze, which means we're in the running for the Erlking's throne. Not my idea, believe me."

"That's absurd," he said. "We can't be contenders."

"We are," I said. "Lady Aiten thinks there's a spy for the Seelie Queen among the other participants, and conveniently, the two of us count as participants because we were first through the doors of the maze."

"Until the binding of the trials unravels, you'll be marked as a competitor," said Swift. "Both of you."

Darrow's face was a mask of disbelief as we walked, once again, to Lady Aiten. Lord Raivan stood beside her, his head bent to listen to her speak.

The sprite flew ahead, fluttering down in front of the two of them. "I have brought you the other contenders."

"A human and a half-blood?" said Lord Raivan. "They cannot be allowed to participate. This will not stand."

"As I said," Lady Aiten interjected, "we need spies on the inside, in case the traitor remains among the contenders."

"But think of the impression we're sending," said Lord Raivan. "That humans and half-Sidhe are our equals."

"Perish the thought," I said, and both of them scowled at me. "Look, I'm not keen on the idea, either. Can't you change the rules?"

"You have no authority to make those decisions, Gatekeeper," said Lady Aiten.

"But you think I have the authority to rule a Court?" I said. "Because if the Seelie Queen meddles in the next two trials and I end up having to use the talisman's magic, I can't control the consequences. I didn't plan this, Lady Aiten. You told me—"

"I told you to go into the maze, yes," said Lady Aiten, her face pinching as though she was in pain.

"I suppose the Erlking's spell assumes that anyone who enters the maze is a contender," I guessed. "We have to take part in the task no matter what, so I guess we're going in as spies."

Lord Raivan looked as though I'd told him he'd been transferred to the Arctic Circle. "This cannot be."

"It is the rules," said the sprite. "All those who exit the maze are elevated to the second stage. The spell doesn't account for their status."

"In that case, we will find a solution," said Lady Aiten. "In the meantime, the celebrations for the victors of the first round of trials will commence."

She and Lord Raivan turned and walked away, leaving Darrow and me alone with the sprite—and a whole room of Sidhe who might kill us if they found out the Erlking's spell had recognised us as their equals.

5

"Of course there's a party." I rolled my eyes. "What's the betting Lady Aiten dives head-first into the fountain to avoid the humiliation of having to admit a human is among the contenders for the Erlking's throne?"

"I doubt it," said Darrow. "She did what she felt was best for her Court."

"You don't seem surprised to have been chosen," I said. "Aren't you worried the Sidhe will smite you for it?"

"There are a number of other, far more pertinent reasons they might turn on me," he said. "My suitability to rule a Court is the least of them."

"How *did* you get into the maze, anyway?" I asked. "I know you could have glamoured the security guards, but the maze was a magical creation."

"Precisely," he said. "It was a simple matter of trickery to get inside, but the other tests will be designed for Sidhe, so the chances of either of us being victorious are slim."

"I bloody hope so, or else I'm dead," I said. "Not only did I claim the Erlking's talisman, I'm in the running for his throne, too. They'd never believe both were total accidents. Imagine that—a human ruler of Faerie."

"There are worse notions," said Darrow.

"The only time a human has sat near a throne has been when a Sidhe ruler has taken them as a pet," I said. "Also, at any point during my training did you ever think I was fit to run anything? I spend all my time getting into arguments with the Sidhe. I have the diplomatic skills of a rabid wolf shifter."

He tilted his head. "You have the right knowledge and skills to work with the Sidhe. You spent your life preparing for it."

"I'm human!" I said. "And proud of it, too. Furthermore, I stole the Erlking's talisman and can't hold a conversation with anyone in this Court without pissing them off."

"I'd say the fault lies with them more than you," he said. "From my observations, the Sidhe get equally angry with each other for perceived faults."

"Won't make diplomatic missions any easier." I shook my head. "You can't tell me you're thinking of playing to win, either. What would Etaina say?"

His mouth parted. "She would not view it as a betrayal if she understood how we came to be in the running, but if I held a position of power in Summer, I would not be allowed to enter my home again."

You might not be anyway, in the end. He'd all but severed ties with his people, and while he hadn't been close to any of his fellow Aes Sidhe in a long while, it must hurt to leave his home behind. I knew how it felt to be adrift between more than one world and not belong in any of them.

Darrow's gaze shifted to a point over my shoulder. "Your sister's here."

I scanned the room. The crowd had thickened, groups of Sidhe mingling with half-faeries and other beings as more of Faerie's inhabitants had arrived to join in the party. Purple-winged piskies flitted above a band of wire-thin fae playing instruments made of what looked like human hair. Nymphs lounged in the fountain, satyrs danced on cloven feet, while two half-Sidhe herded a group of fire-juggling imps off the premises.

Then I spotted two familiar faces heading towards me: River and Ilsa. Darrow stepped back to allow me to talk to them.

"What're you doing here?" I strode forward to greet my sister.

"Did you really think the Gatekeeper's family wouldn't get an invite?" Ilsa smiled. "We arrived a bit late because River had to deal with another zombie situation in Edinburgh."

"How much did you miss?" I asked.

"We saw the wraith," said Ilsa. "Nice job handling that, by the way."

"The Seelie Queen's fault, of course." I dropped my voice. "She has an insider somewhere here, who's probably advanced to the next stage. Whoever opened the doorway to the Vale did it in the middle of the task itself without being seen."

River swore under his breath. "I thought so. The timing was too suspicious."

"Does Lady Aiten think the insider might have advanced to the next round?" said Ilsa.

"She reckons there's a chance they did," I said. "It also turns out Darrow and I are contenders for the throne, thanks to our entering the maze in the middle of the task. So the Sidhe want us to go in as spies and root out the Seelie Queen's person."

Ilsa's eyes widened. "Shit, really? You're in line for the throne? You?"

"Hell, no, and neither is Darrow..." I looked for him, only to find he'd disappeared into the crowd of dancing, laughing Sidhe.

"A Sidhe who isn't from the Summer Court is a contender?" said River. "That seems a major flaw in the Erlking's spell."

"Guess the spell thinks the Aes Sidhe count as part of Summer," I said. "Speaking of whom..."

I told them about the Seelie Queen's attack and Darrow's new mission. He wouldn't be pleased with me for clueing River in on the existence of his Court, but I'd already told my siblings and I had the distinct impression the entire Summer Court would have to face up to the Aes Sidhe's existence soon enough.

River gave a low whistle. "Etaina must be confident he can take down the Seelie Queen."

"That, or she's just angry at him for giving away their existence to begin with," I added. "I mean, the Seelie Queen thought they died out, too. If he hadn't been forced to use his glamour on her in the Vale, she wouldn't have known."

A spasm of guilt struck me. He'd exposed his glamour

for my sake and as a result, he'd drawn his Court into the crossfire of the Seelie Queen's army.

"You think that?" asked Ilsa. "That she might be trying to punish him?"

I screwed up my forehead. "I don't know. We didn't have time to chat about it. Anyway, we're both stuck here for the time being. I don't know anything about the next two rounds of tests, so we're the underdogs in a major way."

"No kidding," said Ilsa. "Hey—your friend is here, and she looks like she needs your help."

Coral made her way across the room, her eyes wide with panic and her cape billowing around her legs.

"Hey." I hurried over to meet her. "What is it?"

"The Sea Kingdom suffered an attack," said Coral. "I have to go. My mother needs me to defend the throne."

Shit. "Is it the Seelie Queen's army?"

"I don't know," she said. "Hazel—you have to stay here. I'll be back as soon as I can."

"Of course." I gave her a quick hug. "Don't hesitate to call on me if you need me. I owe you for all the times you've saved my neck."

"Will do." She gave a smile, then walked away towards the oak doors. River and Ilsa had pulled back, speaking in low voices, while the Sidhe kept a noticeable distance from me. Naturally, nobody wanted to get too close to the talisman. They feared its touch even more than iron, if possible.

I'd never felt less in the party spirit in my life, but I made for the nearest buffet table and grabbed a wine glass, applying the usual test for poison. Darrow approached the table, his silver hair gleaming under the light of the fireflies which had drifted in from outside as night fell. It didn't seem that long since the task had started, but in Faerie, time was malleable, and if the Sidhe wanted a sunset party, the Court provided the atmosphere.

"What was wrong with Coral?" Darrow asked.

"Her kingdom's under attack," I told him. "I don't know if it's the Seelie Queen, but it wouldn't surprise me. First the Aes Sidhe, now the Sea Court. Is she going after all the independent Courts at once?"

His expression turned grave. "It would make sense if her goal was to bring all the other Courts under her submission. It's a given that she'd go after the Sea Kingdom, as she was responsible for luring its heir onto her side and bringing about his death, but the Aes Sidhe are a different matter. They will not bend so easily."

"Nor will the Sea Court." Not if I had anything to do with it, anyway. "You know, I might just go back to the—"

A scream shattered the sound of celebrations. Then a blast of light engulfed the room, and a faerie with long tangled white hair and wings tinted in colours of the rainbow appeared in the middle of the hall.

The memory-eater.

"She should be dead." Darrow's hand dropped to the knife at his waist. "I killed her."

No kidding. I'd seen him stab her with his blade and turn her to mist and fog. Granted, she might have other powers as well as the ability to absorb the memories of anyone who went near her, but death should be absolute. Even here in Faerie.

Her gaze skimmed the room and landed on Darrow and me. With a beat of rainbow wings, she flew in front of us. Clouds of mist billowed from her fingertips. "Hello, mortals."

"I killed you," said Darrow. "You shouldn't be here."

"I returned," she said. "I am here for the Gatekeeper."

Shit. I guess she's come to call in her favour.

I'd promised her a favour in exchange for a memory that turned out to be no use whatsoever. Since Darrow had killed her not long after, I'd forgotten our bargain, but plainly *she* hadn't.

My hands clenched around the staff. "If you want to talk to me, we can do this elsewhere. Your creepy mist is ruining the atmosphere."

"Are you under the impression that I came alone?" A delighted laugh escaped her, and a cold breeze whipped through the room.

Wraiths emerged from the mist curling on the ceiling, and sluagh, and other shapeless monsters. The sounds of merriment turned to cries of outrage; the clank of weapons being drawn echoed off the walls.

Darrow's hands ignited, blasting the memory-eater backwards into a tapestry. She flipped over, shrieking, wings tangled in the fraying fabric. Hissing, she freed her wings and backed into the secret passageway behind the tapestry which Coral and I had once used to flee a group of angry Sidhe.

"Get back here!" I jumped after her into the passageway, brandishing the staff.

"The Summer Court requires a new leader," she said. "But you are not the leader they desire, are you?"

"Quit reading my thoughts and tell me what the hell you want with me." I gave a swipe, sending a wave of shadows at her. Her wings beat, carrying her out of range, and mist flew from her fingertips. Darrow and I dodged her attack, following her deeper into the passage.

"It's me you want," added Darrow. "I'm the one who killed you."

"Oh, but you killed me for her." She cackled, the sound echoing creepily in the narrow passageway. "For this fragile human, who holds so many others' fates in her hands."

"You have no leverage over me," I said to her. "The Court knows the truth. They know I have this."

I lifted the staff and flung a web of shadows at her. The memory-eater dodged, threads of mist curling around my ankles and forcing me to back out of reach.

She laughed. "Why, little mortal, I have such plans for you. You are the first I have met in countless lifetimes whose future I cannot divine. The paths resulting from your decisions are as murky as the shadows you wield."

I batted at the misty tendrils with the talisman's shadowy magic, sending them shrinking towards their owner. "Were you ever really dead, or was it a trick?"

"I walked the paths of the dead, human," she purred. "I passed the sluagh and the restless dead, I heard the howls of the Wild Hunt, and I saw things that would drive you to madness to look upon, human."

"Enough games," snapped Darrow. "Tell us what you want with us, or I will eliminate you again."

"The Gatekeeper knows why I am here." She grinned at me with jagged teeth. "My mistress desires to speak with you."

She's working with the Seelie Queen. Of course she is.

"Tell her I said to go fuck yourself." I raised the staff, blasting a wave of shadows at her.

The memory-eater cackled, her wings beating, carrying her out of the passageway and into the night. I gave chase, ducking out into the back garden. Several Sidhe ran through the exit, doing battle with a group of oncoming wraiths.

"Hang on!" Ilsa ran to the forefront of the Sidhe. The bright blue glow of her talisman shone in her hands, but the memory-eater's misty magic blocked her from view as she flew at Darrow and me.

Then she spoke a word, and pain split my skull in two. The staff fell from my hand, shadows coiling outward— Darrow exclaimed in alarm, reaching for my hand—and I fell backwards into the clouds' embrace.

Catching my balance, I found myself standing on a silver-tinted path below clouds of mist. I was in the Vale… *without* the talisman. She'd spoken an Invocation and brought me directly to her master's side.

Dread gripped my chest at the sight of the Sidhe standing before me. Dark curls flowed past the Seelie Queen's shoulders, while her armoured dress shone with gold buttons beneath woven patterns of green and grey. Magic shimmered in her eyes, and the memory-eater fluttered at her side like a giant, angry piskie.

"That was cheating." My head gave a throb. *She must be more powerful than I thought, being able to speak Invocations.* I'd thought only Sidhe and wielders of the gods' own magic were able to speak them without being torn apart. I swallowed hard and looked up into the Seelie Queen's eerily bright eyes. "What do you want?"

"You owe my assistant a favour."

"You hired the memory-eater?" I forced a laugh. "Damn, you must have been really convincing. She nearly killed me for suggesting she use her powers to intervene in Court affairs."

"Most Sidhe have no respect for my abilities," said the memory-eater. "The true Queen of Faerie will offer me an honoured spot in her Court."

I snorted. "Yeah, right. I can't believe someone like you got played by an ex-queen who couldn't even claim a throne when she was married to the guy who sat on it."

Anger flared in the Seelie Queen's eyes. "Be careful, mortal."

"Or what?" I gave her a challenging stare. However much I might fear her, her own terror of setting off the backlash of the Gatekeeper's curse kept her from doing me harm. Whatever said backlash would do to her remained a mystery even to me, but right now, it was the only thing keeping me alive.

The memory-eater beat her bright wings. "Your curiosity for knowledge remains intact, I see."

Stop reading my thoughts. You don't know anything about me.

"Oh, I know your thoughts," said the memory-eater. "I can show you what you desire most in the world."

"Fuck you," I said. "You know, I preferred it when you lived in your kingdom of clouds and played tricks on people. Now you're just another one of her minions."

A furious hiss escaped her. "Do not judge me, Gatekeeper. Your bastard of a friend cast me into Death, while the Queen returned me to life again."

How? She wasn't Sidhe, and the source of immortality no longer existed. I turned to the Seelie Queen. "You didn't bring your husband back while you were at it?"

"He's long gone," she said dismissively. "I had need of the memory-eater's talents."

"I bet you did." My heartbeat quickened against my ribcage. Not only did she know everything about me, the Seelie Queen did, too. I might not be keeping secrets from the Court any longer, aside from my desire to escape the Gatekeeper's curse, but that didn't mean she wouldn't be able to use them against me—and my family.

"It is time," said the Seelie Queen. "You will take your place at my side in my new Court, Hazel Lynn."

"No thanks." I pulled out my blade. "I think I've outstayed my welcome."

"You assume you have a choice," said the Seelie Queen. "Go on."

The memory-eater bared her jagged teeth. "I call my favour. You will stand at the Seelie Queen's side as Gatekeeper of the Court of the Vale."

6

A sharp tugging sensation yanked on my chest and dragged me towards the Seelie Queen. Then a dazzling light rose to engulf me, blanking out my surroundings. When the light cleared, we stood in a wide hall with arched ceilings.

"I'm not your servant." I tried to take a step away from her, but the vow took hold and yanked me back to her side. "Let go of me, or I'll make you wish you could die."

"I am doing nothing, Hazel Lynn," she said. "Merely seeing you reap the results of your own bargain."

"The memory-eater died," I spat. "If one of the participants in a vow dies, it's voided."

"I bought her back, Hazel," she said. "Along with her magic."

Then I'll just have to kill her again. I'd bet she wasn't immune to my talisman, but I'd been forced to leave it behind. The Seelie Queen had planned this well.

But not well enough. My binding to the Courts had

endured through generations, even the death of the Erlking, and it ought to outdo the memory-eater's vow.

Movement stirred beyond the Seelie Queen, and a wave of coldness brushed my skin, bringing chills to the surface. I glanced up, and a gasp caught in my throat. The ceiling was thick with wraiths, their icy magic casting eerie blue lights over the otherwise pitch-black hall.

"Damn." My teeth chattered, my hands numbed, and even the mark on my forehead lost all sensation. "This is your plan? You want to freeze me to death?"

"No, I simply wish to stop you from running." The Seelie Queen looked me up and down. "I confess, I don't see the need for a Gatekeeper, but thanks to my new assistant, I have a new understanding of your particular situation."

Icy fear that had nothing to do with the wraiths trod cold steps down my spine. The memory-eater had shared everything she knew about the Gatekeeper's curse, from every person she'd met... which might well include whoever had started it.

"Is that so?" I injected false calmness into my voice. "I don't suppose you'd care to enlighten me, since I'm the person who has to suffer the consequences of said curse?"

"No, I don't think so," she said. "Etaina told you nothing, which gives me more of a foothold. I should have known my sister would hoard that knowledge for herself."

Oh, crap. The memory-eater had even shared the details of my meetings with the Aes Sidhe, which might well have given the Seelie Queen clues as to how to find Darrow's home.

The Seelie Queen smiled. "You don't think I'm aware

of your friend's Court allegiance? I have to confess, I thought the Aes Sidhe long dead, including my sister."

"Is that why you sent wraiths to attack them?" I asked. "To recruit them? Because if you just wanted to say hi to your sister, you might have just sent a messenger sprite and not murdered her soldiers."

"I wanted to test the skills of the army my sister has spent the last few centuries building underground," she said. "After all, I may want them on my side in the future."

"Etaina will sooner see you dead," I told her. "Now you've attacked her people."

"I suspect the long years of separation will not have been kind to her," she said. "She remained hidden for a reason."

So she didn't go there in person. Interesting. "She knows I wield the Erlking's talisman and you don't."

"Does she, now?" She tilted her head. "Now you've left it behind, how long will it last before someone else in the Court tries to claim it? You did leave it outside a gathering of hopefuls for the Erlking's throne."

White-hot anger bubbled inside me, but I pushed it down. I would not let the talisman start manipulating my emotions again. "If they don't have the sense to leave it the hell alone, they deserve what they get."

"You have a ruthless streak, Hazel Lynn," she said. "When you and I come to an understanding, you will be a much more useful assistant than Lord Daival was."

"Until you let me kill him," I said. "Do you have an ounce of loyalty in you? Wait, don't answer that question."

My feet twitched. If only the cold would dial down a notch, I might be able to reach my blade. Being dead, the wraiths were unable to strike me with anything other than magic, which I was immune to. I needed to find a way to raise the temperature.

She gave a soft laugh. "These wraiths are much less talkative than my previous subjects have been. You will be the difficult one, I suspect, but you'll soon come to understand my perspective. There has been a rot beneath the Courts for a long time. Even Etaina knew it, though we had our differences. The Sidhe's longevity has always come with a cost."

"You don't mind that the source of immortality has gone?" I felt below the earth for anything living, but not so much as a spark remained. "I suppose you wouldn't, if nothing can counter your healing powers."

She'd be the last true immortal, unless other Sidhe with the same ability existed.

The Seelie Queen continued as though I hadn't spoken. "The Sidhe will be easier to bend to my will. I didn't expect the Aes Sidhe to reappear, of course, but that may work in my favour."

"Oh, please be quiet," I said. "If I have to listen to you monologue at me for the next few years, I'd sooner freeze to death."

Her eyes flared with Summer magic. "Be careful, Hazel. That talisman of yours will not save you this time, and I can do very unpleasant things to you without killing you."

"For the record, the talisman and I have an understanding," I said. "You know, I always thought the Erlking was practising great restraint by not using its magic on you over all those years. I just didn't realise how much."

"There were many occasions where the thought

crossed his mind, but the fool was weak," she said. "He couldn't have done it."

"Did your little rainbow-winged friend rip that out of someone's memory or did you come up with that one yourself?" I reached for the slightest spark of Summer energy, and sensation tingled in my Gatekeeper's mark. I still had my Gatekeeper's powers.

My vow is to serve the Summer Court. I'd sworn a vow to Summer, and it would always come first. If I took a single step out of range of the Ley Line, the vow dragged me back into its orbit. It *must* be superior to my agreement with the memory-eater.

The light grew brighter, and sensation returned to my hands. Then I pulled out my knife and swung at the Seelie Queen.

She whipped out a blade with typical fae speed, blocking my attack. The wraiths swarmed, their coldness bathing me in iciness, but my circlet brightened in retaliation, forming a shield that blunted the cold, made it bearable.

"You can't overcome me, Gatekeeper," she said. "I can cripple you with a single strike. You don't have to be in one piece to act as my servant."

Again and again, my blade clashed with hers, and even when the iron cut her skin, her healing magic sealed the wound in an instant. I, on the other hand, was soon bleeding from a dozen cuts to my arms and hands and one long deep one on my thigh. My wounds throbbed, but the pain also grounded me, kept the wraiths' magic from numbing my senses again.

As I reeled backwards, catching my balance, the shadows turned to mist, and the memory-eater flew in with her spindly hands outstretched. "You made a mistake in trying to deny your fate, Gatekeeper."

"I wondered where you'd crawled off to." I gave a half-hearted swing, seized with an idea. Without the talisman, it might be painful to open a doorway back into Faerie, but it was worth a shot. If I got the Seelie Queen on top of my talisman, maybe I could use its magic to circumvent her healing powers. They must have a limit somewhere. Magic wasn't an inexhaustible resource, even in Faerie.

"You will stay here," said the memory-eater. "Your plan will not work."

"Sorry to disappoint you," I said, with a smile. "But I'm bound to compete in the trials to become the next ruler of the Summer Court. Didn't tell your Queen that, did you?"

The Seelie Queen let out a hiss of fury. "You—?"

"And it's really thanks to you," I added. "If you hadn't set that wraith loose, I wouldn't have had to break into the maze and gate-crash the first trial. I don't suppose you'd like to tell me the name of the person you have on the inside and save me the bother of going through the other two?"

A doorway into Faerie opened beneath my feet. I tumbled out into the middle of the dark lawn, rolling to a halt beside a dark patch on the lawn. The staff stood upright in a halo of darkness, its shadows reaching as though to welcome me home.

Behind me, the memory-eater flew out of the doorway I'd created. At once, a torrent of shadows folded over her head, eagerly seeking life to feed on—and the memory-eater had that in spades.

"Stop!" she screeched. "Gatekeeper, stop this!"

"I don't think I will, considering you tried to have me

enslaved for life." I rose to my feet, ignoring the throbbing pain in my forehead. "You know, those shadows feed on magic and life force. How much will they get from the memories of all the people you met in a lifetime?"

The memory-eater gave another piteous screech, struggling against the shadows' grip, her thrashing growing weaker. The darkness swarmed her, covering her head and reducing her screams to silence.

"Bye, bye." I waved at the outline of the memory-eater as she disappeared into the relentless shadows. "And bye, bye, vow."

That just left the Seelie Queen—wherever she was. I rotated on the spot, searching for the doorway, but found no signs of it. Had the Seelie Queen closed it from the other side? Why not take the opportunity to send more of her monsters into the Court?

Unless she was already in the palace... with my family.

I closed my hand around the talisman's hilt and willed the shadows to disappear. It took several seconds for them to withdraw, as though the staff wasn't happy with me for leaving it behind, but it still answered to me. One enemy down... not that I was any closer to understanding how she'd come back from the dead in the first place.

My leg and forehead throbbed, reminding me of my wounds as I turned back to the palace. When I reached the door, a flash of blue light lit up my vision. Ilsa stood facing off against a wraith, her hands aglow with magic. She caught my eye and relief crossed her face, before the wraith evaporated in her hands. *Good. She's okay.*

"The Seelie Queen?" she said.

"She got away again." I limped over to Ilsa's side. "Where's River?"

"He and Morgan went around the front to deal with a bunch of sluagh."

"Wait, Morgan was here?" I said. "I didn't see him."

"I told him not to come," she said. "Can you find him? I'll deal with these bastards." She held up the book, daring the wraiths to come nearer.

"Give me a shout if you need me to use this." I used the staff as a crutch and limped around the side of the palace. I was lucky the effects of opening a doorway into Faerie without the talisman in my hand weren't worse than a headache.

As Ilsa had warned, shapeshifting sluagh filled the front garden and the palace steps. One of them had Morgan pinned to the grass, and I waved the talisman at it, causing it to release him.

"Hazel." Morgan twisted out of reach of the sluagh, clambering to his feet. "They took Lloyd."

"Who took… you brought a human here?" *Dammit, Morgan.* Not content with keeping his ridiculous shenanigans to himself, he'd gone and dragged his human boyfriend into this mess.

"I thought we were safe," he said defensively. "Because you had that thing."

I used the talisman's magic to turn the sluagh into dust. "A talisman isn't a substitute for common sense, Morgan."

There came an eerie howling noise from somewhere ahead. Then a sluagh shaped like a giant hound bore down on me, a knife sticking out of its semi-transparent hide.

"Hey, that's mine!" yelled a voice. "Get back here, dickface!"

A human stomped out of the shadows in pursuit of the sluagh, dark-skinned with dreadlocks and a second iron blade in his hand. Lloyd hadn't come here unarmed, then, but I'd be giving Morgan a stern talking-to when we got home. Why did my family have to go looking for trouble as though we didn't attract it in spades already?

Lloyd gave a wild lunge at the sluagh and tripped through its transparent form, falling flat on his face. "Ow! What the hell is that thing?"

"A dead faerie ghost," I told him.

"Ghosts can't be stabbed." He picked up his knife from where he'd dropped it.

"Different rules here, mate." I backed up a step to avoid hitting him with the talisman's magic. "Word of advice: find your boyfriend and get out of here."

Lloyd was a necromancer, but that didn't mean much in Faerie, as Morgan himself ought to know. I waved my talisman, sending a jet of shadow at the sluagh's ghostly form. It vanished into the darkness, consumed down to the last particle.

"Holy fuck," Morgan said from behind me. "No wonder the Seelie Queen wants that thing."

I shot him a warning look. Lloyd, meanwhile, backed slowly away from the shadows curling around my talisman. At least one of the pair of them had some common sense.

I used the staff to limp up the steps leading to the entrance hall. "I'm gonna see if there's any more dickheads who need me to teach them a lesson inside the palace."

It seemed Ilsa's talisman had done its job, though. No more wraiths remained inside the entrance hall, though the party had long since broken apart. Sidhe stood among shattered statues and upended tables, wearing aggrieved expressions at having their fun interrupted. Spotting Lady Aiten, I hobbled over to her. "I killed the memory-eater, but the Seelie Queen escaped in the Vale. When my sister is done banishing the dead, can I go home?"

"Yes, you may," she said. "You and Darrow will present yourselves along with the other contenders first thing tomorrow morning for the second trial."

I limped off in search of Darrow, and spotted him helping lift an injured half-Sidhe from the ruins of a collapsed statue. Surprised rooted me to the spot for an instant, until he saw me looking and rose to his feet. His silver hair was covered in dust, his clothes and weapons bloody.

"Hazel." In two steps, he was at my side. "I thought she took you to the Vale."

"She tried," I said. "I killed the memory-eater, but the Seelie Queen got away. We have to come back here tomorrow. The second trial is first thing in the morning."

A dark look passed over his face. "Do the other Sidhe know…?"

"We're contenders? Not yet. But they will."

And then? The next monarch had the power to exile both of us from Faerie for life, but exile was the least of my fears at the moment. While the Seelie Queen might fear the backlash of killing the Gatekeeper, she had no such compunctions about taking Darrow's life.

His fingers brushed my bleeding arm. "Hazel, you're hurt."

"I'll be fine." The grove would take care of my injuries. "Tell you what, you should stay here and help the other half-faeries. Coral's one of the best at brewing up healing potions and she's still not back."

Worry gnawed at me, but I had no way to follow Coral into the depths of the Sea Kingdom without the assistance of her magic and it wouldn't be the first time she faced a challenge to her throne. At the very least, I knew the Seelie Queen wouldn't have gone there in person, not when she'd been attacking the Summer Court at the same time.

Darrow, though? He'd never been friendly with the other half-bloods, holding himself at a deliberate distance from them the way he did with everyone else. It warmed me inside to see him casually helping them out. If he intended to stay in Half-Blood Territory when he officially left the Aes Sidhe, he could do worse than let them get to know the real him, beneath the cool exterior he presented to the world.

"I will do my best to help," he said, "but brewing healing potions isn't my strong point."

"I'd never have guessed." I grinned at him. "I should go. My brother decided to bring his human boyfriend into Faerie, so he's going to get a serious talking-to from me, my sister, and our mother. You might even be able to hear my mum shouting at him from Faerie."

A smile flickered across his lips. "I'm glad you're safe. Get some rest tonight and we'll figure out a game plan in the morning."

A plan to survive the trials without getting killed by the enemy *or* the Sidhe. Not to mention his own Court. "Sure. We will."

He leaned closer and brushed his mouth over mine—so quickly, I might have imagined it—before he was gone.

"Hazel." Ilsa waved at me. "We're heading out."

"Sure." I stepped away from the spot where Darrow had stood, my skin tingling where he'd touched me. Since when did he kiss me in public, without elf wine or faerie magic being involved? Not that I was complaining, but I found myself regretting not asking him to come home with me and help me forget the chill of the wraiths' touch.

That regret evaporated at the sight of Mum waiting by the gates to the Lynn house, twin iron knives in her hand and a murderous expression on her face.

Here we go.

Half an hour later, Ilsa and I sat in the living room of the Lynn house, having updated Mum on the latest turn of events. While a couple of days had passed in the mortal realm as the trial had been in progress, the Sidhe had sent Mum and the others a personal invitation to the party— and since Lloyd had been visiting at the time, Morgan had decided to bring him along. Lucky for him, Mum was more worried about my unexpected status as a contender in the trials, so he'd escaped to fetch a healing spell for his and Lloyd's injuries.

"You're a contender for the Erlking's throne," said Mum. "Do the Sidhe—"

"Nope," I said. "Except Lady Aiten. And one of them already tried to kill me for the talisman, so you can bet we'll face no end of shit in the next trial."

"Darrow's not even from Summer," Ilsa said. "I don't see the Sidhe letting it slide."

"At least Darrow has his glamour." Ilsa had seen us kiss

and doubtless wanted to hear my thoughts on his unexpected arrival, but I wanted nothing more than to sleep. "Also, for all we know, the Erlking's spell will kick in during the next trial and disqualify us for not being Sidhe. Problem solved."

"That's not how it works, usually," said Mum. "There is no spell that can reliably tell if someone is Sidhe or not. We're not talking about a human-controlled spell, but one that works on autopilot. If humans can be chosen by talismans, they can be picked as monarchs, too."

"Because the Sidhe assumed we'd never be in with a shot, so they didn't bother specifying when they set up the spell?" I surmised. "Lady Aiten wants us to catch the Seelie Queen's spy and stop them from opening more doorways to the Vale. That's all. She'd rather eat the crown than bow to a human."

"What happened to the memory-eater?" asked Ilsa. "Nasty creature, she is. I can see why Darrow stabbed her."

"My talisman ate her alive," I said. "She tried to use the favour I owed her to make me serve the Seelie Queen."

"She used her own vow to bind you to another person?" Ilsa raised an eyebrow.

"The Seelie Queen brought her back from Death," I explained. "I hope this time she *stays* dead."

But she'd already told the Seelie Queen all my weaknesses, wants and curiosities. Not only hers, but everyone else's, too.

"No Sidhe can raise the dead," said Mum. "Not even her."

"Well, whatever she did, it convinced her to take the Seelie Queen's side." I leaned back against the cushions.

"I'm guessing it's at least partly because she knows what's coming and she decided to throw in her lot with the person she thinks stands a best chance of winning."

"Etaina can turn the entire Court into her willing servants," said Ilsa. "The Seelie Queen has what, aside from her unlimited healing powers? The wraiths?"

"How's she doing it?" I asked. "Making them do her bidding? I thought wraiths were just... energy."

"Maybe they sense her healing powers," said Ilsa. "Never mind them. There's only two trials left, so you just need to stop her from wrecking everything until then."

"Somewhat tricky when I'm a *contender*." I ran a hand through my tangled hair. My wounds might have sealed up, but even the grove's magic couldn't dispel my bone-deep exhaustion.

"You what?" Morgan walked into the living room again, followed by a wary-looking Lloyd.

"Darrow and I accidentally put ourselves in line for throne when we went in the maze to get rid of the wraith," I told him. "Needless to say, the Sidhe would rather a piskie took the throne than a human, so shit is going down tomorrow."

Lloyd blinked. "I only understood the last part."

I turned to my brother. "When did you come into the palace, anyway? Did you skip the trial and just show up for the party?"

"Ilsa did the same," Morgan said. "And she brought her boyfriend with her."

"River's half-faerie and has been working with the Court for years," Ilsa said. "It might have escaped your attention, but an event like the trials is a prime target for threats even without the Seelie Queen on the loose and determined to make sure nobody but herself sits on the Erlking's throne. It is *not* a suitable setting for a date. In fact, Faerie in general isn't, which I thought you knew by now."

"Are you done?" said Morgan.

"No, I'm not done," said Ilsa. "Do not, for the love of hellhounds, tell the entire necromancer guild that Hazel is a contender for the Erlking's throne."

"Please don't," I added. "One of the Sidhe already tried to murder me over the talisman when I was in the maze and they didn't even know I was a possible contender then."

"Holy shit, you're serious," said Morgan. "*You* could be chosen to sit on the Erlking's throne?"

"No, I bloody well won't be," I said. "It was a mistake, and the only reason the Sidhe are letting me go ahead with it is because they need someone inside the trials to watch out for foul play. Don't go getting any ideas."

"What, about going after a throne myself?" He grinned. "Hey, if even you can do it, anyone can."

"Hilarious," I said. "Even I could do a better job than certain Sidhe, but that's because the bar is so low it's practically below the earth."

"Nobody is sitting on a throne," Mum said, in ringing tones.

Morgan caught Mum's eye, saw her stony expression, and got hastily to his feet. "I'm going back to Edinburgh. Coming, Lloyd?"

"Sure." Lloyd looked quite relieved to leave the Lynn house behind. "Uh, sorry if I caused you any trouble."

"It wasn't your fault," said Ilsa, with a pointed look at Morgan.

Our older brother shrugged. "It's a rite of passage for anyone who wants to get seriously involved with our family, right? Same with meeting the house."

Lloyd startled when the hall lights came on automatically and the door swung open to let him and Morgan leave. Mum rarely asserted her dominance over the house's magic these days, but it couldn't be more obvious she was kicking the pair of them out.

"It could be worse," Morgan added, unable to take a hint. "Ilsa's first boyfriend got turned into a tree when he set foot in here and Mum wasn't around. The house decided he was a threat and refused to turn him back."

"Get *out*," Ilsa said, her eyes narrowing. "Also, who told you that? You weren't even here."

This time, I was the one on the receiving end of her scowl. Morgan retreated, laughing, while I gave Ilsa a sheepish look. "Look, you can hardly expect me *not* to mention the tree incident. It was one of the highlights of our teenage years."

Lloyd and Morgan closed the door behind them, and Ilsa released a sigh. "Next you'll be telling everyone in Faerie."

"I'm not that mean," I said. "What's the betting Morgan's going to avoid the house until he thinks we've forgotten?"

"As good as the chances he won't try it again," said Ilsa. "I had a bet with River that he'd make it six months without bringing Lloyd to a faerie gathering."

"I bet three," I said. "Anyway, the Seelie Queen *didn't* follow me back. I hoped she'd get caught in the talisman's shadows like the memory-eater, but she must have closed the doorway and stayed in her creepy new palace."

"So that's how you got out," she said. "The memory-eater, though? Why would she support the Seelie Queen?"

"Who the hell knows." I sighed. "My only consolation is that the memory-eater told her I'm too unpredictable to figure out."

"No kidding," said Ilsa. "She got that part right. At least you dealt with her before she shared any more secrets."

"Bit late now the Seelie Queen knows everything." I glanced down at my talisman. "I'll be honest, I still don't know how to kill her. She's gonna be a massive thorn in the side of the next monarch, that's for sure."

Ilsa nodded. "Those wraiths she sent... they were aimed at the other Sidhe, weren't they?"

"Exactly," I said. "I have to act as their bodyguard even after they find out I might steal their position on the throne. Better hope they don't kill me first, huh?"

7

I waited in the entrance hall to the palace the next day, feeling antsy beyond measure. After a decent night's rest, I'd recharged from yesterday and spent a while lounging on the sofa before I'd been called into the Court for the second day of the trials. Judging by the position of the sun, either the Sidhe had slowed time down to be closer to the mortal realm for the duration of the trials, or they'd decided to keep a permanent dawn setting. With the Sidhe, it was anyone's guess.

Whatever the case, Darrow wasn't around yet and neither was Lady Aiten. Several Sidhe stood in groups, a mixture of contenders and spectators, but none of them looked twice at me. They didn't know I was a fellow contender yet. *This is not going to end well.*

"Hey, Hazel." A half-faerie with olive skin and dark hair approached me. Willow, Lady Aiten's daughter. "Sorry to interrupt you, but I wondered if you'd seen Coral."

"She's not back?" I said. "I don't know if she told you—she was called to deal with an urgent situation in the Sea Kingdom."

"I know." She chewed on her lower lip. "My mother told me in no uncertain terms that I'm not to see her again, but I wanted to make sure she was okay."

"That's not cool," I said. "Your mother can't tell you who to spend time with."

"It's Lady Aiten's prerogative to decide whether I'm allowed to stay in the Summer Court or not," she said. "I have to win her favour or leave. I always wondered why, but since Coral told me my mother used to work for the Erlking, it makes more sense now. Thanks to all those Sidhe who turned traitor, she's paranoid about being accused of doing the same."

"Then I'll talk to her," I said. "She already hates me but can't get rid of me, it's not like I can fall any lower in her estimation."

On cue, Lady Aiten walked out of the tapestried room and into the hall. "Contenders, come with me," she said. "Gatekeeper, that includes you."

I can hardly wait. Question was, where was Darrow? He wasn't with the other contenders, and the guy was usually early for everything.

Had that kiss yesterday been goodbye, and he'd left me to face the wrath of the Sidhe alone?

No, that couldn't be right. He'd have got tied up somewhere, that was all. Besides, if this was what I thought it was, the Sidhe would be coming after me with pikes in approximately one minute's time.

One of the Sidhe—the female with the scale-patterned

armour I'd seen the day before—cast a disdainful look in my direction. "Did you mean to include the Gatekeeper among us?"

Make that ten seconds.

"Yes," said Lady Aiten. "It seems Hazel's actions in entering the maze yesterday caused her to be marked as a contender."

Thanks a bunch. She just had to make it sound as though I'd chosen to enter the maze with zero input from her. To no surprise, the assembled Sidhe turned on me, their expressions ranging from disbelieving to outright hostile.

"A *human?*" said a male Sidhe with pale, almost translucent skin and bark-green hair topped with a spiked helmet. "This is a mistake."

"A mistake that will be rectified," added Lady Aiten. "However, until we find a way to remove Hazel from the running, she will take part in the trials."

"I'm here to keep an eye out for sabotage, not compete," I corrected. "If the Seelie Queen sends another swarm of death fae to interrupt the trials, I'll handle them."

The helmeted Sidhe drew a long, curved blade. "No human should be allowed to participate in our trials. She has not earned that honour."

"She has." The Erlking's sprite flew into view, hovering in front of the assembled Sidhe. "She has been chosen by the spell cast by the Erlking himself and is bound to take part in the trials."

A furious murmur went through the Sidhe, prompting a spark of magic to run through the room like an electric current.

Why me? "I'm not trying to steal your glory. I don't want a throne."

"You came into the maze yesterday," said a female Sidhe with bark-like skin and eyes with cat-like pupils. "Why would you do so unless you wanted to claim our glory for yourself?"

"To kill the wraith who was trying to interrupt the test," I said, thoroughly exasperated. "The Seelie Queen is the one trying to sabotage the trials to ensure nobody else ends up on the throne of Summer. I nearly captured her yesterday, and I've every intention of succeeding next time. You can ignore one measly human, can't you?"

"Enough," snapped Lady Aiten, as several voices rose in protest. "I will speak with the Gatekeeper alone."

She left the Sidhe grumbling among themselves and walked with me to an alcove in the corner of the room. "You didn't tell me you came close to capturing the Seelie Queen yesterday. Why did you not finish her off?"

"I tried to trick her into getting herself caught in my talisman's magic, but she didn't fall for it," I said. "The memory-eater did, but the Seelie Queen ran away into the Vale."

"This must end," she said, in harsh tones. "She should not be allowed to disrupt our trials any further. Last night's events have left many of the contenders demoralised, and rumours are beginning to spread among the other Sidhe that none of the contenders is fit to rule the Court."

Figures. "When a winner is declared, they'll have to accept them. They must know the damage not having a leader is causing to Summer's territory."

Her expression shadowed. "The rot has only affected

the outskirts of our territory. It has yet to penetrate the Court's centre."

"You didn't tell them." I glanced over at the Sidhe, with their sculpted armour and gleaming weapons. "I realise this is hypocritical of me to say, considering, but if you deny them the truth, you can't blame them when they draw their own conclusions."

"The Erlking himself tasked me with overseeing the trials," she said. "I will not fail."

I thought it was something like that. The Sidhe might not believe in ghosts, but the shadow of the Erlking hung over everyone, including the next monarch. Lady Aiten might not have worked with him for long, but being tasked with running the trials was the highest honour and the weight of that expectation sat heavily on her shoulders.

"Look," I said. "I understand you're under a lot of pressure, believe me. But you can't sweep this under the rug. Odds are, the Seelie Queen's challenge won't end with the ascension of the next monarch. This isn't just about glory, or even about taking the Erlking's place. Whoever takes the throne will need a decisive plan to deal with her, and if she is captured, hand out the appropriate punishment."

"I will not take orders from a human," she said. "Can you imagine what the Sidhe would say if I tell them the Erlking's spell came with a loophole which allowed the likes of you to participate in the trials?"

"You could just tell them I'm a spy." I folded my arms. "You can't stand being out of control, can you? Is that why you're threatening to disown your daughter purely because she's chosen to spend time with someone from another Court?"

Her mouth thinned. "My daughter is half-blood. The

other Sidhe will destroy her if they find out she's passing on our secrets to the heir to the Sea Court. It's safer for her to leave the Court."

"I don't see you falling over yourself to help the other half-bloods." I shook my head. "Besides, it might have escaped your attention that Willow has found a better home among the half-faeries in the borderlands, and I don't blame her an inch."

"My family is none of your business, Gatekeeper." Her melodic voice trembled with rage, and then her gaze fixed at a point over my shoulder. "There is the other contender. I was beginning to wonder if he intended to shirk his duty."

I looked up as Darrow walked in. He had his weapons sheathed, but droplets of blood stained the hilt of his blade. Had one of the other Sidhe attacked him before he even reached the trials?

"Are you going to make a public example of *him?*" I asked. "Or is it just me?"

"If I hadn't drawn attention to you, the Sidhe would have done so themselves," she said. "As it is, they believe you're there to keep the Seelie Queen from disrupting the trials."

"Which is true," I added, for Swift's benefit as much as hers. "I'd like to keep the murder attempts to a minimum, thanks."

"If your presence distracts the other Sidhe, it would be a useful way in which to distinguish those who are not fit to rule," she said. "If the presence of a human is enough to stop them from concentrating on the task at hand, they cannot be trusted to take care of an entire Court."

"Oh, so I'm there to act as a walking target so you can

figure out which Sidhe are more likely to take shots at humans instead of concentrating on the important stuff?"

I rolled my eyes. "Great."

"One last thing," she said. "You will not be permitted to carry any iron, and you must leave your talisman behind."

Even better. "The iron, I understand, but the talisman is kind of a necessity if you want me to get rid of any wraiths," I said. "I've got it under control. Aren't you allowing the other Sidhe to bring their talismans into the maze?"

"Their talismans do not destroy magic," she said.

"Let her bring the talisman," said Darrow, halting beside us. "The other Sidhe have their own advantages, and the rules don't disqualify Hazel from bringing hers."

"He is correct," said the sprite. "Furthermore, it is against the rules for any of the Sidhe to turn against the contestants. If they do so, they will be disqualified."

"I'll try not to turn anyone else to ashes." Unless they attacked me first, that is. "Promise."

"I will hold you to that, Gatekeeper." Her flinty eyes travelled from me to Darrow, and to the other Sidhe gathering expectantly in the room's centre. "Come with me."

Darrow and I walked behind her, remaining at a safe distance from the other contenders. Several of them whispered derogatory comments, but Lady Aiten had one thing right—if my presence distracted them that badly, they didn't have the patience to rule a Court. I'd lay bets on the other Sidhe making trouble before the Seelie Queen did, though.

"The second of the tasks will begin in the garden," Lady Aiten said. "A number of tokens have been scattered outside. You must search for as many as possible. At the end, you will be ranked according to the number of tokens you acquire."

"So it's like capture the flag, except with magical tokens," I said.

Blank stares followed. No surprise there. Darrow didn't look at me, either, and he stood too far away for me to ask how he'd ended up covered in blood, or if he was hurt. It was hardly fair for him to take part in the trial if he was, but nobody expected fairness from the Sidhe. I fell into step with him as we headed for the oak doors leading into the back garden.

"I bet it's not that simple," I said to Darrow. "There'll be trickery to stop us from getting the tokens. Spells, monsters, the works."

He dipped his head but didn't speak, his silver hair gleaming in the sunlight streaming through the doors.

Outside, the field had transformed into a vast forest. Towering trees formed a barrier between us and the world beyond the palace grounds, turning them into a stretch of woodland seemingly without end. I should have figured finding those tokens wouldn't be as easy as picking them up off the ground.

"The last round had man-eating hedges. I can hardly wait for this one." I held my staff in one hand, the other resting on a knife at my waist. I wasn't too worried about magical traps, but if I let the talisman's magic go too far out of control, it might bring the whole forest crashing down.

"Let the task begin," Lady Aiten said.

A bell rang through the air, and the Sidhe surged into

the forest, disappearing among the towering trees. I let them, waiting for the crowd to die down before giving the lawn a cursory scan. No traces remained of yesterday's fight, but since the forest covered almost the entire back garden, I'd have a job and a half tracking any death fae. Especially if someone opened a doorway into the Vale in the forest's midst like they'd done in the maze yesterday. How did Lady Aiten expect me to find it without using my talisman?

Darrow tilted his head at me. "What are you doing?"

"Giving them a head start," I said. "I'm not actually *trying* to take part in the challenge. It's our job to watch out for threats, not find magical tokens, and we're more likely to be able to see wraiths from the outside."

Unlike during the first challenge, however, we stood on the same level as the other trees, preventing us from seeing into the vast forest. I scanned the palace and saw Lady Aiten watching, a disapproving expression on her face.

"Anyone would think she *wanted* us to steal the Erlking's throne." I rolled my eyes at Darrow. "Are you okay? You're bleeding."

"It isn't my blood," he said. "A group of outcasts set upon me this morning."

"You mean those cultists? Or the Seelie Queen's people?"

"No," he said. "They were half-blood."

"*Half-bloods?* Why would they want to attack you?"

"Perhaps they heard I'm a contender." He rested the heel of his foot on a raised tree root at the edge of the forest. "Or the Seelie Queen got to them."

"Like she doesn't already have enough of an army."

Now all we needed was the Unseelie Queen to send an army of redcaps to ruin our day.

"Gatekeeper," said Lady Aiten. "I command you to enter the forest."

Fine. "All right, keep your hair on."

The forest devoured the pair of us like the maw of a colossal beast. Stumps of dead trees stuck up like jagged teeth, while patches of wildflowers in improbable colours filled the air with fragrant smells. Beyond the trees, giant mushrooms the size of houses towered overhead, forming a roof that blocked out every trace of natural light. If not for the ever-present glow of magic, we wouldn't be able to see our own hands in front of us.

"No wonder she didn't want me to bring my talisman in here," I remarked. "I notice she didn't tell us what the tokens looked like, either."

Darrow hissed out a breath. "There's someone up ahead."

I followed his gaze, spotting the limp body of a contender sprawled in a bush peppered with bright purple flowers. I took one step, then halted, a sharp scent tickling my nostrils. The memory of one of Coral's lessons came back to me. "Poison. He must have touched that plant."

"Foolish," he murmured, leaning over the body.

I extended my talisman and gave the purple-flowered bushes a prod, and they wilted on the spot, shrivelling into dust.

"What?" I said, in response to Darrow's raised eyebrow. "There's no rule against killing nasty poisonous flowers. Hope he wakes up. The trials aren't meant to kill people, and I don't have an antidote on me."

"You'd stop the trial to save his life?" he said.

"I'm not *in* the trial, and yes, I would." Darrow came across as human in so many ways, I kept forgetting he and I had been raised in totally different environments and that he'd been taught to view compassion for one's enemies as a weakness. "Not being qualified to rule a Court shouldn't mean instant death."

Darrow turned the Sidhe's body over with his foot, revealing bloodstains darkening his grey armour. *Shit. That changes things.*

"He was stabbed," I murmured. "The killer wanted us to believe he was poisoned."

Question was, why had they killed him to begin with? I'd thought the insider was simply here to make trouble, to open doorways into the Vale and make it look like an accident. A stabbing was harder to blame on an insubstantial nightmare creature, and the cover-up wasn't particularly well done.

Please tell me there isn't more than one traitor among the contestants.

I scanned the surrounding forest for any clues as to which way the killer had gone. Winding trails fanned through the trees and towering mushrooms seemingly at random, and thick undergrowth concealed any footprints. I picked a path at random, and soon, the Sidhe's dead body disappeared from view.

"I reckon the killer took off," I remarked to Darrow. "The forest probably rearranges itself like the rest of Faerie, so the odds of us finding him by accident are slim. Unless there's a minuscule chance I can pull off the same trick as I can in the Vale and make the forest lead us where we need to go."

Darrow gave me a sideways look. "You could try it. You never know."

"Nah, they wouldn't make it that easy." I strode ahead, below the rims of colossal toadstools, and thought, *take me to the killer's location. Take me to find the traitor.*

I rounded a corner, and the world flipped upside-down. My body flipped along with it, and I grabbed the nearest solid object—the side of a giant toadstool—for balance. The blood rushed to my head, my feet tangling in the undergrowth, and something dark swarmed from beneath the toadstool's rim.

Darrow caught his balance. "What is that?"

The solid dark cloud flowed towards us. Not a regular cloud. It had too many legs, for one thing.

"Fucking hell," I said. "Please tell me that isn't what I think—"

The cloud flowed over and around us, as a thousand pairs of spider legs brushed against my skin. I held still, gritting my teeth, until the cloud dispersed, leaving my skin itchy but otherwise unharmed.

"What the hell was that in aid of?" I shuddered.

"Lady Aiten did imply this task was a test of courage," he said.

"Good job I don't mind spiders." I flicked a spider off my shoulder. "What's this for? Picking out random phobias and using them against us? Because those things were miniscule. They didn't have any weapons, either."

The ground trembled. Darrow lifted his head. "I think you spoke too soon, Hazel."

Another tremor shook the toadstool in my grip, and then a round, bulbous body crawled into view, its huge hairy legs kicking up the undergrowth.

"It's their mother." I flicked another spider off my arm. "Sorry, I think I trod on a few of your offspring."

Darrow conjured magic to his palms, green and blue light intertwining. "Stay back."

"I don't think it's gonna listen." I held up the staff. "I'd recommend getting the hell out of here. Go on, Shelob, go and chase the person who left the guy dead back there. How about that?"

The spider raised its huge head, and a jet of viscous black liquid shot out from its gaping mouth. I threw myself behind a toadstool, while Darrow darted around the other way, blasting the spider with magic. It flailed back, its legs sprawling, and one of them kicked me in the face. I lashed out with my blade, severing it, and the spider let out a screech. Another two swipes had it staggering away into the undergrowth. I advanced forward, raising the staff. "Didn't your mother teach you manners?"

"Hazel." Darrow pointed to the spider's bulbous head. In place of what I thought had been eyes was a large, glinting coin-like shape.

That couldn't be a token, could it?

"Damn." If I used the talisman, it might well blow the token away along with the spider. And I wasn't one to back away from a challenge. "All right, then."

I switched my knife to my right hand, hacking and slashing at the spider's legs. Darrow went on the attack, too, blasting its maw every time it opened to spew venom at us and dealing well-timed strikes with his blade. When it collapsed into a flailing heap, I climbed the nearest toadstool, using the momentum to leap onto the spider's giant hairy head.

My knees slammed down on either side of the large coin. With one wrenching motion, I yanked the coin from the beast's head.

At once, it vanished. My legs flailed at thin air. I caught hold of the side of a toadstool, my knife driving a track down its side as I skidded to a halt at Darrow's feet. The coin bounced to a halt beside me.

"Go ahead and pick it up," I said, breathless.

"You earned it," he said. "I should have known it was an illusion. Its venom left no mark."

I turned to look where he pointed, and he flicked the coin with his heel, causing it to fly into my hand. "Now you're just showing off." A grin slid onto my mouth. "Good job you gave me so much training at seeing through glamour, huh?"

"We should leave," he said. "If anyone didn't know we were in this part of the forest, they will now."

"Better find that killer. I won't get distracted by the next shiny object."

As fun as it'd been to fight alongside Darrow once again, I had a conspirator to catch.

We resumed our path through the winding tracks, but I didn't see a soul. Either our battle with the spider had scared off the competition, or the forest's magic had intentionally split everyone up.

Darrow's steps halted in the middle of the path, and he raised his head. "There's someone close by."

I frowned, but I didn't have a Sidhe's enhanced senses. Darrow slowly drew his weapon, his ears pricked, his body dropping into a combat stance. I looked ahead, and did a double-take.

Several pointed-eared figures stood concealed behind

the trees. If Darrow hadn't pointed them out, I'd never have spotted them. They didn't move as Darrow trod softly towards them through the undergrowth, his weapon at the ready. I didn't have a hope of being that stealthy, so I held my talisman in both hands and marched into the trees.

A rustling noise whipped past my face, and I stopped mid-step. Ahead of me, the figures weren't there anymore, as though they'd never existed.

Huh? How'd they move so fast?

Darrow's eyes narrowed, scanning the undergrowth. Then he pounced.

A choked noise escaped his target and the body of one of the hidden people fell beneath his blade, blood gushing from his mouth as he crumpled to the earth. I barely had time to register my surprise before the second one was on me, aiming a knife at my back.

Nice try. I swung the talisman around, deflecting his blow. Threads of shadow washed over him, but when they cleared, he was still standing.

My talisman didn't affect him.

"What the hell are you?" I gave another spin of the talisman, but while I blocked his attack, the magic-eating shadows did him no harm. If he was a creation of glamour, they should have eaten him alive, and even if not, they'd have turned him to dust. They *should* have.

Darrow's hands lit up with magic, blasting a torrent of blue light into the trees. Three more hidden assailants toppled out, their bodies frozen with Winter magic. He lunged and slit one of their throats, while I moved to his side, drawing my blade and stabbing the second assassin in the chest. He finished off the third one, letting his neck bleed out into the undergrowth.

"Darrow, what the hell are they?" I said.

"They aren't from Summer," he said. "They're Etaina's soldiers. They're Aes Sidhe."

8

The undergrowth rustled on our right, and I raised my staff to block another assassin's strike. His blade clattered to the ground, and I kicked him hard in the chest, sending him crashing into the assassin Darrow was duelling. Darrow's knife swiftly dispatched both targets.

A final attacker jumped out of the bushes at me. Like the others, he had long silver hair and wore a dark uniform that downplayed his otherwise striking features. My blade swung around, sinking through his chest to his spine.

The bushes rustled to silence as his body fell, his silvery blond hair splaying over the blood-soaked earth. I shook crimson droplets from my knife and turned to Darrow. "Is that the last of them?"

"I believe it is." His dark gaze swept the bushes. "I see no traces of how they got into the challenge without being spotted."

"Nor me." I sheathed my knife and gave the nearest

body a prod with my foot. "Wish we'd kept one of them alive to question. Why'd they attack you as well as me? Do they know we're working together?"

Did that mean Etaina knew, too?

Darrow didn't answer. He reached into the bushes and grabbed one of the assassin's shoulders, moving the dead Sidhe onto the path. Then he did the same to a second.

That's when I noticed the obvious. All of the attackers were male, though their long silvery hair hadn't made it immediately clear, and were of a similar tall, lean build. I looked from one to another, taking in the angular features, the vibrant green eyes. "Are they related to one another?"

Even my siblings and I didn't look that much alike, and back when Ilsa and I were kids, people had frequently confused the two of us. A third Aes Sidhe soldier joined the others, as Darrow moved his body out of the undergrowth. His face looked the same as his companions, down to the last angle and curve of cheekbone.

"In a way," he said. "They're Etaina's elite unit of assassins."

"Not your relations." No, his aquamarine eyes set him apart. These Aes Sidhe were all Summer, and utterly identical. "Are they *clones*? As in, copies of the same person?"

Like when Darrow used glamour to create copies of himself… but these guys were as solid as I was, and, it seemed, immune to the talisman's power. *Etaina used glamour to create living beings?*

"Etaina only sends her elite assassins when she wants to dispatch someone without leaving a trace behind." His mouth tightened. "I trained with them myself. If I hadn't, I wouldn't be able to predict their movements."

"Holy shit," I breathed. "Did Etaina create them herself?"

"She did," he said. "They might be creations of magic, however, but they are living beings capable of experiencing the same senses and emotions as we do. The one thing linking them is their undying loyalty to Etaina. They will do anything for her, so only she could have sent them here."

No wonder nobody had kicked up a fuss when Etaina had brainwashed her entire congregation, with an army of elite clones keeping everyone in line. I hadn't known it was possible for illusion magic to create real living beings, but it explained a lot about how so many Sidhe had survived underground.

"They couldn't have meant to attack you, too," I said. "She's the one who sent you into the Summer Court, right? Why would she then order her assassins to eliminate us both?"

"She wouldn't," he said. "I suspect they saw the two of us together and struck without thinking. They can be quite literal in how they interpret orders."

Despite the certainty in his tone, his brow pinched with worry. The bodies of the fallen Aes Sidhe creeped me the hell out, but I made myself examine each one, marvelling at their identical features. Then I peered through the bushes, spotting another body lying in a clearing.

"I don't think we need to worry about the Seelie Queen's insider any longer," I murmured.

A Summer Sidhe lay dead in the undergrowth, his body split open from throat to chest to expose the organs glistening inside. Behind him lay the sprawling body of a dead ogre, almost concealing the slash in mid-air which marked a partly open doorway into the Vale.

"Etaina's assassins killed the Seelie Queen's insider," I remarked. "And then we killed them in return. Really, they did us a favour."

"The doorway is still open," said Darrow.

"Not for long." I trod up to the gaping slash in the air, seeing nothing on the other side but empty space and the blankness of the Vale's paths. One touch of my talisman and it folded shut. "That's our saboteur dealt with."

But Etaina had sent her own form of sabotage, and her assassins hadn't seemed to care about targeting their fellow soldier. Either they'd been told to kill everyone they came across and she hadn't meant to include Darrow among them... or she knew, somehow, that we were working together.

Darrow released a slow breath. "We can't leave the bodies here. If they do, the Summer Court will realise there's more than one enemy."

"But—there is." I looked at the fallen Aes Sidhe. "If we don't tell them, they won't know there's another threat to their Court."

Damn Etaina. What the hell was she doing?

Darrow's mouth pressed together. "It may not count as a threat to the Court. The assassins targeted the Seelie Queen's insiders and the two of us, not the other Sidhe. If it turns out they *did* attack the other Sidhe, then by all means, tell Lady Aiten—but remember that exposing the Aes Sidhe also means exposing my own ties to that Court, and I may well be executed for treason. I can't permanently glamour the entire Summer Court into sparing my life."

"Shit." Putting him in the spotlight was the last thing I wanted to do, but why had the assassins targeted the two of us? If they'd just been sent here to eliminate the Seelie Queen's people—as revenge for her attacks on the Aes Sidhe's realm—then I'd have no issues with keeping their interference quiet, but this was different. "I'd use my magic to destroy their bodies, but..." I indicated the shadows curling around the hilt of the staff, somehow unable to touch the fallen Aes Sidhe. "How are they all immune to my talisman? Are they carrying those stones?"

"Let's find out." He lifted one of the bodies into the air, and I dug my hand into the pocket of his coat in search of the stone he must be carrying. All I found were knives, each engraved with a swirling symbol on their hilts. The mark of the Aes Sidhe, perhaps.

Darrow removed the assassin's cloak and swore under his breath. Beneath the Aes Sidhe's torn sleeve, marks were visible on his arm, a swirling complex of lines that reminded me of my Gatekeeper's mark.

"She gave them magic that made them immune." I touched the mark on my forehead with my fingertip, my heart thumping at I took in the similarities. The symbols' meanings whispered through my mind, speaking of bindings and power barely within my comprehension. "That... isn't faerie magic."

The marks were Invocations. The language of the gods.

I dropped my gaze to the staff, which gleamed with similar glyphs. Darrow did likewise, letting the assassin fall into the undergrowth. "Hazel, what spell is it?"

"I don't know, but I don't like it a bit." Shivers ran up

my arms, and I tightened my grip on the staff. "I can't destroy their bodies while they're wearing those marks."

Darrow drew his knife, and with a methodical motion, sliced off the assassin's arm. "Will that do?"

"Maybe." I raised the staff. This time, the instant the shadows touched his body, it disintegrated into dust. The knot in my chest eased slightly, though a new pang of guilt struck me at the knowledge that we were removing the evidence of an attack, and Lady Aiten would have both our heads if she knew. "What about his arm? I mean, we can't exactly walk out of here carrying a sack of dismembered limbs without arousing suspicion."

Darrow pressed the tip of his knife to the severed arm, cutting a diagonal slash through the symbols. "Try now."

I did so, and this time, the arm disintegrated into ashes. "Nicely done."

Moving on swift feet, we did the same to the other assassins, leaving the body of the murdered Summer Sidhe beside the dead troll in the hope that it would look as though the troll had gutted him and not the assassins.

"Why does it feel like we're covering up a crime?" I let the last body crumble to dust. "If I'd known we'd be dismembering corpses, I'd have asked one of my siblings for advice." The odd look Darrow gave me compelled me to add, "Because they're necromancers. Not because they secretly murder people on the weekends."

"Right," he said. "You have a strange family. Has anyone ever told you that?"

"Several times a week, yes." I ducked around a towering toadstool and led the way along yet another path. "Etaina's people wouldn't have killed the other competitors, would they? The ones who didn't open doorways into the Vale, I mean."

"You're forgetting, I *am* one of Etaina's people," he said. "And she would never have ordered me to do anything which might draw attention to our Court."

"Unless she doesn't care if it goes public now," I said. "She might assume the Seelie Queen told everyone she knew that the Aes Sidhe aren't as dead as everyone thinks, so she wants to make a statement."

"After centuries of secrecy?" Darrow's expression was bleak. "No. There's something else she wants."

"We all know what that is." I prodded a wall of poisonous-looking toadstools with the talisman's base, causing them to shrivel on the spot.

Darrow didn't speak for a while. For a wonder, neither did I. It felt like hours had passed while we walked, but time held no meaning here. Silence held the forest in its grip, punctuated with faint rustling noises, and not another soul appeared within sight.

The gleam of water caught my eye, and we halted at the edge of a river bisecting the forest through the centre. A single bridge ran from one side to the other, wooden but sturdy-looking.

I glanced at Darrow. "What d'you reckon? Should we look for a way around or walk right across and hope nothing eats us?"

"Walk across," he said. "There is no way around."

"You sure about that?" I said. "Because that has 'troll bridge' written all over it."

Bridge trolls were territorial as hell and didn't like anyone using their chosen bridge without paying a tribute. For some, coins would suffice. For others, the tribute tended to be of the flesh-and-blood variety. I had zero desire to be a snack for a troll, even an illusory one. The river extended both left and right without an end in sight, and with no other obvious bridges, either. A gleam on the opposite side caught my attention. *Another token?*

Darrow went still. A moment later, so did I. A Sidhe emerged from the bushes on the other side of the river, a gleaming token in his hands. His skin was ebony, his hair blue-black, and he wore armour decorated with crow feathers.

"It's safe to cross," he called across the river to us. "The bridge troll is unconscious. I dropped some of those deadly flowers into the water."

"Why should I believe you?" I called to him.

"Feel free to take a look." He lowered the token, amusement gleaming in his bright green eyes. "I thought I'd even the odds."

A likely story.

Darrow, however, climbed onto the bridge. "Then we'll hold you to your word."

Striding across the narrow wooden bridge, he left me with little choice but to step up behind him. My nerves jangled at every creak beneath my feet, and when I glanced at the water, dark shapes moved below the surface. My grip on the talisman tightened.

Another alarming creak made my body tense, but Darrow took my arm to steady me. "Better?"

"Nope. Get me off this bridge." I startled when his grip tightened around my upper arm. He wasn't usually so open about touching me, but I wasn't about to complain about having an extra hand to steady me as we crossed the bridge. "Where's this troll?"

"There." He pointed over the edge with his free hand, where the huge lumpy body of a troll lay sprawled half-under the bridge. *The Sidhe wasn't misleading us after all?*

Then the wooden planks gave a sudden, alarming creak. Darrow's pace quickened as cracks began to appear in the wood below our feet. "Of course there'd be another catch."

The bridge split in two directly in front of me, leaving us stranded on the wrong side, suspended above the water.

"Hazel!" Darrow shouted. "We have to jump."

"I'll never make it." I didn't have a Sidhe's ability to jump impossibly long distances. If I tried, I'd fall into a watery grave.

Darrow leapt across the gap, easily catching his balance on the edge. "Jump. I'll catch you."

"You'd better." Cursing myself for trusting the word of a Sidhe, I backed up, and then jumped, sailing over the water.

Darrow's hands grasped mine, pulling me tight against him. "Told you I'd catch you."

"Yeah." I leaned closer, feeling his heart racing against mine. "Damn close call, though."

His hand cupped my chin. I startled at the unexpectedly intimate moment of contact. His lips brushed mine, his body moulding against me. I felt his beating heart, and the soft silkiness of his hair tickling my face.

I opened my eyes to find him looking back at me, his green eyes—

Green?

Darrow turned away, his face flickering.

It wasn't Darrow. He was a glamour. His eyes were

slightly the wrong colour, the angles of his face minutely wrong. I jerked out of his grip, my skin prickling.

"How long have you been following me?" I demanded. "Where the hell is the real Darrow?"

Had he been left on the other side of the bridge? Shit, I never should have taken my eyes off him for an instant.

Darrow's face melted away, revealing another of the Aes Sidhe clones, and he swung a blade at me with blinding speed. I dodged his strike, and the bridge disappeared beneath my feet, pitching me towards the water.

My hand snagged the wooden edge, splinters digging into my fingers. Holding the talisman awkwardly in one hand, I struggled to catch my balance. A green glow came from beneath the bridge in the spot where it'd broken. *He did it. It was him all along.*

The Aes Sidhe kicked a booted foot at me, and I swung the staff at his ankle. He pivoted—while I couldn't disintegrate him, he could still fall into the water, same as me—and I seized my chance. With a desperate lunge, I dragged myself back onto the bridge, the sharp wooden edges digging into my arms and chest.

"You've *really* pissed me off now," I said, blasting him with the staff.

The shadowy magic bounced off him, dissipating as though no target existed. I drew my knife instead, swiping low, but he dodged with wicked speed. His expression was blank, as though he gained no enjoyment from our conflict. With mechanical motions, he drove his knife towards my heart.

I deflected the blade with the edge of my staff, wielding it one-handed and stepping around him until our positions were reversed, and he stood with his back to the river. It was tempting to throw his body into the water and leave him for the fishes, but what if his corpse washed up somewhere in the Summer Court and was discovered by one of the Sidhe? I had to dispose of him like the others, or else risk Darrow's safety. The real Darrow, that is.

"Who are you?" I stabbed at him, my knife clashing with his. "Did Etaina send you?"

Our blades locked against one another, and he broke first, the tip snagging the edge of my hand. I gritted my teeth against the sharp pain and swung the staff at him with my other hand. The shadows had no effect, but a giant staff was harder to dodge than a knife. My talisman slammed into his elbow with a satisfying crunch, causing his grip to loosen on his weapon. Teeth bared in a snarl, he went on the attack again. Damn, the bastard was persistent. I gave another swing with the staff, this time knocking his knife out of his hand. In the same instant, he drew a second one with his free hand, narrowly missing my arm.

"Tell me who you are," I growled. "Did Etaina send you to kill me?"

The staff hit him hard in the chin, sending him sprawling onto his back. He spat out blood. "You will not convince me to break my vows."

"You're a disposable clone, but I suppose it's a waste of time trying to convince you she's screwing you over." I gave him another thwack, this one on the forehead. The back of his skull hit the ground, his limbs twitching. "Tell me."

"I would sooner die, Gatekeeper." He bared bloody

teeth at me. "I enjoyed pretending to be your lover. He will die a traitor's death."

"Have it your way." Dropping low, I sank my knife under his ribcage. His eyes—green, not aquamarine—widened as I yanked the knife free with a firm tug. Blood gushed out along with the knife, and his body stilled.

My hands itched to unleash the talisman's magic and devour every particle of him until I was rid of the shiver of his fingertips on my skin, his lips on mine, his hair on my face. I sank my fist into his limp face, pummelled him over and over again.

"Hazel?"

Darrow. My hands froze mid-punch. "This isn't what it looks like."

"Another one?" He strode to my side. He *looked* like the real Darrow this time, but then again, so had this dude. "What are you doing?"

"Redecorating his face." I stepped aside as he leaned over the body, examining the impact of my knuckles on the assassin's angular features.

"If he wasn't alone, there may be others." Darrow sliced off the clone's arm, his blade coming so close to me that I instinctively raised the staff and knocked his arm away. "What is it, Hazel?"

I opened and closed my mouth. How to get a reaction that would bring out the real Darrow or expose him as another fraud? For once, my imagination failed me. I became aware my hands were shaking. I'd kissed the fake Darrow, let him touch me, and he looked so much like the man beside me that it sent my thoughts in a tailspin. Darrow's comment about love being a weakness might not have been far off the mark after all.

I lowered the staff. "I'm a little jumpy. That dickhead pretended to be you for a bit."

Shock transformed his harsh features. "Did he hurt you?"

"No." I raised the staff again, and shadows swept from the talisman to the body, eagerly devouring his every particle. I spat in the spot where he'd vanished, turning back to Darrow. "If you're not real, I'll do worse to you."

"If you want me to prove I am, then I will do so," he said. "Ask me any question."

My throat closed up, my heart continuing to beat too fast. *How can I prove who he is? I didn't even know his Queen had a crack team of cloned assassins until today.*

"Go on," he added, a smile flickering at the corner of his mouth. "You can't pretend you haven't been waiting for this opportunity."

"Definitely not." I felt better in an instant. "Okay, tell me one thing only Darrow would know. Anything."

"You're going to have to be more specific," he said.

"Why, because you haven't told me anything about yourself?" I said. "What's your sprite's name?"

"Hummingbird," he said.

"Where does he live?"

"In my quarters, in the realm of the Aes Sidhe," he said. "But any Aes Sidhe might tell you the same."

"All right." I racked my brains. "Where did you find Hummingbird the last time you and I went into your room?"

"Ah—he was sleeping on a book," he said.

"Which book?" I pressed.

"The complete works of Shakespeare."

Relief swept the last traces of doubt away. "All right, let's destroy the rest of this fucker and get out of here."

Darrow sliced through the symbols on the Aes Sidhe's severed arm, and I destroyed the remains. "Have you read Shakespeare?"

"A little," I said. "My sister's more studious than I am. The only play I liked studying at school was *A Midsummer Night's Dream*."

He arched a brow. "Because of the faeries? I'd have thought you'd dislike it for that exact reason."

"Nah, Ilsa and I were cast as Hermia and Helena in the school play, which meant we got to wrestle one another on the stage." I grinned. "I reckon Shakespeare must have met some of the Sidhe, personally. Titania reminds me of a certain Queen. And Oberon..."

"Oberon was the Erlking's name."

"How the bloody hell do you know that?" Even the Gatekeepers were hard-pressed to access information on the Sidhe's real names, as I'd found out when Mum had attempted to compile the Erlking's family tree.

"I inferred it from when Etaina spoke of the talisman's previous owner," he said. "Oberon's staff."

"Hmm." My mood sobered. "The assassin wouldn't admit Etaina was the one who sent him here."

Darkness flashed across his face. "We know it was her. She had two goals: remove the talisman and destroy the Seelie Queen's accomplices."

"They didn't even need to kill me." Not with the markings she'd given them, anyway. *Invocations.* Since when could the gods' language bestow powers on *Sidhe*? If they spoke a word aloud, its meaning became literal, but while the gods' symbols were frequently carved into talismans and other objects of power, I hadn't known the words themselves held hidden magic.

I kept on eye on Darrow as we walked in case another sneaky assassin tried to take his place. My own reaction unsettled the hell out of me. If the assassin had pretended to be my sister, I'd have punched him in the nuts for it, but that the Aes Sidhe had used my attraction to Darrow against me made me furious for a whole other set of reasons. Not least of which was the fact that they knew I was attracted to him at all. Which meant Etaina must know. Like all Sidhe, little escaped her attention.

The resonant sound of a bell echoed through the forest. "Was that the end of the challenge?"

We only had the one token between us. We weren't going to win this challenge—not both of us, anyway.

The forest began to warp and spin around us, the trees merging, the giant toadstools folding back and then vanishing. I kept my eyes on Darrow to make the dizziness less intense. "What are we supposed to do? We have one token."

The honourable thing to do was to take the token for my own and let Darrow walk away free without the Sidhe believing him an interloper who wanted to steal their throne.

Except if those Aes Sidhe assassins *had* been out to kill him—if he truly had lost his place among their Court—then if he dropped out of the race, there was nothing stopping Etaina taking him back, and not letting him go this time.

My gut tightened. I held out the token. "Take it."

"I'm not from Summer," he said. "I have more of a

claim on Winter's throne, even, because my Winter ancestor was at least from their Court."

"I have zero," I reminded him. "On account of me being an annoying human who keeps messing up their plans. You need the protection of the trials, I don't."

"I beg to differ," he said. "The trials didn't stop the enemy from coming after us. Besides, if anything, one token won't be enough for either of us."

The remains of the forest vanished, leaving us on the lawn behind the palace. The other participants stood around us, some holding tokens, some not. Others, like the bodies of the two dead Sidhe—the one who'd been hidden in the bushes and the one who'd been beside the troll—lay unmoving on the grass.

Among the living Sidhe, the Sidhe with blue-black hair and the feathered armour held the most tokens, at least four or five of them. I never did thank him for his help, though hell if I knew why he'd given it. Maybe he figured I'd owe him a favour later down the line.

"Those of you with less than two tokens are disqualified," Lady Aiten said. "You are to head back into the palace while I speak with the winners."

Disappointment spiked, swiftly followed by relief. "We're out, then."

Darrow and I joined the other losers and walked back into the palace. For once, I didn't mind the stares, because it brought a decisive end to my participation in the Erlking's trials. I was more than happy to leave the contesting up to the Sidhe and focus on the more important matter of keeping the Court safe from its enemies.

More importantly, no traces of the assassins had followed us back. Darrow's secret was safe… for now.

9

Darrow and I walked through the entrance hall of the palace, leaving the rest of the Sidhe to celebrate their victory alone.

"What're you going to do?" He held the front doors open to let me pass through.

"Now?" I said. "I planned to go home, clean up, and build an effigy of that face-stealing dickhead to set on fire. If my sister's there, I'll ask her about those symbols, too."

"You're planning to tell your family about the assassins?" he asked.

"Of course I am," I said. "I told them pretty much everything else. They already know Etaina has my name on her hit list."

His eyes widened. "You told your whole family about my Court?"

"Uh... yes?" I frowned. "Even if I hadn't, they'd want to know if assassins are after me. Especially as my enemies make an annoying habit of targeting them, too. Look at Lord Daival and the Seelie Queen."

Had he really assumed I wouldn't confide in the people I was closest to? I supposed he wouldn't, not if he didn't have anyone with whom he shared everything. He hadn't grown up close to anyone. Except…

The image of the girl I'd seen in his memories came to mind. Reyna. He'd loved her, I was sure, and my heart ached not with jealousy but with sadness. Despite my exhaustion and emotional upheaval, I didn't want to leave him alone in Faerie. If he was attacked by assassins, he wouldn't be able to dispose of their bodies without my talisman, which would expose his Court to Summer and leave him to deal with the fallout.

At least that's what I told myself when I said, "Come back with me and I'll introduce you to my family."

"I've met your family," he said.

And… he still wasn't getting it. "The Aes Sidhe assassins targeted you as well as me. The Seelie Queen might want revenge on you for interfering in her plans. The Lynn house isn't theoretically safer than the palace, but I'd rest easier knowing they weren't trying to slit your throat in your sleep."

"You think me so easily overcome?" he said. "You're forgetting Etaina taught me the same tricks as her elite assassins. I know how they operate."

"Yes, I know," I said. "But I don't like knowing you could turn into one of those freakish assassins at any given time. Can you teach me to tell the difference? Another glamour lesson, just for old time's sake?"

His mouth lifted at the corner as the implication seemed to finally sink in. "It would be my pleasure."

Mine, too. Just as long as Mum doesn't ambush us in the garden and spring the sex talk on us.

I found myself watching Darrow's movements closely as we walked to the gates to the Lynn house. As much as I'd have taken any excuse to get him out of the Court, the end of the test didn't mean Etaina's assassins would give up, and for all I knew, they were lurking elsewhere in Faerie. Yet from the way they'd acted in the test, they hadn't wanted to rig the results. Their orders were clear: kill me and take the talisman.

I opened the gate and led Darrow into the grounds to the Lynn house, some of the tension easing out of me at the sight of the familiar bright lawns and ivy-cloaked house. It was daytime here, though later than ideal, and the sun had begun its descent over the trees beyond the gate.

"Do you want to start the lesson right away?" asked Darrow.

"Better see who's in first." A hammering noise from the shed answered that question. "Mum's gonna be in there for a while, but I'll check if Ilsa's around. She's still working on that damned family tree. Hell if I know why. She already has a full-time job and a PhD application to contend with, but she's always been the overachiever of the family."

I led the way to the back door and unlocked it. "You've already seen my house… in the dark, anyway. The night we met."

"I remember." He entered the kitchen behind me, eyeing the shiny appliances. "This is all created by the Summer Court's magic?"

"You've got it. No idea what used to be here before Faerie's magic created the house. I've never asked." I walked through the kitchen and out into the hall, peering through the open door into the living room. Nobody was in there, but the remnants of the Erlking's family tree lay strewn around the tables.

Darrow, however, was more interested in the portraits in the hall. His gaze paused at the crayoned drawing Ilsa had pinned to the blank stretch of wall at the end. "Is that supposed to be you? Riding… a unicorn?"

"My sister drew it when we were kids," I said. "My actual portrait is meant to hang there after I retire as Gatekeeper, assuming I live that long."

"And there's your mother," he noted, his gaze skimming along the line of portraits. "Does every family member have their own portrait?"

"Nah, just the Summer Gatekeepers," I said. "We're the only ones who get fancy portraits. Tradition. And the lack of wall space."

Darrow studied the end portrait, a man with dark hair and brown eyes. "Who is he?"

"Thomas Lynn." I peeled off the fake moustache Morgan had stuck on his face. "The man who started this madness."

"He doesn't look much like you," he observed.

I shrugged. "He vanished after his twin daughters were taken into Faerie, so nobody has an accurate picture of him. Even his grave's empty. I'd offer to take you to see it, but the sun's going down. We should get on with our lesson, unless you'd prefer it to take place in the dark."

"No…" His gaze travelled over Thomas Lynn's portrait, a frown puckering his brow. "No, we'll do it now."

I went out via the front door, circling the house to find a clear spot on the lawn, and stood facing him. His aquamarine eyes shimmered with magic, and shame tightened my chest for falling for that clone's absurd trick. I jerked my gaze away. "Okay. Let's go."

"How do you want to do this?" he asked. "Do you want me to use glamour and ask you to pick out which is the real me?"

I drew in a breath. "Okay. I'll turn my back. I won't cheat."

Two more Darrows appeared, each identical to him. My gaze panned from one to another, looking for clues to tell them apart, but only keeping the one on the left in the corner of my eye allowed me to remember it was really him.

"Can you make them talk?" I asked.

"Yes," the three Darrows chorused.

"And hold a conversation?" I laid the staff down, wanting to do this without the talisman's magic interfering.

"To an extent," said the Darrow on the left.

"But it requires concentration," added the middle one.

"And if the caster becomes distracted, they lose their grip," the third put in.

"So it is like necromancy," I observed. "Except instead of piloting dead bodies, you're controlling pieces of yourself."

"Not exactly," said the left Darrow. "I'm not tied to the clones, but they're tied to me."

"We're independent of one another," added the middle guy. "We can walk around and do whatever we like."

"But if we're killed, we disappear," the third finished. "The real person doesn't, for obvious reasons."

"If I use iron, you disappear, too," I said. "I guess that's one way of handling it. If I'm not in the trials, it shouldn't matter if I'm carrying an iron knife or not."

"No, it shouldn't, but I'd prefer it if you didn't use iron on me," said the real Darrow.

"Don't worry." A mischievous smile tugged my mouth. "I like you in one piece. Even if your clones do look freakishly alike. I'm gonna turn around. When I do, feel free to rearrange your clones or otherwise try to confuse me. Then I'll see if I can tell the difference."

I rotated on the spot, counted down from twenty, then turned around again. No fewer than seven Darrows fanned out across the lawn, all identical down to the last detail. Silver hair, aquamarine eyes, angular features. Even the smears of blood on their clothing matched. It was uncanny.

"Where'd you learn how to do this?" I scrutinised the first Darrow, who didn't move. "Did you spend hours in front of the mirror learning to create a double of yourself?"

"No," said the first Darrow.

"I practised on animals at first," added the second.

"Uh-huh." Attempting to tell one Darrow from another based on physical appearance alone was an impossibility, and while I might joke about using iron, the last thing I wanted was to cause pain to the real Darrow. "Like the squirrel you vanished during our first glamour lesson."

"And the horse," said the third Darrow. "I didn't see a horse until I was sixteen."

"Right, you didn't set foot aboveground until the meadow."

A sharp exhale from my right drew my attention to the fifth Darrow along. "What meadow?"

"Aha." I pointed. "That's the real you."

He frowned. "What do you know about the meadow?"

"Nothing." I wished I hadn't brought it up—but apparently, the trick to finding the real Darrow was to bring up random childhood memories. "I saw it in one of the memory-eater's tricks. I gathered it was your first time leaving the realm of the Aes Sidhe."

"Yes, it was." His voice was quiet, his eyes layered with emotion, which made it easy to identify him as the real Darrow.

"You saw some of my past, too, didn't you?" I asked. "Which memories?"

"The day you woke as Gatekeeper," he said. "A lot of memories of you getting into fights at school, arguing with your siblings, conjuring up an illusion of a vehicle…"

"Which vanished when I tried to drive it," I added.

"I know it did." His mouth twitched. "I don't recall seeing a single memory where you remotely acted as you were supposed to."

"I don't know why you're so surprised." Closing the inches between us, I rested my hands on his shoulders, tilting my head to meet his eyes. "I reckon I have more incriminating things in my history than you do. You *didn't* see the strip poker incident, did you?"

A spark grew in his eyes. "I take it you were the one stripping?"

"I lost a bet with a goblin." I let my hands fan through the silky strands of his hair and forgot about the clones surrounding him. I only had eyes for the real deal; the grim set of his mouth and the stormy currents in his eyes, both of which I wanted to kiss away, to draw him into me until he forgot all about the chains that bound both of us.

My lips touched his, then I kissed him harder, winding my hands into his hair. His hands came around my waist, pulling me tight against him. My skin burned white-hot under his touch, and I moaned against his mouth. Lifting me off my feet, he laid me down on the lawn without breaking off the kiss. Grass tickled my bare skin, and his gleaming eyes made the stars in the darkening sky look dim. My core tightened with need as he lay astride me, his legs on either side of my body.

Breathing heavily, I became aware of the silence hovering over the lawn. The noise of Mum hammering on the target had ceased.

"What is it?" he said, noting my pause.

"I think," I said, "my mother has realised we're here and is waiting to ambush me with another lecture."

He pushed to his knees. "Another lecture?"

I lifted my head. "About the Gatekeeper's curse and why dating faeries is a big no-no."

"I don't believe you ever explained," he said. "Why does the curse forbid you from romantically associating with the fae? I assume it isn't because we're mercurial and untrustworthy."

Ah, crap. I pulled my body into a sitting position. "It's the Courts' age-old rivalry again. Essentially, they don't want a half-faerie Gatekeeper because it'd upset the power balance between Summer and Winter. Somehow that morphed into a rule telling Gatekeepers not to get romantically involved with the Sidhe, as if that's somehow going to stop us from fornicating with them. It's not a literal part of the vow, and they don't care what we do when we're not in the Courts, besides."

Darrow climbed to his feet. "A half-faerie Gatekeeper? Will one of your children be the next Gatekeeper?"

"That's how the curse works," I said. "It picks someone from each generation. Might be my siblings' kids, might be mine. Holly has it even worse than I do, because she's an only child and there aren't any surviving Winter Lynns aside from her."

He looked stricken. "So if you have children at any point—"

"I already told you nobody volunteered for this," I interjected. "I meant what I said—I'm intending to break the curse as soon as there's a new monarch on the throne and the Sidhe stop trying to kill me and each other."

"And if not?" His voice was clipped, tense. "What would happen if the curse found no target?"

"I don't know," I said. "The curse wasn't supposed to end up like this. It's only because Thomas Lynn was mortal and the Sidhe didn't take that into account when they cast their spell. Once the curse was enacted on him, that was it. There's always a Gatekeeper. But it doesn't change anything between us."

His jaw clenched and unclenched. "Hazel, I can't take the risk of starting a relationship with you for a multitude of reasons. This curse of yours is only the latest of them."

My heart sank in my chest. "You mean because Etaina wants me dead. You do realise that if it turns out she *does* know you've defected, we'll both be in equal danger from her assassins, right?"

"That doesn't make it worth the risk," he said. "That curse of yours is the most complex I've seen. There's no telling what it might do if we become closer than we already are."

Angry words exploded onto my tongue. "Then, by all means, run away. Just like you're running from Etaina. You never wanted a relationship with me, did you? You just wanted an excuse to get away from that miserable shithole she calls a kingdom without confronting her directly."

That wasn't it. I *knew* it wasn't it, but the words poured out like a faucet and I was powerless to stop them. Darrow's mouth opened, then closed. "That isn't it at all, Hazel."

He turned and walked away. I could have followed, but in an instant, he was gone, through the gate and back into Faerie.

10

"Way to go, Hazel." Suppressing a sigh, I turned to the house and saw my sister approaching.

"Hazel?" Ilsa caught up to me. "I thought I heard your voice outside. I was in the shower. Was that Darrow?"

"I told him about the curse," I muttered to the grass. "The *you have to volunteer your future offspring* part. I thought he would have already worked it out, but I guess not."

"Damn." Ilsa winced. "What was he doing here, anyway? Is the trial over? It's been more than a day here, but I wasn't sure."

"I wanted him under my eyes because of Etaina and her trickery." I pushed to my feet and told her about the trial in the forest as we walked back to the house and into the living room.

"So let me get this straight," said Ilsa, moving a stack of notes from the sofa so she could sit down. "The Seelie Queen isn't the only person trying to interfere in the contest over the Erlking's throne. Now Etaina wants in on it, too?"

"Not sure she does," I said. "Her assassins didn't attack any of the Sidhe except for the ones who were conspiring with the Seelie Queen. Then they tried to kill us both, and frankly, I've no idea if they were aiming for Darrow because they saw us together or because Etaina knows he's defected."

"Damn." Ilsa shook her head. "He's playing a dangerous game if he's still planning to pretend to be working for her after this."

"So am I, considering I helped him destroy the bodies instead of reporting them to Lady Aiten." I twisted my hands together. "If I hadn't, the Summer Court would have found out and might have put Darrow on trial for treason. After all, on paper, he's still working for Etaina. Hence why I wanted him to stay here at our house, before I screwed it all up."

"No kidding," she said. "I mean, you didn't screw it up, you told him the truth."

"What do you expect?" I said. "He doesn't think we have a future, but he's honourable enough not to want to risk bringing a child into the world who might end up enslaved to a Court. But he doesn't think I can break the curse, or he doesn't want to risk it anyway. Can't really blame him for that."

How could I contemplate any kind of a future with Darrow, if I remained tied to the Gatekeeper's curse and he belonged to a Court that wanted me dead? I'd never expected to be in with a shot at a normal relationship, and until now, I'd been fine with short-term flings. None of them had made my chest ache as though someone had pressed a heavy boot against my ribcage. The idea of cutting Darrow out of my life felt like carving a chunk out of my own chest.

Ilsa's lips pursed. "He'll see sense. Want me to call for takeout?"

I arched a brow. "Whatever happened to avoiding Mum's wrath by not ordering delivery people to come to the house?"

"You look like you need it." She rose to her feet and made the call.

My mood improved substantially at the arrival of the Chinese takeout, due in no small part to the delivery man's confusion at being called to an address in the literal middle of nowhere. Ilsa and I returned to the house to find Mum sitting in the living room. She gave the cartons of takeout a disapproving look, but all she said was, "Glad you're back in one piece, Hazel. How did the trial go?"

"Knocked out of the running." I opened the carton and dug in. "I bloody hope so, anyway, since I spent more time killing Aes Sidhe assassins instead of looking for tokens."

"Aes Sidhe assassins?" said Mum. "Now Etaina's after the throne?"

"Nah, she's after the Seelie Queen." I chewed a mouthful of lemon chicken and rice. "Oh, and me. The assassins were armed with some kind of magical marks that made them immune to my talisman."

"Shit, Hazel," said Ilsa. "You didn't mention that. What marks?"

"I can't draw them from memory, but they looked like the ones on my talisman."

"Invocations." Ilsa laid down the carton and pulled her Gatekeeper's book. "I did wonder… look at this."

I peered over her shoulder at the page, which gleamed with similar symbols. The text inside the book changed depending on what Ilsa's talisman wanted her to know, so it must have thought she'd need to see those symbols.

"Looks similar," I murmured. "It was like a protective spell, drawn onto their bare skin like a tattoo."

Ilsa's hand clenched. "I've seen humans with the same marks. There was an epidemic in Edinburgh not long ago among the witches."

"The Aes Sidhe can't be working with humans," I said. "Etaina lived in the time of the gods herself. She probably learned how to write in their language at school or something."

Mum's expression shadowed. "I would have thought someone who lived in the times of the gods would not use their language lightly."

"We're talking about the same person who wants to steal this." I tapped the staff, which leant against the end of the sofa. "We already knew Etaina has those stones which make her people immune to my weapons. Shouldn't really be a surprise that she has another way to make my life difficult."

"How did they get into the Court, anyway?" asked Ilsa. "The Aes Sidhe's realm is supposed to be outside Faerie, right?"

"I think they must have followed the Seelie Queen's trail when her insider opened the doorway into the Vale," I said. "The Seelie Queen's wraiths already found her realm once, so there might be a way underground from the Vale, too."

"Makes sense." Ilsa picked up her takeout carton again.

"It seems odd that Etaina would risk exposing her Court at a time like this."

"Yeah, I still don't get that part." I laid down my carton. "Only the Seelie Queen knows the Aes Sidhe exist. Nobody else in the Court does. Either Etaina had absolute faith in her people not to show themselves in public, or…"

"Or she wants the Courts to know," finished Mum.

Unease skittered down my spine. "Why would she? The Aes Sidhe's Court is a fraction of the size of Summer. I've seen them assembled in one room."

On the other hand, what better time to stir up trouble than during a leadership changeover? Without a monarch on the throne, there'd be no better time to try to grab some of the power she'd lost to the Erlking. All she needed was my talisman.

Ilsa and Mum exchanged glances that told me they'd shared the same thought.

"If she wanted the throne, she'd have to go through the trials in person," Ilsa said. "Right?"

"Yes, she would," I said. "I don't think that's her goal. Maybe it's a revenge thing. She and the Erlking weren't fans of one another, from what I gather. And the Seelie Queen is her sister, so there's some definite bitterness there."

"What does Darrow think?" Mum looked at me. "I saw you two on the lawn."

I dug into my food again to avoid making eye contact. "He went back to Faerie."

"And he doesn't think he might be attacked by more of those assassins?" she said.

Anger sparked, then fizzled out just as instantly. "According to him, dealing with assassins can't be worse than spending time in the same house as someone who's under a lifelong family curse."

Mum frowned. "I thought he knew about the curse."

"He does." I addressed the takeout cartons. "The implications took a while to sink in, that's all."

"That sounds familiar." Mum's gaze travelled between Ilsa and me. "I never told you how your father took the news, did I?"

Well... no. "How did you and Dad handle it? When the truth came out, I mean?"

"We didn't," she said. "He fell in love with me while we were at school, thinking I was an ordinary human. Back then, supernaturals didn't live out in the open, so I had to decide how and when to reveal the truth to him. I decided to start with Foxwood. A town with a mostly supernatural population seemed a safer introduction than taking him into the Summer Court."

"You aren't wrong," said Ilsa. "So how'd he react to Foxwood?"

"He was fascinated, of course," she said. "Your grandmother encouraged our relationship, for obvious reasons. I liked him, I enjoyed his company, and I thought my misgivings were due to the worry about revealing my identity as Gatekeeper."

"Did it go badly?" I asked.

"Not at all," she said. "I kept our interactions to the Lynn house and did my best to shield him from the rest. The fae at the house and in the garden annoyed him a little, but he didn't have the Sight, so he couldn't see the worst of it. After Morgan was born, we hit a rough patch, but we got through it. And then, two years after I gave birth to you and Ilsa..."

"The invasion happened," said Ilsa. "The faeries attacked earth."

She dipped her head. "He left at once to find his family in Ireland and make sure they were safe. And he never came back. He reasoned that it would be easier for the three of you to grow up closer to Faerie than torn between two worlds like he would have been if he'd stayed."

I blinked, my eyes burning. "So you don't mind…"

"It's easier that way." She smiled. "You needn't pity me, Hazel. I didn't love him, not in the way he wanted. It would have inevitably come out sooner if I hadn't wanted so badly to make it work. I think part of him always knew that what he felt for me would never be reciprocated, but he let himself look past it. I don't want for companionship, not when I have you three. You're the one good thing that came out of this curse."

"And I thought we annoyed the hell out of you." Ilsa shot me a grin, her eyes as damp as mine. "Guess we can't be worse than the Sidhe are, huh."

"Definitely not." I stole Ilsa's abandoned takeout container, feeling a little better despite my growing suspicion that the only two people who might know how to undo the curse were the two Sidhe who hated me most in the world.

———

Despite my bone-deep exhaustion, sleep eluded me until dawn, and I woke up restless and irritable and wishing I'd stayed in Faerie after all. Dread knotted my chest as I walked through the gates, crossing my fingers behind my back that no more of Etaina's assassins had attacked Darrow on the other side. It'd only be an hour or two at most since the trial in Faerie, but that didn't mean he'd be any safer.

At least with the Seelie Queen's insider dead and my name removed from the list of contenders, I was officially out of the running and free to do some more meddling in my own way. Once I found Darrow and apologised to him, that is.

The Erlking's sprite flew over to me as I approached the palace, his semi-transparent wings beating frantically. "You must come, quickly!"

"What's going on?" I readied my talisman, one hand on the knife at my waist. "It can't be time for the third trial already?"

I climbed the steps into the palace two at a time, bracing myself to fight. Instead, I found a considerably smaller group of Sidhe than yesterday gathering in front of Lady Aiten. I halted, lowering the staff, as she strode over to meet me. "Two participants were disqualified for cheating when we examined the results of the second trial, which leaves a gap. The magic of the trials dictates that you should return to the contest, Gatekeeper."

"What?" I looked between her and Swift, disbelieving. "That can't be right. Cheating? In what way?"

"Lord Anther saw fit to try to poison another candidate."

"Lord Anther? As in the guy with the wing-patterned armour?" The Sidhe who'd helped me in the maze? He'd come across as one of the few decent contenders, but with the pressure mounting, it might have got the best of him.

"Look, I can't be in the running. I split my only token with Darrow."

"A number of the other Sidhe found no tokens," she said. "Two were also found dead, which I wished to discuss with you, Hazel. The bodies we found inside the second trial did not bear the marks of your talisman. How did they die?"

Crap. What was my cover story again? "The first guy—the one we found in the poisonous bushes—was killed by the Seelie Queen's people, hidden in the bushes to conceal the cause of death. Further in, we found the body of a Seelie knight beside a fallen troll and a partly open doorway into the Vale. I assumed the troll trampled him to death."

"We found marks of weaponry on the bodies, including the troll, but not the cause." Her sharp gaze skimmed over me. "None of the other Sidhe claimed to have seen either of them."

Oh, hell. I should have tried harder to hide the cause of death. "I can only tell you what I saw. I closed the doorway. Perhaps the first Sidhe who the Seelie Queen's people killed was the one who slaughtered the troll."

"If I see any act of sabotage in the trials, I must question it, Hazel," she said. "Now we're almost at the final round, which will be the Seelie Queen's last chance to intervene before the new monarch takes the throne."

My heart gave an uneasy flip. I shouldn't be in the running at this stage, but that wasn't the reason a mounting sense of foreboding lay over me. This wasn't just the Seelie Queen's last chance to intervene, but Etaina's, too. Even the iron I carried didn't soothe my suspicion that I'd overlooked some obvious error.

"Should I fetch Darrow?" I asked. "I assume he doesn't know he's back in the running, and he's on the Seelie Queen's hit list, too."

"I sent a messenger to Half-Blood Territory, so he should be on his way here now," she said. "The trial begins at dawn."

That gave me a few hours to find Darrow... assuming he'd made it to Half-Blood Territory at all. *Dammit, why did I drive him off yesterday?* I should have kept my mouth shut and let him sleep on the sofa.

Cursing under my breath, I followed the path to the meadow where Lord Raivan hung out, close to the one path in Faerie that connected Winter and the borderlands with Summer.

Up close, I was sure it was the same meadow I'd seen in Darrow's memory, formed of bright green strands of grass swaying in a gentle breeze. Lord Raivan wasn't there, but the sound of voices drifted from further down the path bordering Half-Blood Territory. Shoulders tensing, I pulled out one of the iron knives I wore strapped to my belt and advanced down the path.

A circle of Aes Sidhe surrounded Darrow, at least five of them, all wearing the same black-green armour.

"You will come back to Etaina to stand trial for your crimes," said a male warrior with silver hair. "Do not deny that you have forsaken your vows and brought the former Queen of Summer on our tail."

"I have not," said Darrow. "The Seelie Queen was alive in the days before the Aes Sidhe split from Summer, and I assume that is how she tracked our people down. Rest assured, I am doing everything in my power to find and kill her."

"Then why are you participating in the trials of the Erlking?" asked a second Aes Sidhe soldier, this one female. *They're not the same clones as yesterday.* While they might wear the same uniform, they weren't identical.

"That was a mistake, and it is now rectified," he said in calm tones. "However, several of your kin tried to kill me during the second trial. Did Etaina give the order?"

"Everyone knows you turned traitor," said the silver-haired male Sidhe. "You gave us all up for a pathetic mortal who stole our magic and made a mockery of our Court. I suppose it's fitting for one who betrayed us once before. I always knew Etaina was wrong to trust you, Darrow."

Okay, enough games. I raised the talisman above the speaker's head. "This pathetic mortal thinks you ought to work harder on your stealth skills. Knock it off. Darrow doesn't need to join your creepy league of clones, and he doesn't want to go back to the boring underground hole you call a kingdom. Etaina might call herself a leader and not a queen, but as far as I'm concerned, if it quacks like a duck, it sure as hell isn't a monkey."

The assassins gave me blank looks, as though they couldn't fathom what the hell I was talking about. "If you're insulting our leader—" the male Aes Sidhe began heatedly.

I jabbed my knife in his direction. "Go on. Either attack or get out of here. Do you want the whole of Summer to know your Court exists? Is that what Etaina asked you to do?"

"Etaina told us to bring the traitor back to her," said a third Aes Sidhe, a male with glittering silver hair and darker green eyes suggesting he had human heritage somewhere.

Darrow gave them a contemptuous look. "The only traitors I see before me are yourselves. I am here on my mission from Etaina, and I have not betrayed her trust."

"Why did the human suggest otherwise?" said the first Aes Sidhe.

"Because that's what I do," I said. "Say shit I don't mean and jump to conclusions."

Hey, I had to get an apology in there somewhere.

"At dawn, the final trial to select a leader of the Summer Court will begin, and I will be there to ambush the Seelie Queen if she tries anything," Darrow added. "Which I'm sure she will do. What I would like to know is why Etaina risked compromising our secrecy at a time like this."

"Because she wants the throne herself?" I interjected.

"Be careful of the accusations you make, Gatekeeper," said the silver-haired assassin in soft tones. "The Lady of Light has been generous in sparing your life so far."

"Yeah, right," I said. "Several of your people tried to kill me during the last trial. I bet if I look closer, I'll find you're all marked with the same symbols which make you immune to my talisman's magic. And you should know, if you're wondering why none of your pals came back yesterday, those marks of yours aren't enough to stave off death. If your *Lady of Light* told you they were, she lied to you."

"Careful, Gatekeeper," said the first Aes Sidhe. "You'll face a reckoning for your crimes at our Lady's hands, make no mistake."

"I can hardly wait." I folded my arms across my chest.

"Get out or I'll be forced to call for reinforcements to chase you down. You should also know that since this path falls on the border of neutral territory, both Summer *and* Winter can kick you out."

The Aes Sidhe's eyes gleamed with hate, but he ignored my words. "You have been warned, Darrow. Betray us again and you will face death at our hands."

He and his companions turned and walked away down the path, vanishing from sight among the trees.

I turned to Darrow. "Lady Aiten is already suspicious about the deaths during the second trial. They aren't going to Half-Blood Territory, are they?"

"No, but the longer I spend there, the more my presence will put the others in danger," he said. "I should have stayed in the palace."

"You should have stayed at my house," I corrected. "We have spare rooms, you know. Three generations of Lynns lived there once."

He shook his head fiercely. "Hazel, don't ask me to risk your family's lives."

"Have a little faith in me, would you?" I said. "Mum would have it a lot easier if she decided to leave the Lynn house, but she stayed for my sake. Because we care about one another. Same as I care about you. Ignore the bullshit I said yesterday. I know you're not only here because you're avoiding Etaina."

His mouth tightened. "Hazel, you should go to the palace. I'll handle the Aes Sidhe."

"Uh, no," I said. "There's a time and a place for heroics, and this isn't it. Stick to your word and come back to help me deal with the Seelie Queen, and if the Aes Sidhe *do* attack Summer, you won't be blamed for conspiring with them."

Raised voices drifted through the trees, followed by screaming.

Darrow lifted his head. "I believe we're already too late, Hazel."

Crap. I about-turned, heading down the path towards the palace. The sounds resolved into the clashing of weapons, and panic spiked, driving me forward. Darrow ran on my heels and overtook me at the palace entrance, his hands alighting with magic.

A sluagh reared above us, its semi-transparent form undulating like a giant shadowy serpent. Darrow's attack slammed into it, knocking it into my talisman's path. Turning it to dust without breaking stride, I kept running through the gate and into the grounds. Outside the palace, Coral stood arguing with Lady Aiten.

"Whoa." I skidded to a halt beside her. "What happened now?"

Coral met my gaze, her eyes wide with terror. "The Seelie Queen's forces are decimating ours. My mother is injured, and she's locked herself in her palace so nobody can get in. We're all going to die if the Summer Court doesn't help us."

11

I caught my breath. "The Seelie Queen sent her armies underwater?"

"Wraiths and sluagh don't need to breathe, do they?" She gave Lady Aiten an imploring look. "They're overwhelming the Sea Kingdom. Most of the sea fae have never seen one before."

Oh, damn. I turned to Lady Aiten. "We can spare some people, right?"

"Certainly not," she said. "The next monarch of Summer will be chosen after the final trial. It cannot be delayed."

"They're *dying*," I said. "I'm going with Coral. There's several hours until the trial starts, so nobody has to stay here."

"The Sea Kingdom is the heir's responsibility." If I didn't know better, there was triumph in her expression, as though she was pleased Coral wasn't around to draw away her daughter's attention any longer. "We have no armies to spare, given the imminent threat to the Summer Court."

Cold air whispered across the garden, bringing the stench of decay. Several sluagh drifted into view, warping into grotesque shapes as they did so. Coral cursed under her breath. "They followed me here."

Lady Aiten's face became a furious mask. "Get them away from the contestants."

I resisted the impulse to thwack her over the head with the talisman and headed towards the attackers. The sluagh slithered through the air, forming transparent beasts with sharp teeth and deadly claws. With a wave of the talisman, I sent them reeling backwards, their insubstantial bodies collapsing in on themselves and disappearing into a haze of shadows.

Darrow caught up to me. "Where are they coming from?"

"They must have followed me through the portal I unlocked in the pond," Coral said. "It'll close when I go back through. Can one of you tell Willow I'm okay? I think she's worried about me, but I don't have time to run back to Half-Blood Territory."

"Wait," I said. "I can't dive into the ocean without a breathing spell, but I meant it when I said I'll help you. Darrow, can you watch the portal while I go back to the Lynn house?"

Darrow reached into his pocket, then his hand brushed mine. "I'm going to warn the half-bloods and ask for their help on the Sea Kingdom's behalf, then I'm coming after you. Take this."

He pressed something into my hand, and then he vanished, striding out of the palace entrance.

"Dammit, Darrow, I told you not to run off alone." I glanced down at my palm. "Berries?"

"For breathing," she said. "Where'd he get those?"

"Half-Blood Territory," I said. "Maybe he thought we might go to the memory-eater's place again."

Not that there was anything left of it, in all likelihood. When a Sidhe died, everything that was left of them disappeared. Even wraiths did, in the end.

I wouldn't let the same happen to Coral's home. Not on my watch.

Shoving the berries into my mouth, I chewed, grimacing at the soapy taste. Wearing my thick armoured clothes would slow me down, as would my iron weapons, but speed had never been my strong point and at least it'd be harder for the Vale beasts to claw at me with little bare skin on display.

I swallowed the berries. "Where'd you come in?"

"This way." Coral indicated the pond in the corner of the garden. "Hazel, please be careful. I know you have that talisman, but she means to drive us to extinction."

"I bet the Seelie Queen never intended to show her face. I can deal with her army." Gripping my staff in both hands, I followed her to the pond.

The surface churned, dark and murky, and the smell of saltwater rose from within. Then a wave cascaded over my head, sending me plunging into the ocean's depths.

The shock of the cold on my skin drove the breath from my lungs, while my clumsy limbs kicked and flailed. My heart lurched against my ribs, my hands clutching the staff by sheer instinct. Blinking against the stinging in my eyes, I followed Coral's tail, and we descended into a battleground.

Dark shapes moved beneath the water, sprouting limbs, warping from one shape to another. Armoured merpeople did battle with them, wielding shields and swords, while selkies either fought in the shape of humans or used their seal forms to create a barrier preventing the enemy from getting into the village's houses below.

But it wasn't enough. The village hadn't been put together to withstand a siege, and while stones were piled in the windows of the houses, they couldn't keep out the dead. Sluagh floated around, shape-changing at will, while wraiths drifted through the middle of the village in clouds of malevolent magic.

Ice flew from one wraith's hand, forming a spear that caught a merman in the throat. His blood darkened the water and his limp body floated beside his stricken companions.

I raised the talisman and took aim. Clouds of shadows whipped through the water and dissolved the wraith on contact. The merpeople and other fighters backed away from me, allowing me a clear path into the village.

"I have to find my mother," Coral said in my ear. "We need to deal with the armies, but I don't know where they're coming from."

"There must be a doorway open somewhere." I blasted another wraith with shadows, clearing the way for me to swim up to the other selkies. "Did any of you see where the army came from?"

A selkie shifted into the form of a frightened-looking young teenage girl. "They came from the land. The coastline is just over that way."

"Damn." I'd need to get *out* of the water to close the

doorway, which would leave the village undefended. "Hang on. I'll take care of these bastards first, then I'll close that doorway."

Clouds of darkness swirled around the staff, disposing of any wraith they touched. When the path was clear, I swam out into the gloom, unable to see any signs of the coast. I didn't know what the time limit on those berries was, and they didn't come with buoyancy or the other effects of the spell I'd used last time. Or night vision, but I had an alternative.

I tapped into my Gatekeeper's powers, the circlet's glow bathing the waters in an eerie light that made everything look twice as creepy but at least let me see more than a few inches in front of me. Swimming with the staff slowed me down even with its comparatively light weight, and the armoured clothes I wore didn't help, either. Ragged breaths escaped with every kick, and when my head broke the water's surface, the sunlight blinded me for an instant. Salt stung my eyes and caught in my throat. *Where's that blasted doorway?*

I trod water, my gaze snagging on the waves lapping against a beach on my right. I let the currents' momentum carry me over to the beach, depositing me on the shore.

Without a wet suit, my soaking clothes clung to my skin and left me shivering and salt-sticky. The briny smell of the coast filled my nostrils, and my limbs felt clumsy, weighted by more than just weapons. I used the staff as a walking stick to cross the beach, feeling more like a weak human than I had in a long time.

There it is. The doorway into the Vale lay open, a jagged slash against the sand. I shuffled towards it, limbs numbing with cold. Even in June, an unforgiving breeze swept off the coast, freezing the salt to my lips and seeping under my clothes. Gritting my teeth, I reached out and pulled the threads of the doorway together, erasing it from view.

Now all we had to do was get rid of the rest of the Seelie Queen's army.

Teeth chattering, I waded into the shallows, wishing I could shapeshift into an aquamarine creature just to make swimming bit easier. Not so much as a splash disturbed the ocean's surface, and a chill settled over me. Where had the Seelie Queen gone? Had she abandoned her armies, or directed them at the Summer Court instead?

I swam into the sea with strong kicks that propelled me into the path of a large wave. Despite the shock of submerging myself in the cold water again, I adjusted to the temperature quicker this time, moving with the currents instead of against them until I found myself pushed towards the darkness of the village below the water. I needed to find Coral so I could get the hell out of here and back into Summer before the Seelie Queen interrupted the third trial and declared war on everyone.

Even with my Gatekeeper's light, finding my way down was tough going, and it took several confusing minutes to realise I'd somehow bypassed the village altogether and was swimming above the Sea Queen's palace. Coral should be down there, so I descended over the hulking shape of the giant abandoned ship.

"Coral?" I called out, touching down on the bed of sand outside the door. It hung off its hinges, and there was nobody around. Had the Sea Queen been attacked and fled the place?

"Coral?" I called, louder.

I pressed on the door with my hands, pushing it inward. Movement stirred the waters, then a pale hand reached out of the shadows. The Sea Queen's fingers closed around my ankle, pulling me after her into the gloom of the abandoned ship.

12

"Ow!" I kicked out, but her nails dug in, sharp as iron, her free hand slamming the door behind me. "What the hell are you doing?"

With difficulty, I angled my talisman so that its shadowy magic came within inches of touching her. The Sea Queen released me at once. "You're the one they're after. You're the reason my people are dying."

Her hands reached for my throat, and I swung the staff at her, hitting her in the forehead. She fell back, her head bleeding, her eyes dazed.

"Watch it," I warned. "I'd rather not have Coral lose another family member. Why the hell are you attacking me? Who's after me?"

"Who isn't?" She gave a brittle laugh. "One wants your blood, the other wants you at her side, the others want you dead or a pawn, or both."

"Tell me something I don't know." My gaze went to the dark shape of the throne at the back of the hall. "Where's your talisman?"

"Gone." She let out a hiccoughing sob. "They took it."

"What?" I swam over to the throne, but her claw-like hand caught my ankle again, bringing a fresh bite of stinging pain. "Ow! I'm not your enemy. If the Seelie Queen has your talisman, I can get it back."

"It is not she who concerns me, and she'll be dead before she can use it."

I gave another firm kick, and her grip broke, her mad eyes staring into mine. *I thought her son stopped poisoning her.* I tasted bile at the back of my throat, mingling with the salt taste of the water. "What do you mean?"

"I told you," she croaked. "The false Queen wants you because she cannot undo your curse and guarantee her safety. The other Queen wants you to disappear because she knows what you are, what you may become. She saw to it, after all."

"What the hell do you mean?" I leaned away from her mad eyes. "The other Queen? Are you talking about Etaina?"

Questions swirled around my thoughts like the water currents, and I became aware of a mirror standing against the wall that hadn't been there before. The shimmering glass reflected my face back at me, and the glowing light of the Gatekeeper's mark on my forehead made me look like a ghost.

"I'm sorry you were attacked," I said, through gritted teeth, "but if you don't want the Seelie Queen to use that talisman to kill half the Court like she did to the Erlking, you have to let me go."

"She won't, and it's not hers to claim." A bitter smile tugged at her lips. "I am not long for this realm, Gatekeeper, but both you and that talisman you carry have the power to turn the tides of the war, and I will not allow either of you to leave."

Damn her. Not only did she want the talisman away from the warring queens, she wanted to keep me locked up in here so the Seelie Queen couldn't claim me.

"Yeah, no thanks," I said. "Where's Coral?"

"My daughter is fighting the invaders," she said, in dismissive tones. "I never wanted her to rule, you know. She's too soft-hearted, as kind as my son was foolish and self-centred. I made a mistake in not raising them myself, but I always knew my own end would spell the closure of our rule over the kingdom."

"If you want me to end you myself, just say so."

Shadows swirled around the staff's hilt. Her gaze followed the movement, her eyes sad, clouded. "That weapon should never have been allowed to endure."

"Believe me, if I ever get a spare moment, I'm going to find out if there's a volcano I can toss it into," I said. "Despite everyone wanting to get their hands on it, including Etaina. You *do* know who Etaina is, don't you? How? I thought you'd been stuck down here for decades."

I'd also thought she was half or quarter blood, close enough to human to live a normal lifespan, but surely that made it impossible for her to have known the leader of the Aes Sidhe back before the Courts had split several hundred years ago.

"The Lady of Light craves the power she felt she was denied." The Sea Queen gave a coughing laugh. The water reddened around her. "She sees the talisman as her right, the fool. Of all of us, she was the hardest for Oberon to contain. Harder even than her sister, if possible."

"You're older than you seem, aren't you?" I said. "You're not really half-blood at all. Are your children?"

She began to cry. Tears mingled with the water on her face, and the blood blooming around her mouth. *She's sick. Really sick.* But if she was full-blooded fae... she couldn't lie.

"I could not have children of my own," she whispered. "I adopted Coral and her brother and loved them as my own. After all, if I did not produce an heir, those hateful merpeople would claim leadership over the kingdom again upon my demise. I did what was necessary to secure my position. And now... now it seems we must die out after all."

"You can't have children," I said. "That's not an uncommon issue with the Sidhe, is it? Could the Erlking?"

"This is our curse," she said. "The curse of eternity has taken our lives one by one, and now we suffer and die for it. And you carry a curse of a different kind entirely, Hazel Lynn."

Damn. No wonder the Sidhe were sore about losing their immortality, if none of them could have biological children with one another.

The door opened with a clicking noise, and Coral swam into the hall. "Mother!"

"I don't know what happened—she's dying." I kicked back to give her space as she swam to her mother's side. "She was like that when I came in."

"She—she poisoned herself. I smell it in her blood." Coral pressed her hands to her mouth, a sob escaping.

My throat closed up. "Did you—did you hear? What she said to me, I mean?"

She nodded mutely, and shifted into her seal form,

releasing a howl of anguish. I trod water on the spot, my thoughts whirling. Coral knew her mother hadn't been her biological parent. She knew she wasn't the heir. Not by blood, anyway, which didn't matter when there were no other contenders—but would the rest of her Court see it the same way?

Several figures swam through the open door of the palace. Most were merpeople, with seaweed-like hair and gills rippling on their necks.

"The Queen is dead!" one of them howled.

The words travelled throughout their group, echoing away into the haze surrounding the Sea Kingdom's village. Within seconds, the merpeople surrounded me, their long hair wild, eyes hostile, and their weapons sharp.

"Neither of us killed her," I told them. "She poisoned herself."

"Where is her talisman?" Coral shifted into human form again, her voice choked.

Shit. "Gone. The Seelie Queen's army took it."

A mermaid with glimmering silver-blue hair swam up to me. "If that's the case, the two of you must leave this kingdom at once. You no longer have a claim to leadership."

"Give her a moment to grieve," I snapped. "Besides, Coral is the heir."

"She is not," said the mermaid. "This kingdom was ours first, and without that talisman of hers, you are nothing."

"All right." I raised the staff. "Coral, do you want me to turn them to ashes? Just say the word."

She shook her head. "No... if you do, there'll be nothing left of the Sea Kingdom."

I pointed the staff at the merpeople. "Back off, all of you. This is your last warning."

The merpeople shrank away from the shadows in my hands. Then cold hands closed around my throat, cutting off the air from my lungs. For an instant, I thought someone had grabbed me from behind, but the burning sensation came from within.

The effects of the berries were wearing off. I was drowning.

Coral swam up to me, an expression of alarm on her face. I felt her arms close around my shoulders and pull me out of the palace door. I struggled to cling onto consciousness, despite my lungs screaming for air—and then we were floating upwards, through the water and towards the spark of light in the distance.

13

I emerged in the palace garden in a shower of saltwater, to the sight of Darrow and several other half-bloods doing battle with the Vale's monsters.

Coral released me, and I staggered onto the lawn, shivering uncontrollably and coughing up mouthfuls of water. Using the staff to prop myself upright, I looked into Darrow's concerned eyes.

"Are you okay?" he asked.

"Yeah." My teeth chattered. "I wondered where you were. Glad you didn't follow me."

"So am I, considering I can't swim," he said.

"You can't? Seriously?"

"Where would I have learned?"

"Fair point." I scanned the lawn, which was strewn with the bodies of the Vale's beasts. "The Sea Queen is dead. The Seelie Queen's forces took her talisman, and now the merpeople want her throne."

Coral sank into a sitting position beside the pond, her expression dull and her eyes streaming. "They have as much of a claim on leadership as I do. More, if anything. They are prepared to fight for the crown. That talisman was the only leverage my family had left."

"Coral!" Willow left the other half-bloods and hurried over to join us. She knelt beside Coral with a comforting expression on her face. "It'll be okay. We got rid of the Seelie Queen's forces, and now the doorway is closed, there's no other way for them to get in."

"Gatekeeper!" The Erlking's sprite flew towards me, his expression panicked. "The third trial will start soon, and you should be with the other contestants."

"Oh, no." I coughed, shivering. "I dropped out. I never should have made it through to the third round to begin with, and besides which, I'm freezing cold and I just dropped half my weapons in the bottom of the ocean."

"You must, you must!" Warm air bathed me from head to toe, drying my clothes in an instant.

"Thanks, but really—I can't." I looked around and spotted Lady Aiten crossing the lawn behind him.

"Gatekeeper." Lady Aiten halted, her gaze landing on Willow and Coral embracing by the pond. "What is the meaning of this?"

I barred her path. "Coral just lost her mother and her Court at the same time. Besides, it might have escaped your attention, but your old king is dead, and you have nobody left to impress. If you're really that scared of being cast out as a traitor, you'd be in there watching the trials, not policing the choices of your adult daughter."

Her gaze cut to me. "You swore to use your talisman in defence of our Court, yet you abandoned us at the first opportunity."

"To help a friend!" I exploded. "Speaking of talismans,

the Seelie Queen just stole the Sea Queen's talisman—you know, the bow that's enchanted so it can't miss a shot—which is pretty damned relevant to your trials." Didn't mean she'd be able to claim it, but with the way my luck was going at the moment, she'd have it pointed at the next monarch of Summer before the third trial was over.

The blood drained from Lady Aiten's face. "I cannot leave the palace at a time like this. The Seelie Queen is still in the Vale, is she not? You will find her, Gatekeeper. That's an order."

Willow walked up behind me. "Do you need us to come with you to the Vale?"

I looked past her to the other half-bloods on the field. The only people who'd come to my aid in the end had been my former bodyguards. "I wouldn't ask you to risk your lives."

"We have to get that talisman," said Coral. "Even if it doesn't let me claim it—we can't let someone else use it to kill Summer's next leader. Not again."

"I won't let them," I vowed. "I'll use my own talisman to get it back, one way or another. Can you stay here and guard the doorway? I can pretty much guarantee the Seelie Queen will send more of her monsters through the instant I follow her."

"Doorway?" said Lady Aiten.

"Yes, doorway." I was done playing nice with her, or anyone else, for that matter. "I can't cross into the Vale without one, you know."

"Then you will do so at your own risk," she said. "All of you."

"Fine by us," said Willow, prompting a furious look from Lady Aiten.

As she swept away, I turned to Coral. "What do you want to do?"

"I want to retrieve my mother's body before those merpeople leave her to rot at the bottom of the ocean." She pushed to her feet, trembling. "Then I'm coming with you, Hazel."

My eyes stung, and not just from the saltwater. It seemed bitterly unfair that Coral had to lose so much at once and wasn't even allowed to grieve her mother in peace. Getting her mother's talisman back wouldn't solve all the problems in Faerie, but it'd remove a weight from all of our shoulders, especially hers. "I'll be back before you know it."

I found a clear spot on the lawn to open a doorway. While the water had vanished from my clothes, my skin felt salt-sticky and a persistent chill gripped me. I wasn't doing myself any favours by going into the Vale, either, but I was at the crux of the war in Faerie, whether I took part in the trials or not. I always had been, for as long as the Sidhe had pushed me between these ancient monarchs who cared nothing for the damage they did.

Even the Erlking. He was as much to blame as the others, for arrogantly assuming he'd live forever and that nobody else would have to deal with the talisman after his death. Like the others, who couldn't take responsibility for their own decisions if their lives depended on it. I might resent the hell out of them for leaving me to deal with the chaos they'd left behind, but that didn't mean I'd let them bring about humanity's end.

A doorway into the Vale opened at my command, allowing me to step through onto the silvery path.

Darrow entered beside me, his silver hair glowing as bright as the paths.

"The Seelie Queen didn't steal it in person, did she?" said Darrow.

"No, so I hope it's here," I said. "The Sea Queen didn't tell me who took it. She was dying. She poisoned herself, in fact. I guess she didn't see a way out, because her talisman was taken and the merpeople were beating down the doors of the palace."

"They drove Coral out?" he said. "Isn't she the heir?"

"No." I suspected everyone in Faerie would know soon. "The Sea Queen adopted her and her brother because she had no biological heirs and didn't want to lose her kingdom to the merpeople."

Darrow's eyes widened. "She did?"

"She told me before she died," I explained. "Turns out she was an immortal, not half-blood, and she couldn't have children of her own. Can't say I know why she told *me* that, but she wasn't exactly in a rational frame of mind. She's from the Erlking's generation, so she knew both Etaina and the Seelie Queen and knows they're both after me. Pretty sure she hasn't left the water in years, so I'm inclined to believe she was telling the truth."

Confusion furrowed his brow. "What did she know of Etaina?"

Of all of us, she was the hardest for Oberon to contain. If Oberon was the Erlking, then… was he the reason she'd ended up trapped underground? I'd thought her decision to split from Summer had been her own choice.

"She told me Etaina—or the Lady of Light—is out to claim power she was denied, which fits with what she told me herself the last time I spoke to her. Etaina implied the

Erlking tricked her out of securing the talisman, so we all know why she's so thrilled that I wound up claiming it myself."

Darrow wore a troubled expression. It couldn't be easy to hear the truth about the one person who'd been his unwavering supporter even when he'd lost the respect of the rest of his Court.

"She seemed to think the Seelie Queen's days were numbered," I added. "That she'd be dead before she had the chance to use the talisman she stole. Which I guess means she thinks Etaina will challenge her directly, and soon."

As for what else she'd said? *The other Queen wants you to disappear because she knows what you are, what you may become. She saw to it, after all.* Those words might be the rantings of a queen losing her grip on life and sanity, but whatever truth was within them was lost to the depths of the sea.

Darrow's body tensed, a knife sliding into his hand. "Someone's coming."

A dark shape crossed our path, the outline of a slight figure holding a crossbow appearing on the silver path of the Vale.

Aila. I'd thought she was dead, marked for execution after she'd aided Lord Daival in his attempt to murder the potential heirs to Summer.

"There you are," Aila said. "I wondered if you'd drowned along with your pathetic friend, human."

"Give Coral's talisman back," I warned. "Now."

"That would ruin the fun." She pointed the crossbow at me. "You've always thought you were better than us, haven't you? The lone human, blessed with the power of the Sidhe. You think you have the right to strut around here like you own the place."

"I never said that," I said. "I think you're a vain, self-centred bitch, but that has nothing to do with being human or not, or your magical talent. And I'm here because the Sidhe ordered me to find the depraved piece of shit who stole the Sea Queen's talisman and drove her to suicide."

"Killed herself, did she?" she said. "She had no right to wield this talisman. It wasn't the Erlking's to give away."

"What did the Seelie Queen offer you for it?" I said. "Let me guess... a chance at a bit of power? You know she's as likely to screw you over as anyone else in Faerie, right?"

She raised the bow and aimed an arrow at my chest. "Time for you to die, Gatekeeper."

An arrow arced towards me, and the world slowed down. Darrow pushed me out of the way, and I opened my mouth to shout a warning—but my own talisman got there first. Shadows burst out, turning the arrow into ashes.

Aila gave a startled yell, jumping away from the shadows. The bow trembled in her grip.

"You haven't claimed it, have you?" I held out my free hand. "Give it here before it kills you."

"You're no match for my talisman," she said. "I claim its magic as mine!"

The talisman glowed white-blue, and she dropped onto her back, her body convulsing. Blood and spittle flew from her mouth, along with cut-off cries. Darrow and I watched in silence as she flailed and struggled. The talisman had rejected her, and the price for failure was death.

The bow's brightness grew blinding, and Aila gave one final gasp before falling silent.

"Don't touch it!" I warned, as Darrow took a step forward. "It might think you want to claim it, too."

"Think?" he echoed. "The bow isn't alive."

'It was." I paced towards Aila's fallen body. "Some talismans—like mine, and the bow—were created using the magic of one of the Sidhe's predecessors. They were worshipped as gods, once, and because of that, part of them is still conscious even inside the talisman itself."

"Did you say *god?*"

"You bet. Etaina knew it, too," I said. "I hope my talisman is enough to stop it from doing the same to me."

My hand closed around the bow's edge, and at once, a shock jolted through my limbs, throwing me onto my back.

No. I'm not trying to claim you.

Darrow shouted my name, but I locked my hand around the bow again and lifted it off the ground. Images exploded behind my eyes, violent and stark.

An arrow slammed into the chest of a young half-Sidhe, sending him toppling onto his back. Another hammered into the heart of a huge tusked beast—one arrow, two, three—and it fell into a pile of trees with a tremendous crash. An arrow flew from the bow, arcing towards a throne of tangled, rotting roots.

The Erlking.

"Stop!" I screamed, but the Erlking didn't look up until the arrow found its home in his heart, sending him sprawling into the dirt.

Bile seared my throat. *I just saw the Erlking's death.* A

shiver racked my body, vibrating beneath my skin and trembling in my nerve endings. The Sea Queen had lived beside this talisman for years? No wonder she'd seen death as her only way out.

A jolt of disconnected anger shot through my blood as the glowing light of the bow made contact with the shadows in my other hand, followed by pain so all-encompassing that its light extinguished the darkness.

14

Water lapped above my head, lulling me to wakefulness. The hedges of the grove spun like a merry-go-round. I took in a gulping breath of clean air, then the darkness took me again.

The next time I woke, it was to my mother pushing a mug into my hand and ordering me to drink. Voices murmured around me, indistinguishable. As I drank, a rush of warmth spread to my fingertips, and the mug drooped in my hand as I fell into sleep once again.

When I opened my eyes again, it was to the incongruous sight of Darrow standing beside my bed, his silver hair gleaming in the bands of moonlight creeping across the floor through a gap in the curtains.

"Are you okay?" Darrow tilted his head in my direction. I blinked, disorientated as hell to see him in my childhood bedroom.

"What are you doing here?" I mumbled. "In fact, what am *I* doing here?"

"Your mother ordered me to bring you upstairs," he said.

I squinted suspiciously at him. "Isn't she concerned about leaving us alone in the same room?"

"You were unconscious and drooling all over the pillow when she left," he said. "Besides, we're not alone." A sprite flew into the light. Hummingbird blinked his large eyes at me, his pointed ears poking through his transparent hair.

"You brought your sprite here?" I pushed into an upright position. "Wait, the bow. The talisman. It rejected me, didn't it? How am I not dead?"

"That." He pointed to the staff leaning against the bed. "It opened a doorway back into Faerie and I got both of us through to the gate. I saw to it that Lady Aiten took the Sea Queen's bow safely to the palace and hid it before the trial started."

Right... the trials. It felt like an age since I'd dived into the Sea Kingdom to help Coral. "What time is it here?"

"Midnight," he said. "You should rest. The Court will call you when they need you."

I leaned back on the pillows. The bow was safely back where it belonged. Aila was dead, but I didn't pity her in the slightest. And Darrow... had brought me home. After our last major misunderstanding, I didn't want to drive him away again. "Thanks for getting me out of there."

"You're welcome." The human response made me blink, and he took a step backwards, making me very aware of the not-exactly-pristine state of my room. Most of my possessions hadn't been touched since I'd taken up my job as Gatekeeper, and when I recalled how spartan his own quarters had been, mine looked a total mess by comparison. Moonlight shone across stacks of paperbacks, discarded clothes, weapons, and other relics from an unconventional childhood.

"You could have cleared a space on the floor to sit down." I leaned over to push a stack of books under the bed and unearthed my annotated copy of *A Midsummer Night's Dream*.

"So you did read it," he said.

"You didn't think I read Shakespeare?" I said. "I did, back before I was Gatekeeper. I'd have more time to read if I wasn't always picking up after the Sidhe. I'm guessing you don't have a lot of time either."

"Etaina never encouraged me to learn to read," he said. "In fact, I asked Hummingbird to bring me the books so I could teach myself. She preferred her soldiers to focus on battle arts, not poetry."

"She didn't want you thinking for yourself," I surmised.

His gaze dropped. "I suppose I wasn't as good at following the rules than I thought I was."

"What, and it's not just me being a bad influence?" I winked at him.

He didn't smile back. "I spent my life following the rules of the Aes Sidhe and gained nothing in exchange but regret. Now I have no Court to call my own."

"You can call your mind your own." I met his eyes, wishing I could reach past Etaina's influence. "You taught yourself to read? That's awesome."

"Are you making fun of me?" he said.

"Of course not," I said. "I'm impressed. Really."

"I'm less good at writing," he said. "Terrible, actually. I

learned by copying from my own books, which is why they're covered in notes."

My mouth parted. I could read between the lines that that was one of many things he hadn't wanted me to see in his room. Part of me was doubly impressed, another part of me wanted to give Etaina a thorough lecture and then punch her in the nose.

"I didn't mean what I said before," I said. "I know you're not here because you're running away from her. Though I have to admit I'd like you to tell me why you stayed."

"I was hardly going to leave you in such a state, Hazel." He turned to Hummingbird, who'd settled to sleep on a pile of cushions. "Can he stay here? He might not be safe in the realm of the Aes Sidhe any longer."

"Sure, but you're not leaving," I said. "Grab some of those cushions and clear a space on the floor. Or you could join me on the bed, if you wanted to."

He frowned. "On the bed? I thought humans didn't practise such intimacy with strangers."

"Have you been reading up on us like we're an alien species?" A smile curled my mouth. "Besides, you're hardly a stranger."

He didn't look convinced, but he climbed into the bed next to me. A chill breeze swept under the covers, so I wrapped my arms around him.

He tilted his head. "What are you doing?"

"Snuggling. I'm cold."

He made a noise of protest, at least until my hands circled his hips, pulling me against him. Then a sharp exhale escaped. "Hazel, you can't expect me to believe you would touch every stranger you meet in this manner."

"How do you know? Besides, I have a reputation, remember?"

He rolled smoothly onto his back, deftly escaping my grip. "I regret that comment. It would be remiss of me not to admit I've been wanting to do such things to you that would make you forget all those past lovers."

I laughed. "There weren't *that* many. Besides, you wouldn't be that confident in yourself if you didn't have any experience to draw on."

He tilted his head to look at me, a smile playing on his mouth. "I'm fae. There's little we don't know about the application of pleasure."

Tension hummed between us like a current of electricity. I let my lips tease his, my nipples tightening under my shirt. A shudder went through his whole body,

"The things I want to do to you, Hazel Lynn," he murmured.

"Go on." I kissed him, hard, nipping at his lower lip.

Then his hands were all over me, under my shirt, bringing sparks of heat to my bare skin. I tugged impatiently at his clothes, my hands tangling in his armoured coat.

"You're not just wearing a glamour?" I freed my hands and pulled my own shirt over my head. "Pity. There'd be fewer layers to remove."

He shrugged out of his coat, his aquamarine eyes alight with mischief, then leaned in, kissing me fiercely. Heat exploded in my core, and I ground against him, drawing a moan from his lips. "Hazel—the curse—"

"I'm taking a contraceptive potion." I tugged his trousers down around his lean hips. "Alternatively, you could let me do the work here."

His breaths turned ragged as I slid my hand down his hardening length. Grinning, I quickened my pace, figuring out which movements made him writhe against me and beg for more, and how to draw out the pleasure until he was gasping. When I had him speechless on the bed, his aquamarine eyes dazed, I straddled him and let him pull my underwear down. "Your move."

At the first touch of his tongue, my whole body tensed. I guided his hands at first, then let him take over. He flipped me onto my back, sucking and licking until waves of pleasure jolted through my core. My back arched, and I gasped, collapsing into boneless bliss.

He released me, moving to my side. "Now I know another way to make you quiet."

"Quiet?" I grinned up at him. "Next time I'll make a point to scream loudly enough that the Sidhe can hear me on the other side of the gate."

"Next time?" A smile played on his lips. "How soon would that be?"

A spark entered the corner of my vision, then the window clicked open and the Erlking's sprite flew into the room.

"Hey!" I grabbed the covers. "Can you at least knock?"

Bloody faeries. Darrow didn't move, not self-conscious about his nakedness. Well, he wouldn't be. Every inch of him from his silver hair to his lean, muscular build was flawless.

"My apologies for interrupting, Gatekeeper, but the third task is over," said the sprite. "The next monarch of the Summer Court is ready to be declared."

I forgot all about my annoyance. "Who won?"

"Lord Talthain," said the sprite. "The crowning ceremony will be at high noon, as is custom."

Lord Talthain. I mentally ran through the list of contenders, and recalled a male Sidhe with pale, almost translucent skin and a spiky helmet who'd pulled his blade on me. Great. Well, it was probably too much to ask for the new monarch to be someone who actually liked humans.

I sank back onto the bed. A new monarch of Summer, who the Seelie Queen and the renegades wouldn't be able to deny had a right to the throne. It should be a victory, but a hard lump of dread settled in my chest.

At the sprite's expectant look, I attempted a smile. "There, you don't have to call me 'my Queen' anymore. Ever." *Thank the gods.* "I'll see you later."

"My pleasure, Gatekeeper." The sprite bowed, then flew out of the open window.

I scooted across the room to tug the window closed and pulled the curtains firmly shut. "That's it, then. The third trial is done, and we have a new monarch."

"You do." Darrow pushed to his feet. "Or you will, anyway. Do you want to discuss it with your family?"

"Hell, no." I let my arms circle his waist, pushing him onto the bed. "The sprite will tell her. I have other plans for the night."

His aquamarine eyes sparkled. "Such as…?"

I told him.

―――

I opened my eyes to find myself alone in the room. My body ached, in a good way, though that wasn't what had woken me up. The staff, leaning against my bed, was glowing, the runes on its length shifting and warping before my eyes.

I slid out of bed, padding to the bathroom. Despite my skittering nerves over Darrow's absence, it felt entirely too long since I'd had a proper shower. Unless you counted bathing in the pool of the Inner Garden, anyway. I tugged on a clean shirt and trousers, figuring I'd glamour them into a fancier outfit when the time came to head to the coronation.

Downstairs, I found Ilsa lay sleeping on the sofa in a pile of cushions and books. When I entered the room, she opened her eyes. "Good. You're awake."

"What are you doing here?" I said. "It's over. The new monarch took the throne. Or he will, in a few hours. You don't need to work on the family tree anymore."

Ilsa made an indistinct noise and shoved a handful of hair out of her face. "The Gatekeeper's family has to come to the coronation."

"Doesn't mean you had to camp out on the sofa. You do have a bedroom upstairs." I conjured up breakfast for both of us, wondering where Darrow had wandered off to, and grabbed a mug of coffee, propping my talisman against the side of the sofa.

"I offered to donate it to Darrow," she said. "Guess he decided not to take it."

"You don't seem surprised." I bit into an apple.

"Hazel, when you want something, you don't let a little thing like a lifelong family curse stand in your way," she said.

"Damn right I don't," I said. "Speaking of curses, you don't agree with Mum and think our curse is going to go haywire when the Summer Court's leadership switches over, do you?"

"I don't know, but something feels off." Ilsa reached into the pocket of her hoody and pulled out her talisman. A faint glow lit the book's cover from underneath, giving the raven's wings a brighter sheen than usual. "It's been doing that all night. Since the trial finished."

"Huh." I swallowed my mouthful and jerked my head at the staff. "Mine's been glowing, too. Not sure how long. I was asleep."

"Asleep, huh," she said. "Like Darrow wasn't in there with you all night."

"Where'd he go, do you know?"

"I saw him go outside." She yawned. "I asked if he was going back to Faerie, and he said no."

"Good. I bet Etaina will have to change her strategy now Summer has a new leader."

"Hmm." Ilsa pushed her plate away. "I'm more concerned about her sister. I find it odd that she didn't show up at the trials in person. And what did she have to gain from attacking the Sea Kingdom, anyway?"

"A bow that couldn't miss. Which the other Sidhe have now." Given their track record, though, perhaps I should have taken it myself. If it hadn't tried to kill me, that is. "Maybe she didn't want to risk being rejected. Aila tried to claim it and it killed her."

Ilsa's mouth pressed together. "Does it feel to you like all the gods' talismans are coming to the surface at the same moment? Do you think that's strange?"

"You've had yours for over a year," I pointed out, grabbing my plate. "I'm going to find Darrow. He can't have gone far."

I didn't see him in the garden, but when I drew closer to the Summer gate, I spotted a flicker of movement over the hedge. I headed that way, ducking into the Inner Garden. Darrow sat on a rock next to the pool, the same rock Ilsa had sat on when she'd stripped the talisman's magic out of me the first time, with Hummingbird perched on his shoulder. He lifted his head when I walked in and laid down my plate between us.

"Hey." I sat down next to him and tossed him an apple, which he caught. "If I was kicking you in my sleep, you could have just woken me. I wouldn't mind."

He turned the apple over in his hand. "I couldn't sleep, and I didn't want to disturb you. Besides, I haven't seen this pool of yours in its normal state. Where did its magic come from?"

I looked into the clear waters. "The Sidhe. Like everything else in our house, pretty much. Why?"

He bit into the apple. "It seems a generous gift, water that can heal any wound."

"Considering the faeries are the ones who inflict most wounds on me, it's fair compensation." I tossed my apple core into the bushes, where the Summer Court's magic eagerly swallowed it up. "It can also counter the magic of a certain staff."

Darrow's gaze flickered over the talisman. "Why is it glowing like that?"

I turned the staff over in my hand, admiring the play of light on the swirling symbols. "I don't know. Ilsa's is doing the same. She thinks it's a bad omen. Or a reaction to Summer's change of leadership."

Despite my light tone, Ilsa's words had worried me. My sister's hunches were rarely just that. She'd carried her talisman for longer than I'd had mine, and she'd even met the god whose magic was contained within it, giving her an insight few others had. Granted, Ilsa's talisman was different than most, since it had more power in the mortal realm than it did in Faerie, and the god who'd created it hadn't been an amoral force of destruction like the Devourer.

"Have I seen Ilsa's talisman?" he asked. "What does it look like?"

"The Gatekeeper's book," I said. "A book with a raven on the cover she carries in her pocket everywhere. It's a bit less destructive than mine. Well, if you count opening the gates of Death as less destructive, anyway."

"I thought you were embellishing the truth when you said that," he said. "How did she come by the talisman?"

"Inherited it," I said. "Another family member of ours —not a Gatekeeper—made a deal with the god in order to fight a bunch of angry wraiths and bound its power to the book. That's why Ilsa can banish them."

"Wraiths are dead Sidhe." He threw his apple core into the bushes.

"Only those who die in the Vale," I said. "If Ilsa ever looks super stressed out, it's probably because she's one of the few humans who *can* banish them. She's forever having to drive faerie ghosts out of Edinburgh, and now she's being dragged into doing the same in Faerie. I don't know why the Seelie Queen decided an undead army was her best bet of winning the throne. It won't win her much support in Summer."

"No, but if few people can fight the wraiths, she may plan to win her throne by sheer force," he said. "Did you say she wanted to rule the Vale?"

"That too," I said. "She only wants to win Summer to stick it to her dead husband, from what I figure. She called herself Queen of the Vale when she tried to force me to stand at her side."

"Where did the Vale come from?" he asked.

"You're full of questions today," I commented. "The Vale was created when the Sidhe kicked their gods out of Faerie. After stealing their magic to put into their talismans, that is."

His eyes widened. "So what you said yesterday... your talisman..."

"Why do you think Etaina wants it?" I said "She and the Erlking have a feud going back hundreds of years. It all goes back to their little group who screwed over their own gods to gain power. Yes, I include the Erlking among them. He was no saint, that's for damned sure."

But if that was the case, how had the Gatekeepers wound up entangled in their feud? One lone human who wandered into Faerie by accident a few centuries back shouldn't have ended up caught in a war between the most powerful Sidhe in the realm, those who coveted and wielded the power of the gods. Not only were the Sidhe unable to get rid of us, Ilsa and I had both claimed talismans. Surely the Sidhe who'd bound us hadn't planned for that to happen.

"Who's that?" Darrow pointed through the hedge to a figure crossing the lawn, a woman with dark hair and a bright blue light emanating from the circlet on her head.

"My cousin. Hang on." I stepped out of the grove. "Holly?"

Holly jumped, spinning around to face us with a half-unsheathed blade in her hand. "Don't sneak up on me like that, Hazel."

"Figured it was me you wanted to see," I said. "What is it? Bit early for a social call."

On Holly's brow, the Gatekeeper's circlet gleamed with bright Winter energy, while the swirling symbol beneath matched the one on my own forehead. Her plain dark clothes were laced with armoured padding and edged in silver and blue. She was dressed, in fact, as though she was ready for battle.

"Someone just broke into my house," she said. "And it's your sister I'm looking for, actually. The thing that broke in... I'm pretty sure it's a wraith. I can't see it all that well, but it's loose in the garden and I think it's following me."

Great.

"All right, I'll get Ilsa." I headed back to the house to find Ilsa standing in the doorway expectantly. "Wraith, coming this way."

"Oh, bloody great," Ilsa said, whipping out her talisman. The book's glow brightened, the raven on the cover shifting position as she advanced across the lawn.

A tiny winged shape zipped past her, his wings beating fast. The Erlking's sprite. "Danger!" he shouted, flying in circles above our heads.

"What's wrong?" I asked.

"*She* plots to take the throne," he howled, "and terrible things will happen at the coronation if we don't stop her."

"Hold up," I said. "You mean the Seelie Queen? What's she doing, planning to kill the monarch?"

He shook his head. "I am bound to serve the next monarch from the instant they put on the crown. This is your last chance... the last chance to stop him."

"Him?" I echoed. "You mean her, the Seelie Queen. Right?"

Then it hit me. The next monarch...

Ilsa swore. "She rigged the contest. One of her people is going to take the throne."

The next king of the Summer Court was working with the Seelie Queen.

15

For an instant, we all stared at one another, including Holly. After everything I'd done, everything we'd sacrificed... the Seelie Queen was going to take the throne anyway.

"Shit." My heart lurched. "It's my fault he was able to get away with it. I went off to the Sea Kingdom and then the Vale when I should have been in the trial—not that I'd planned to get involved anyway, because I thought we were safe."

"Even if you hadn't gone to the Sea Kingdom, he'd have still been in the running for the throne," said Darrow. "If I hadn't got distracted in the second trial—"

"Distracted? Assassins came after us." I scuffed the ground with my foot. "Okay, forget the blame game. How the hell do we prove the guy's working with her? I bet he framed those two other Sidhe for cheating, too."

"You're probably right," said Ilsa, white-faced. "Swift... any ideas?"

"You must stop him!" he insisted. "Two are already dead."

"Two…" I trailed off. "He killed that Sidhe in the second challenge. It wasn't the assassins."

The next monarch of Summer had killed two of his fellow Sidhe. Anger gripped me. How dare the Seelie Queen drive the Summer Court into chaos without even showing her face in person? She treated even her fellow Sidhe like pawns. Look at Lord Daival. And they still served her.

Ilsa hesitated. "I think I know how we can prove it, but it won't be a popular idea."

"Ilsa, I thought you said you wouldn't raise the dead in Faerie," I said. "You refused to raise the Erlking for the same reason."

"Yes, I know," said Ilsa. "But all spirits go into the Death Kingdom after they die. I should know, I nearly went there myself."

"Wait, you want to go and find the ghosts of the Sidhe she murdered in the *Death Kingdom*?" I said. "Don't you remember how it went last time? I seem to remember Lord Raivan insisting ghosts weren't real."

"They might say differently with wraiths attacking the Court every other day," said Ilsa. "I don't know, it's all I've got. I'll go there, and you go to the ceremony, Hazel."

"It's not for a few hours still, in Faerie's time," I said. "Besides, if we find the ghosts first, there won't *be* a ceremony."

Why am I agreeing to this? Going into the lands of the dead had not been on my bucket list, but I was out of ideas on how to prove Lord Talthain's treachery before the Seelie Court furnished him with a crown.

"The Death Kingdom?" said Holly. "You know that's in the Winter Court, right?"

The sprite let out an anguished howl. "She has the dead on her side, and if she gathers any more, the living will fall."

I looked between the sprite and Holly. "*She* isn't in the Death Kingdom, is she? Is that how she raised the memory-eater from death?"

The sprite shook his head. "I know nothing of those dark magics, Gatekeeper. I would not ask you to walk down the path of the dead, but if you wish to stop her... you may have no choice."

The Path of the Dead. The place where I'd been crowned as Gatekeeper.

"Maybe..." Ilsa trailed off. "Morgan, you can come out now."

Morgan stepped out from behind a hedge. "I didn't mean to eavesdrop. Pepper wanted to find a piskie to chase and found a sprite instead."

The cu sidhe barked in agreement, running in circles around the lawn. Hummingbird flew into the air with a squawk of alarm, and Darrow let him land on his shoulder out of reach of the puppy.

"A likely story," said Ilsa. "Let me guess, you want to tag along."

"I raise the dead for a living, too, remember?" said Morgan. "Also, Pepper's a tracker dog who's trained to attack ghosts. You want me on your team."

"Did you say he's trained to attack *ghosts?*" said Holly dubiously.

"Yeah, he is," said Ilsa. "Morgan, you're free to come,

but only if you promise not to bring your boyfriend. Just the puppy."

"Hey!" Holly said. "I didn't promise anything, least of all a free trip to the Death Kingdom. If the Morrigan catches me, she'll have her crows strip my flesh from my bones."

Ilsa looked at her. "Don't you need me to banish a wraith for you? Let us use your gate and I will. We'll make our own way from there."

"I can't let you do it alone," she said. "You'll need my help to get from Winter's gate to the Death Kingdom without being caught by the Sidhe. And even then, I don't know what you'll face over there."

Like the Seelie Queen. I couldn't think of any reason for her to take an interest in the furthest region of Winter, but the Death Kingdom was one of the parts of Faerie that lay closest to the Vale, aside from the borderlands. For all we knew, she'd been travelling back and forth from there ever since she'd escaped from jail.

"We'll risk it," said Ilsa.

Holly sighed. "If the Unseelie catch you, you're dead. You can use the gate, but please, try not to draw attention."

As Ilsa and Morgan followed her, I turned to Darrow. "Still want to come along? This is your last chance to drop out."

"The Death Kingdom," he said. "I've heard nothing good about that place."

"Leave it to my sister," I said. "She's Gatekeeper of Death. This is her area of expertise."

I hope. My talisman might be enough of a deterrent to

keep the dead from attacking us, and Ilsa's, too, but if the Seelie Queen was lurking over there while she waited for her ally to be crowned, we'd have a whole other battle on our hands.

He dipped his head. "Hummingbird will watch your house. If we end up in trouble, call his name, and he'll come to aid us."

We left through the front gate and walked down the country lane towards the second Lynn house. The home of the Winter Gatekeeper had stark white walls the colour of ice, contrasting the ivy-covered walls of my own house visible on the other side of the fence in Holly's back garden.

Darrow glanced over his shoulder. "Didn't we just leave your house? How can it be over there as well?"

"We're close enough to Faerie that the usual laws of space-time don't apply," I answered. "This is a liminal space, so it loops around in a circle. If we walked across that field, we'd end up right back where we started."

"Oh, there's the wraith." Ilsa stepped forwards as a shadow passed over the fence in a cloud of cold energy. "Go and bother someone else."

"Or else I'll disintegrate you," I added, waving the staff. Holly gave me a suspicious look, edging away from me, but Ilsa's magic did the trick. A wave of icy energy smashed into the wraith and it disappeared, leaving us alone on the path.

Holly led the way past bare trees, their arm-like branches swaying in the bitterly cold breeze, and down the side of the whitewashed house into her back garden. Unlike ours, there was no grove, no pool of healing water, and the snow-covered lawns seemed desolate in comparison. Despite that, there was a cold beauty to the jewelled snowflakes clinging to the bushes and the sharp twigs jutting from the hedges like broken bones. Beautiful and terrifying pretty much summed up Winter. Summer hid their treachery behind their smiles. When Winter smiled, people died, generally in unpleasant ways.

Holly halted beside the Winter gate. Its hawthorn points glistened with ice rather than moss and weeds like ours, but the same swirling symbol marked the top. *Gatekeeper.*

Holly ran her fingertips over the edge of the gate. "It's said that Thomas Lynn went into Faerie this way."

"They say the same about our gate," I said.

"They can't both be true, can they?" said Morgan.

"This is Faerie," said Ilsa. "So I'd say yes, they can. Are you coming with us, Holly?"

She shot Ilsa a frown. "You all owe me for this."

"Yeah, it's not like we're preventing a war or anything." Morgan peered through the gate, while the faerie dog whimpered at the cold. Holly's dark hair and ice-white circlet blended into the bare scenery on the other side, but even glamouring my circlet didn't take away the greenish edge to its sheen.

I still glamoured my clothes, darkening the colour and giving the illusion of armour. Darrow, meanwhile, wore a glamour that made his clothes look like the armoured outfit he'd worn to train me as Gatekeeper.

"Want me to glamour you?" I asked Ilsa.

"If we're going to the Kingdom of Death, we'll stick out no matter what," she said. "Pretty sure the only living creatures there are banshees and redcaps."

"Please try not to bleed on anything," said Holly. "Those redcaps can take you apart with their bare hands."

"We know," I said. "We *have* dealt with Faerie ourselves, you know."

"Not the Death Kingdom." Her gaze lingered on Darrow. "You're a hybrid, right? Do you have a contact in Winter?"

He shook his head. "I never knew my father."

"Well, that's inconvenient," she muttered. "This way."

The Erlking's sprite tugged on my collar. "I cannot go with you, not if I don't want to draw the Court's suspicions about my absence. I should not have left them for so long."

"Don't put your life in danger," I told him. "Go back to Summer… maybe find Lady Aiten or Lord Raivan. Someone who we know isn't working with the enemy."

Not on purpose, anyway. Damn, the situation was a total clusterfuck.

"Good luck, Gatekeeper." The sprite flitted out of sight, and I slipped after the others through the gate.

A cold breeze drifted down the leaf-strewn path, but not as cold as Holly's garden. I knew this part of Faerie, which consisted of a single path connecting both Summer and Winter. The borderlands lay somewhere in between, though as in all of Faerie, only the general directions stayed the same.

"Are you sure you can find the way?" I asked Ilsa.

"Maybe." Her doubtful eyes scanned the path, which led to the Winter Court on the right-hand side. "This isn't quite how I remember."

Holly made an impatient noise. "Do *not* draw any attention, that clear?"

She marched down the path towards Winter territory. In no time at all, the trees turned leafless and dry, their branches twisting into sinister patterns like contorted limbs, while the temperature dropped with every step.

Ilsa pulled out her talisman, letting its bright blue glow spread over the path. "Damn. I can see them, but I wouldn't know which of them was the murder victim."

I halted. "Wait, you can see ghosts? Here?"

"Sure," said Morgan, his gaze flickering among the trees. "I thought you all could."

Not me. Not Darrow or Holly, either. "We don't all have the spirit sight."

Darrow met my eyes. "The ghosts aren't like wraiths, are they? They can't harm us?"

"Regular ghosts?" I said. "They're as harmless as you can get, assuming you can see them."

"How do you expect the ghosts to testify if nobody can see them?" asked Darrow.

"They can use glamour to make themselves visible to anyone," I explained. "If they know we're looking for them, that is. Ilsa, try calling their names. Lord Walvein and Lady Horell."

In the mortal realm, Ilsa just needed to say a dead person's name to draw their attention, but I doubted anyone had ever tried the same in Faerie.

She repeated the names, then shook her head. "I think we're going to have to go deeper into the Death Kingdom."

"Great." I walked alongside Darrow, whose evident confusion prompted me to add, "To summon a person from Death, you need their name. You also need candles and a bunch of other preparatory crap if you're in the mortal realm and it might not work even then. Unless you're the Gatekeeper of Death, that is."

Holly walked ahead of our group, not speaking. I wondered if she remembered she'd once tried to take Ilsa's talisman for herself, believing she was the rightful owner. She'd been trying to stop her mother's wraith from escaping at the time, but we'd come damned close to a world-destroying family feud ourselves.

The path angled uphill, weaving between shadowy trees. Spiked plants flanked the path, their leaves crimson like bloodstained knives, while a chill breeze swept overhead. Every exhale fogged the air, and I buried my free hand in my pocket, the other gripping the staff. Darkness swirled around its edges, symbols shifting up and down its length.

"Someone's tap-dancing on my grave," Morgan muttered, and the faerie dog whined in agreement. "Who rules this place, anyway?"

"The Morrigan, a nasty shapeshifting faerie who can turn into a giant crow," I said.

"She's in good company." Ilsa held up her book to show the image of a raven on the cover, which had moved to spread its wings as though it wanted to jump off the page and fly away.

"The Morrigan eats souls," said Holly. "I don't doubt she'll have seen the spirits you're looking for, but she claims to remember everyone who passes through her territory."

"Eats souls," said Morgan. "Not living people's souls, right?"

"Not as long as you don't insult her," said Holly. "The Winter Court keeps her in check. She's bound so she can't leave her lair, but that doesn't stop others from visiting her."

"Let's just hope they aren't working together, then," said Ilsa. "Her and the Seelie Queen. I wouldn't put it past her to convince the Morrigan to take her side."

It was just the kind of trick the Seelie Queen would pull to gain yet more allies, and it fitted with her sudden interest in gathering an army of the dead from the Vale.

Maybe we shouldn't have come here after all.

An eerie wailing noise came from within the trees. Holly drew a sharp iron knife—clearly, Winter hadn't forbidden her from carrying iron—and faced the bushes, from which a feminine figure with long hair trailed towards us. A banshee.

She bared her sharp canines in a smile. "Human prey walks willingly into my lair. Three humans, no, four humans. I will feast well today."

I whipped the talisman out, sending a jet of shadows towards her. The banshee danced out of range, unleashing out a shriek that pierced my eardrums and vibrated through my whole body. *Ow.*

Holly raised her hand and threw her knife. It sank into the banshee's chest, cutting off her scream. "We'd better move. Banshees can't die. They always come back."

"Not in the same body, though." With the Sidhe's immortality source gone, the only true immortals left were banshees, who were reborn into a new body after their demise, sometimes several years down the line and often with no memory of their past. It shouldn't surprise me that the Seelie Queen would take an interest in their domain, yet I saw no signs of the her, only the dead and those who fed upon them.

The memory-eater's realm must be closer to Death than I'd thought, though, given the odd mist seeping through the trees. That, or all of Faerie's outer edges came with the same creepy scenery. At least gravity stayed the same, but a foul smell grew in intensity the further we walked. Crimson soaked the mud, and further off, a group of redcaps tore the wings off some small creature, bathing their pointed hats in its blood.

"I understand why you don't get much tourism here," Morgan said, wrangling the cu sidhe back onto the path and away from the bloodthirsty creatures. "C'mon, Pepper, you aren't scared of ghosts. This place isn't that scary, either."

"Famous last words," Ilsa muttered.

Ahead of our group, Holly crested a hill. "We're here."

I caught up to her at the hill's peak. Ahead of us lay a moat, but instead of water, it was blocked with bodies piled high enough that those below were crushed into a mass of limbs. Bones jutted out at angles, and blood filled the gaps in a gory current. Inside the centre of the moat was what appeared to be a giant mound of earth and stone.

I held my breath, swallowing bile, while Morgan retched into the bushes. "What the hell is this?"

"That," said Holly, "is the Morrigan's lair. I hoped she'd redecorated since the last time I came here, but I guess not."

"You came here voluntarily?" I said incredulously.

"Mostly to deliver messages between the Morrigan and the Unseelie Queen," Holly said, her mouth twisting with distaste. "Angry ones, judging by the temper tantrums she throws. Don't piss her off, and for god's sake don't feed the birds."

"I'm more worried about something eating us," said Morgan, wiping the back of his mouth on his sleeve. "This is fucked up even by Faerie's standards."

"It's the Kingdom of Death," said Ilsa. "What did you expect, an inflatable pink bouncy castle? Let's get this done."

I averted my gaze from the gory currents of water, holding my breath as we crossed the bridge over the moat to the Morrigan's lair. When we touched down on the other side, a towering ogre lumbered into view, his mossy green skin caked with gore.

"Who are you?" he growled.

"Hazel Lynn," I said. "Gatekeeper. Three of us are, actually. Summer, Winter and Death."

"There is no Gatekeeper of Death," he said, baring bloodstained teeth.

Ilsa cleared her throat and held up the Gatekeeper's book. "I'm Gatekeeper of the humans' Death, not Faerie's. May we please speak to the Morrigan? It's a matter of urgency concerning the whole of the faerie realm, including the Courts."

The ogre's gaze travelled across our group. Morgan hid behind Ilsa, while the faerie dog hid behind his legs. Darrow, meanwhile, stuck out even more than the two humans did, with his fine silver hair and astonishingly bright eyes. The ogre, however, stared at the staff in my hand, a growl slipping between his teeth.

"That is a creation of dark magic," he muttered. "If you use it against my mistress, you will lose your soul."

"No danger of that happening." I held my breath, waiting, and he lumbered aside to allow us to enter the tent-like heap of earth and stone.

As we walked into the gloomy cave, a flock of birds flew overhead, squawking loudly. Clouds of firefly-sized faeries hovered beneath the domed ceiling, alighting on a throne in the centre of the cave. A human-sized figure sat there, dressed all in black. As we drew closer, she snatched a glittering crown from the beak of one of the birds and replaced it on her head with a muttered curse.

The Morrigan looked like a crow shifter had got stuck halfway between forms. Her pointed ears and jagged face were human, but her jet-black hair and wing-patterned armour mirrored the feathered animals flitting around the room. She had wings of her own, too, large ones, pinned behind her back by the same chains that bound her body to the throne.

Darrow came to a dead stop. "That's iron."

I'd heard the Morrigan was one tough creature, but I hadn't expected to see human-style iron chains wrapping around her body and locking her ankles together. When her eyes met mine, cold fear locked me to the spot. The talisman jumped to attention, shadows whirling around the hilt.

"Control that thing," she growled. "Have you come to threaten me?"

"Nope," I said. "We have questions. Have you seen two Sidhe from Summer who recently died pass through here?"

"I see many Sidhe," she said. "Many others, too."

"Lord Walvein and Lady Horell," I went on. "They were murdered, and I need to borrow their ghosts to testify to Summer. Urgently. Like, within the next two hours."

"Borrow?" she echoed. "I cannot return the souls I have devoured, mortals."

"You ate them." No shit, Hazel. *Now what am I supposed to do?* "Have you seen the Seelie Queen recently, then? She's building an army of wraiths in the Vale and I wondered if she'd paid you a visit."

"I wouldn't know." She adjusted her position on the throne, her chains clanking. "I am not permitted to leave my cave, by the orders of the Unseelie Queen. I have not seen the traitor of Summer. If she came to my kingdom, she did not speak with me."

Damn. "Well, she brought the memory-eater back from death. How?"

"That one?" she said. "The souls of her kind are poison to me. Too many memories create a bitter taste. I did not devour her soul, so perhaps the Queen found a way to ensnare her."

"I used this to kill her the second time." I raised the staff. "She'd better not come back after that."

The Morrigan hissed. "Keep that abomination to yourself, mortal. I have no involvement in the Gatekeeper's arguments, nor will I get involved in your struggles over the remnants of the gods' magic."

"The Seelie Queen threatens more than just Summer," I told her. "She won't stop with our Court. In a few hours, a monarch will be crowned, someone who doesn't deserve to be on Summer's throne. There'll be war and bloodshed that might consume the whole of Faerie."

"Why would I object?" she said. "The more souls I gain, the better."

Ugh. "She might try to kill you, too. Or replace you."

"Is there a point to this warning?" said the Morrigan. "Many have threatened my rule in the past, but none can displace me. I am eternal, after all."

"There are others who would say the same," Darrow said.

The Morrigan gave him an appraising look, and a wicked grin curled her lip. "You're one of *hers*, aren't you? Oh, this is interesting. How I wish I could see *that* unfold."

"What's she talking about?" Holly hissed.

Nobody answered her.

"Just what I thought," Darrow said. "You know of her. You're old enough. What if the person threatening your position was her, and not the Seelie Queen?"

"You think I fear the Lady of Light?" She cackled. "If you cross her, mortal, it will not be I who devours your soul."

Darrow took a step closer to her, the outline of his body glowing brighter than the fireflies on the ceiling. "Tell me. Why would the Seelie Queen amass an army of the dead? What is her goal?"

"Her goal?" said the Morrigan. "The dead can get into places the living cannot, and as the Huntsman rides no more, perhaps she means to take his place. Whatever her goal, it holds no interest for me. She was always the weaker of the two sisters."

"What does she mean?" said Ilsa. "What *is* he doing?"

"Glamouring her," I whispered. "Etaina's last order was for him to kill the Seelie Queen. I guess he wants to know whose side the Morrigan might take if this comes to war."

"What the hell is going on?" Holly said.

"Your guess is as good as mine," said Morgan.

Darrow. Stop glamouring the goddess of Death. I gave him a look to convey the same, but his eyes were on the Morrigan.

"The Seelie Queen is weak," said the Morrigan. "The Lady of Light might believe herself eternal, but it is I who will endure beyond all others. Leave now, mortals."

16

"Are you out of your mind?" I whispered to Darrow as we left the Morrigan's territory behind. "What was that?"

"A gamble," he said.

"She knows Etaina," I said. "You guessed?"

"With her being as ancient as she is, I suspected they would have met."

And he'd thought it was worth pulling his glamour on her. I was no longer sure I knew him. He was something else, something strange and... well, fey. It set my blood rushing in my veins.

"The Huntsman," I said, recalling her words. "Wasn't he the guy who led the rebels who attacked Earth?"

"You've got it," said Ilsa. "Originally, he carried the souls of the dead into the afterlife. Don't ask me why the Seelie Queen would want to take his role for herself, though. I can't picture her riding a horse around collecting souls. Besides, the Path of the Dead is abandoned now."

The Path of the Dead. Chills sprang to my arms. The path had once been the route the Sidhe had travelled in order to become immortals, but it haunted me for a different reason. On that path, I'd claimed the title of Gatekeeper and my fate had been sealed.

I turned to Holly. "I guess you know it all now, but… if the Seelie Queen wins the throne, I bet she comes for Winter's next. Is there the slightest chance anyone from Winter might work with us to stop the coronation?"

"Winter doesn't interfere in Summer's disputes," she said. "No exceptions."

"It won't just be Summer's problem if this goes on," I reminded her. "And that's assuming Etaina lets the Seelie Queen take her throne without a fuss."

"Who's Etaina?" she said.

"Someone even worse than the Seelie Queen, if possible," said Darrow.

"She has an army of evil clones," I added. "They have Summer eyes and all of them look exactly the same. They're also masters of glamour."

"Hold up," said Holly. "They're *not* the Seelie Queen's? How many evil queens are we dealing with, then?"

"Just the two, unless the Morrigan and the Unseelie Queen want to make it a quartet," I said. "At least we know the Seelie Queen didn't come to speak with the Morrigan."

Or Etaina either. But that didn't mean she wouldn't take their side if necessary. The old crow was out for herself alone.

Holly came to a halt at the edge of the path leading from Winter territory back to the Summer Court. "I doubt the Unseelie Queen will want to send any of her people to help, but Lord Lyle has battled the Vale monsters alongside Summer before. I might be able to persuade him to cooperate."

"Thanks," I said. "If you can get anyone from Winter to help, you might just save all of Faerie."

"No pressure, huh." Holly gave a brief half-smile, then she walked away.

"Are we going home?" Morgan turned on the spot. "Wait, I know this place. I remember coming this way when River and the other half-faerie got into a fight."

"The borderlands," I said. "They're not far off. I suppose Raine and Cedar might help... but we'll have to move fast if we want to make it to the coronation."

"Are you sure?" said Ilsa. "Hazel, you said the borderlands were dangerous."

"Times change," I said. "Their territory now belongs to the half-faeries. It's not quite their own Court, but they're the only people likely to ally with us against Summer."

Darrow and I led the way, not speaking. The stench of the Morrigan's cave seemed to cling to my skin, while the eerie quietness of the borderlands made my body tense. It was a relief when we came to the half-bloods' palace. A fence surrounded the perimeter, and thankfully there wasn't a troll in sight.

"I like this place more than the Morrigan's already," said Morgan. "No rivers of blood or dead things in sight."

Two armoured half-faeries stood outside the gates, one of whom I recognised from last time.

"Hey," said the dark-haired female guard I'd seen the last time I'd been here. "You're here to see Raine and Cedar, right?"

She beckoned a sprite to her side, who looked us up

and down before flitting over to the palace doors and entering.

"How d'you know we aren't invaders?" Morgan wanted to know.

"Because no other humans would be foolish enough to wander around the borderlands at a time like this," answered the guard. "Raine, they're here to see you."

The door opened, and the sprite flew out, followed by Raine, a female half-Sidhe with long, white-blond hair and the shimmering blue eyes of an Unseelie. She wore a silver crown atop her head, her armoured clothing decorated with silver and blue. "Oh, hey, Hazel. Who are these humans?"

"My siblings, Ilsa and Morgan. And Darrow, you've met." The faerie dog barked, chasing his own tail in a circle. "That's Pepper. We can bring pets in, right?"

"If not, I'd have to kick out Volt here." The guard held out her hand to catch her sprite.

Raine nodded. "Come on in. There's someone here who's going to be glad to see you're alive."

We walked the short distance to the palace doors and followed Raine inside. A number of half-Sidhe filled the main room, including...

Ilsa stepped forward. "River, what are you doing here?"

"Looking for you," he said. "I checked the ambassadors' palace, but I didn't see you there, so I thought you might have come here. Is that blood on your shoes?"

"Sorry," she said. "We had a situation. Which is now escalating. I think you need to talk to your father." She walked over to him, talking urgently. From River's aghast expression, she'd just told him about the Morrigan.

"Oops," I said. "I guess she didn't have time to text him before we went through Winter's gate. Mum's going to kill us."

"Bet she thinks it was all my idea," said Morgan, restraining Pepper from chewing on the edge of a tapestry. "Wait, Mum's supposed to be at the coronation, right?"

"Shit," I said. "What time is it?" In Faerie, time was fluid, but the tangled trees of the forest made it hard to pinpoint the position of the sun even when it was imitating the one in the mortal realm.

"Two hours until noon," said Raine.

Two hours to prevent Faerie from falling. "Can I talk to you alone?"

"Sure." She walked through the hall to a door at the back, leading the way into a room decorated with tapestries. Cedar stood on the other side, speaking to another half-Sidhe. Like Raine, he wore an armoured coat and a simple crown atop his silky dark hair, which flowed past his shoulders. He didn't look surprised to see Ilsa or River, but his brows arched at the sight of Morgan pulling the faerie dog away from the tapestries before the door closed behind Darrow and me.

"Your missing human showed up, then?" He dismissed the other half-blood with a nod of thanks. "Lord Torin's son tried to recruit half my people to rescue your sister."

"Why'd you let him come in here?" I asked. "I thought you and River hated one another."

"We were at cross-purposes once. Now we are not."

That was faeries for you. Even for half-bloods, loyalties shifted like their mercurial tempers, and friends one day might be foes the next. Okay, perhaps humans weren't that different, but still.

"Did he come here to tell you about the downfall of the Summer Court, or do I have to give you the bad news?" I addressed both Cedar and Raine.

"Bad news?" echoed Raine.

"Really bad," I said. "To put it mildly, things have gone to shit. The Seelie Queen is about to put one of her puppets on Summer's throne. There's also another rogue queen out there who might declare war on her before or after, and who also happens to be after my talisman. The Morrigan won't help us, nor will the Unseelie Queen, and most of the Summer Sidhe think they're electing a genuine leader. So, if any of you are willing to volunteer to help us fight, I'd appreciate it."

Raine's mouth parted in surprise, and a gleam at her waist pointed to the sceptre she wielded as her talisman. "The Summer Court's Sidhe were fooled so easily?"

"Of course they were." Cedar's tone was calm, but his hazel eyes shimmered with magic. "If their former monarch was involved, it's no wonder."

"The Erlking picked out the potential heirs before he died," I explained. "No doubt you heard. The trials were supposed to be a fair way to assess their abilities, but the Seelie Queen had spies among the contenders who rigged the results."

"There are spies among the half-Sidhe, too," Darrow added. "One of them attacked us in the Vale, and several others set upon me in the forest."

Raine's expression clouded. "We had a few people choose to leave us this week. We always allow them to come and go as they please, but in cases like this, where they're defecting to join the Seelie Queen, it's hard to explain that she's not going to give them what they want."

"I think they have to make that choice for themselves," I said quietly. "But now the Seelie Queen is a couple of hours away from taking the throne of Summer. She already killed the monarch of the Sea Court, and it wouldn't surprise me if she targeted the borderlands next."

"I'd like to see her try." Raine's voice was laced with steel. "This puppet of hers is one of the Sidhe. Can they be persuaded to step down?"

"By persuaded, you mean threatened?" I said. "I doubt it. She has her people eating out of her hand. I wanted to prove she killed the competition, but the Morrigan helpfully ate their souls before my sister could bring them back. She also refused to offer us aid."

"I've met the Morrigan twice," Raine said, "and it doesn't surprise me that she wouldn't help. She's one of the last true immortals, but she's also a miserable hag who does whatever she feels is best for her. Doesn't give a toss about anyone else."

"I got that impression," I said. "I wondered if she might be working with the Seelie Queen, but apparently not. Why's the Morrigan chained up like that, anyway?"

"She fought on the wrong side in the last war," said Raine. "She's a conniving bitch and not someone you want to cross, but I doubt she'll make the mistake of aiding the enemy again."

"By war, you mean the one with the mortal realm?" I said. "She sided *against* the humans?"

"She was bound into service by the enemy," said Raine. "Or so I hear."

"Even without her, the Seelie Queen has an army of the dead on her side," I said. "She even brought back the memory-eater from death to gain intel on her enemies. Granted, I used my talisman to kill her, but the Seelie Queen is immune."

"Your talisman," said Raine, her gaze dropping to the staff in my hand. "You didn't have that last time."

"It used to belong to the Erlking." There was no point in hiding the truth, not now. "Then I accidentally claimed it. It can destroy any magic and any living thing if I want it to… except for the Seelie Queen."

"I *knew* my sceptre sensed something different about you," said Raine. The sceptre gleamed with blue-white light as she pulled it out, glimmering with runes similar to mine. "Your sister, too. She has a talisman."

"Don't get too excited," I said. "Ilsa can banish wraiths with hers, but even between the two of us, we can't deal with the Seelie Queen. She might not wield a talisman herself, but she has unlimited healing powers. That's a more irritating ability than coming back from the dead, if possible."

Raine's mouth pressed together. "I might be able to help. My own talisman allows me to displace the magic of another and replace it with my own."

"Shit, really?" I stared at her. "Want to come to the coronation?"

She nodded. "All right. I'll ask Viola—my captain—to assemble an army. And I'll keep an eye out for defectors. They can expect no mercy from me."

"Nor I." Darrow looked at her. "I will go with Hazel and attempt to warn the Sidhe, but if we're forced to go to war, I will stand with your armies."

"All right," said Raine, striding to the door. "I'll speak to the other half-Sidhe."

She and Cedar exited the room, while Darrow leaned closer to me. "I hope it's okay, my fighting with the others.

"No, it's great." I gave his hand a squeeze. "I'm all about encouraging you to make friends. Half-fae ones, not weird humans with faerie magic."

He smiled, brushing his mouth over mine. "Let's go and check on your family."

As soon as we re-entered the main room, Ilsa walked up to me. "River is going to tell his father to amass a group of Sidhe to stand up in the coronation and prevent it from going ahead, but most of them will flat-out disbelieve him. He's become unpopular among his fellow Sidhe for helping humans so often."

"Figures." I swore. "That's not enough. People from Summer will fight on the Seelie Queen's side thinking they're in the right. They'll die for her."

One way or another, she would win.

"Then we'd better delay that coronation," Cedar said.

An instant later, Coral walked in, following Willow and several other half-faeries. "There you are, Hazel. The Erlking's sprite was looking for you."

"Did he tell you?" I asked.

"That the next monarch is a traitor?" said Coral. "At this point, I have to admit I was expecting it."

"What was that about delaying the coronation?" Darrow looked at Cedar.

"They need the crown to perform the coronation," said Cedar. "That's why it was delayed before."

Raine made a tutting noise. "Cedar."

"I once tried to steal from the Erlking." A smile

touched the corner of his mouth. "I will see what I can do."

He's going to steal the crown?

"Lady Aiten has the crown somewhere in the palace, but I'm not sure where," I said to him. "The Erlking's sprite won't betray you, but he might not be able to help you either. If you see him, tell him I sent you and you're on my side. He'll be bound to serve the next monarch as soon as they take the throne, but until then, he's an ally."

"Wait." Willow stepped forward. "I know where my mother will have hidden the crown. I can help."

The two moved in to talk to one another, while Coral looked on anxiously.

Darrow leaned closer to me. "Can he pull it off?"

"For all our sakes, I bloody hope so," I said. "I can't believe I'm backing up someone stealing the crown for a second time."

Cedar left the hall through the front doors. Willow exchanged one last hug with Coral, then followed him. I walked over to Coral, whose hands were shaking. "If Lady Aiten catches either of them—"

"She won't," I said, with more confidence than I really felt. "Cedar will make sure of it. He once tried to steal from the Erlking himself and damn near came close to succeeding."

"Yeah." She exhaled in a shaky breath. "I wish I hadn't left my mother's talisman there in Summer. It shouldn't be theirs, but every time I look at the cursed thing, I think of what my brother—what he did with it." Tears trembled on her eyelashes.

I hugged her. "You don't have to claim it. You could

drop it in the ocean, in fact. Let it rot there among the fishes."

She gave a brittle laugh. "I would, if I wasn't sure it'd wash up on shore a few months later and end up in some poor fisherman's hand. Those talismans have a mind of their own."

Recalling the vivid memory of the Erlking's death I'd seen through the talisman brought a shiver to my skin. "They do. You're still better off without it."

"I hope so," she said. "I never expected or wanted to rule the Sea Court, and given the lies my mother told, it's for the best that the talisman stays far away from anyone who might use it to rule."

"Yeah, I think the only halfway decent person to wield a talisman might have been the Erlking, and he had major issues." To say the least. "Oh, and Raine. My sister, too, but she prefers to keep a low profile."

"There's something to be said for that," said Coral. "I like this place. I'm glad you told me about it. The other half-faeries appreciate having somewhere to stay where they aren't forced to swear loyalty to a Sidhe lord."

"Good," I said. "If I were you, I'd stay here with the others while I tell Lady Aiten. I'm going to have one attempt to warn her, and then..."

And then? Either the Courts would stand, or they would fall.

"Good luck," said Coral, moving over to the other half-bloods. With obvious practise, the raven-haired half-faerie—who must be Viola—called the half-bloods into line, giving out orders.

I found Darrow standing next to one of the tapestries, his gaze preoccupied.

"Do you like it here?" I asked.

He looked up. "I do, but I confess to not being optimistic about the Sidhe continuing to allow this place to exist."

"Hey, you never know. They let me walk in here with this." I raised the talisman. "Though when the monarch is crowned, I'm supposed to hand it over to Lady Aiten."

Perhaps if I asked her to delay the coronation, she might assume I was just making excuses. It wouldn't surprise me. Without proof, I'd have a hell of a job convincing her, and even stealing the crown wouldn't be enough for her to cancel the coronation altogether. I needed to talk to her and hope that all our arguments wouldn't stop her from doing the right thing.

"Reckon Cedar's had time to steal the crown by now?" I asked.

"If he's as good as usual, yes," said Raine.

"What're we supposed to do?" Morgan asked. "Join the army? Raise the dead? Come back to Summer and make trouble?"

"Stick with Ilsa and River," I said. "I don't want any of you to face the backlash if the Sidhe turn on me again. River is going to get his dad to find some Sidhe who are likely to support our cause, but even if I warn the rest of Summer, there's no guarantee the Seelie Queen isn't waiting to ambush us."

"If that's the case, we should speak to Lady Aiten at once," said Darrow. "I'm more than a little suspicious that Etaina hasn't made her move yet."

"Don't even," I said. "I have my plate full enough with the Seelie Queen as it is. Ilsa, let me know if you have news."

"I will do," she said. "Hazel, please try not to get exiled again."

"I think that's the least of my problems." I waved her off, leaving the palace with Darrow at my side. Guards stood at intervals all around the fences surrounding the half-bloods' palace, and the tense atmosphere pursued us through the tangled woods back to the path leading to the Summer Court.

Morgan and Ilsa are safe, but is Mum at the palace? She'd have been invited to the ceremony, of course, but it was anyone's guess as to whether she'd show up with all three of her children missing. As long as she hadn't gone into the Vale again…

Darrow caught my arm as the ambassadors' palace came into view. "They're expecting us."

Lady Aiten stood outside the gate, wearing a long dress of shimmering gold and a murderous expression on her face.

"Well?" she said.

"I know you're not going to believe me," I said, "but the coronation needs to be put on hold. The trials were sabotaged."

"We have already found the saboteurs," he said. "These people tried to kill our next monarch on his way down to his own coronation." She gestured through the open gates at the palace.

I looked past her, and my heart plummeted. Inside the grounds lay the bodies of several Aes Sidhe with identical features.

And they all looked like Darrow.

17

"They're not Darrow," I said. "I mean, he's not like them. They used glamour to disguise themselves."

"I am aware of that," said Lady Aiten. "As I am aware that he belongs to their Court, which has been thought extinct for countless years."

Shit, shit, *shit*. We didn't have time for this. Darrow himself had gone rigid, his gaze fixed on the nearest mirror of his own face. While he might be able to glamour Lady Aiten, if she'd already told everyone in the Court, they'd all know the Aes Sidhe existed. There was no hiding this.

"Darrow isn't a villain, and he's not working with those assassins," I told her. "We need to stop the coronation—"

Lord Raivan marched over to us, his antlered hat askew. "The crown is missing."

Lady Aiten gave him a cutting look. "Send a team to

search the area thoroughly. In the meantime, bring the former Gatekeeper here at once."

Dammit. I should have known she'd pin the blame on my family.

"She's already here," said Lord Raivan. "She's been here since the ceremony started, and the crown was in your quarters the whole time."

Silently sending thanks to Lord Raivan, I said, "Apparently, we're not the only people who think this is a trick. The Seelie Queen rigged the results."

"And these assassins came out of nowhere, did they?" She faced Darrow, who looked stonily back.

"They're a distraction," I said. "The Seelie Queen picked a fight with another Court, yes, but she's still coming for Summer first."

"The Court is already assembled for the coronation," said Lady Aiten. "It will not wait."

Sure enough, the sounds of merriment drifted through the doors Lord Raivan had left open. *The assassins failed.* Which meant the false monarch was inside that very room, waiting to be crowned.

"Fetch the past Gatekeeper," she told Lord Raivan. "As for you, Darrow—"

Mid-sentence, she froze, her mouth parted. I glanced at Darrow, saw his eyes glowing, and looked away before his glamour could ensnare me, too.

"Damn," I murmured. "How long will it last?"

"As long as I'm here, which can't be for long," said Darrow. "If anyone else saw the assassins, I can't erase their memories of the attack. They know. No doubt as Etaina intended."

"We can at least deal with the bodies." I approached the

dead assassins, feeling for the threads of their glamour. It took several seconds for me to peel away Darrow's face to reveal the familiar clone's appearance beneath. Darrow stepped in to help, and before long, the clones all wore their true faces.

"It won't change a thing," he said. "They were already spotted by multiple witnesses. This is too big to cover up."

"Doesn't mean you have to take the fall." I looked up, spotting Lord Raivan exit the palace with Mum behind him. They descended the steps towards Lady Aiten, who stood frozen in place.

Lord Raivan frowned and started to speak, then stopped, his mouth half-open. The shadow of Darrow's magic trailed ghostly fingers along my skin.

"What's wrong with them?" Mum eyed Lady Aiten, then Lord Raivan.

"Darrow." I nodded to him. "Glamour paralysis. Not permanent."

Mum looked between us. "Hazel, what did you do this time? The Erlking's sprite showed up in my room this morning and told me all *three* of my children had disappeared. Now I hear the crown has gone, too."

"There was no time to warn you," I said in apologetic tones. "Ilsa and Morgan are safe in Half-Blood Territory, don't worry. I forgot the Sidhe were likely to blame you for the crown's disappearance, even though Lady Aiten herself was the one who asked you to hide it last time."

She raised an eyebrow. "And you don't have anything to do with it, do you, Hazel?"

I grimaced. "Believe me, there's worse going on here than an attempted coup. Etaina sent assassins to kill the next king and frame Darrow."

"And they won't be alone," Darrow put in. "There'll be more of Etaina's people waiting elsewhere in the Court, whether the ceremony takes place or not. I need to find them."

"Like hell," I said. "You aren't wandering off alone. And the Seelie Queen will still be on her way to the coronation—"

"Never mind the coronation," he said. "Etaina did this to send a message to me. She knows I've taken your side over hers."

"Etaina isn't here yet, but the Seelie Queen's pawn is inside the palace, and we only have until the crown is found to get rid of him," I said. "I'll be honest, I'd rather go with your approach than introduce him to my talisman in front of the whole Court. Can you use glamour to make him step down as the new monarch?"

"Perhaps, but I can't glamour everyone in the room for longer than a few seconds at a time," he replied. "Besides, it's the Seelie Queen who needs to be taken care of, and she's not here. I can glamour the false king for long enough for him to give a public confession, but if I do so, the glamour will wear off Lady Aiten and Lord Raivan and they'll order the guards to arrest me."

I swore. "Mum—Ilsa and Morgan are with River. They went to find River's dad and get some of the Sidhe on our side. You'll be safer with them than at the Lynn house."

Mum's lips compressed. "Hazel."

"This is going to get ugly no matter what," I went on. "We have to force a public confession. Darrow and I will take care of it, but I don't want you caught up in this."

"I've been caught up in this my whole life, Hazel." She

eyed Lord Raivan and Lady Aiten. "I'll distract those two and buy you time to get a confession from the false king."

I didn't argue. With the crown gone, we wouldn't get a better shot at thwarting the Seelie Queen's plan.

I walked up the palace steps towards the oak doors. "I'll go in as me, but you might want to hide your face, Darrow."

Darrow's visage changed into Lord Raivan's, complete with his lopsided hat. "Will that do?"

"Perfect."

We entered the hall to find the interior of the palace had changed yet again. Gold drapes festooned balconies that hadn't existed before, while twin spiral staircases curved around each side of the main entrance hall. The tapestries had turned into gilt-framed portraits of Seelie knights clad in armour. Past monarchs, maybe.

I scanned the crowd for Lord Talthain and spotted his spiked helmet. He stood arguing with a winged Sidhe with long golden hair. "This will *not* do. I must be crowned at high noon, and the time is almost upon us."

"Excuse me." Darrow stepped between us, affecting Lord Raivan's deferential tone. "May I speak with the future king alone? Lady Aiten and I have a lead on the person who may have taken the crown, but it will require a small delay."

His glamour was so subtle one might overlook it, but the two Sidhe stepped aside, allowing Lord Talthain to follow us. The Sidhe didn't know anything was wrong, but one misstep and we'd all be royally screwed.

Where is the Seelie Queen? I kept expecting to see her stunning face among the other courtiers, but either she trusted her pawn to fulfil his role, or she had another plan brewing.

Darrow took Lord Talthain aside and spoke to him in a whisper. Even with his power focused on another person, the echo of it stirred my blood, compelled me to bow down and worship him. I gritted my teeth, keeping my eye on the Sidhe. In the corner, River and Ilsa stood with Lord Torin and a number of others. *They moved fast.* Ilsa caught my eye, and I gave an encouraging nod to tell her we had the situation in hand.

Lord Talthain ascended the stairs onto the raised platform of the front of the room. The murmur of voices ceased as the Sidhe realised their future monarch stood before them, without a guard or a crown. His translucent skin gleamed in the light of noon, while his spiked helmet sat at an angle atop his mossy green-brown hair.

"I have chosen to postpone my coronation," he said. "Because I am not the true king of Summer. I lied and cheated during the trials and framed my fellow Sidhe for crimes they did not commit. I even murdered Lord Walvein and Lady Horell and opened doorways into the Vale on the orders of my Queen."

Gasps echoed through the room.

"Then who is the true king?" said several voices. "You serve the Seelie Queen, do you not?"

"I do," he said, "but she is not our true ruler."

My heart missed a beat. Darrow stiffened at my side, horror flickering across his face.

Lord Talthain grinned as he faced the audience. "Our true leader was robbed of her throne by the treacherous Erlking, and she has come to make this right."

A flash of light in the corner of my eye drew my attention to the balcony. Time slowed, each second dragging out as an arrow arced towards Lord Talthain, soaring through the air and hitting him in the heart.

After all, the bow couldn't miss.

Etaina descended the spiral staircase, her dress streaming behind her, and her entire body glowing with iridescent light. Even among royalty, she stood out like a rose in a bed of weeds. Her piercing silver-white hair shone as bright as her Summer-green eyes and the silver trimmings on her armoured battle coat.

All gazes turned to her as though they couldn't help it. The false king's body crumpled off the stage, while she took his place, holding the Sea Queen's bow in both hands. The entire room held their breaths, caught in the irresistible spell of her glamour.

"So easy," she murmured, soft yet loudly enough for me to hear, as though the words were meant only for me. "So easy to manipulate. My sister was a coward and a fool not to show her face in person. One would almost think she doesn't want Summer's crown at all."

She can't make herself queen. Not as long as the crown was missing, at any rate, and I hadn't the faintest clue where Cedar had taken it. On the other side of the room, River and Ilsa stood frozen among the courtiers, unable to catch my eye.

Etaina turned to me, and I forgot to breathe. Her green eyes swam with mesmerising light, and my breath whooshed out as her gaze shifted to Darrow.

"I do wish you hadn't let the Gatekeeper poison you against me," said Etaina. "You were my most promising prospect, Darrow, yet you were unable to finish the simplest of missions."

Darrow's face was expressionless. "You must know the former Queen can heal from any injury, Etaina. I did the best I could, but I have not yet been able to devise a way to take her life."

"Yet you left no mark on her." She shook her head. "I've let you fool around with this human for long enough. I command you to seize that girl using the full extent of your powers."

Darrow had looked into death without batting an eyelid, fought monsters which terrified the Sidhe, lost everything more than once and even faced down a death goddess... but this was the first time I'd ever seen him look scared.

Then his eyes brightened, his skin glowing, his whole being turning radiant. At once, the world ceased to exist.

Everything except for him.

18

"Hazel," said a voice. A familiar one, but not one I could immediately place.

I blinked, my vision hazy. I lay on a hard, wooden bench inside a room the size of a cell. It should have hurt my back, but my senses felt muted, slow to recover from the impact of Darrow's magic.

I didn't recall a single moment of anything that had happened since, but somehow, my clothes had reverted to the plain trousers and shirt I wore beneath my glamour. Nobody else was in the room except for the person who stood next to my 'bed', a stocky man with longish shaggy dark hair, pale skin and dark brown eyes. Definitely not a Sidhe, so he had to be human. The curving earthen walls told me I was in the realm of the Aes Sidhe, but why the bloody hell would Etaina have a human living in here?

I ran my hands over my forehead. The circlet was still there, thank the gods, but she'd taken all my other weapons… including the Erlking's talisman.

"What the hell?" I blinked a couple of times. "Is this

what she decided to do with me? Lock me in a cell? What's she doing now, declaring world domination?"

"I believe the Lady is addressing her subjects," said the man. "You haven't been here for long. An hour at most. She told me to watch you, that's all."

"Who…" I'd heard his voice before—I was sure of it. "I know you."

I'd heard his voice in the vision I'd had of my past. The vision where I'd been picked out as Gatekeeper. I hadn't made the connection at the time, but I was almost certain the other voice had been Etaina's.

"The Lady told me the glamour should have lasted longer," he said, "but you have more resilience than most."

I pushed into a sitting position, scanning the room for anything I might use as a weapon. However curious I might be as to why Etaina had a human living here—a human who'd featured in a vision of my past, no less—I needed to get that talisman out of her hands and save Darrow from her clutches before she used it to bring the Courts crashing down.

Aside from the tree stump the stranger sat on and the clusters of luminescent mushrooms on the walls and ceiling, the room was bare save for a wooden door. The man noticed the direction of my stare and raised a hand, displaying a glittering knife. "You are to wait here until the Lady calls for you."

That implies she's staying here. I still had time to stop her from attacking the Courts.

"I take it Darrow is with her?" I said.

"Yes, she has all her subjects ready to take orders," he said. "I know nothing of what they discuss."

"I don't doubt that." I ran my fingertip over the Gatekeeper's mark. The man's gaze lingered on the swirling symbol below my circlet, something glinting in his eyes. Something... familiar.

I sprang to my feet. A wave of vertigo hit me, and I grabbed the wooden bench to steady myself. Why had she brought me here? Why did this man remind me so much of... no. It was impossible.

He held up the knife. "I wouldn't try to escape."

"She hasn't blasted you with glamour," I said. "Any reason why?"

"It pleases her to keep me aware of my condition," he said. "Those she glamours are utterly in her thrall. Thoughts and feelings are irrelevant, for nothing exists to them but her. I am no servant of hers, so she has nothing to gain from turning me into one of her puppets."

"Not a servant," I murmured. "What are you, then?"

"One who cannot be saved, Hazel Lynn."

I staggered against the bench, my heart thundering. There was no sign of anyone—not Etaina, not her Court, and not Darrow. Just this stranger, this stranger who looked too much like a portrait on the wall of the Lynn house.

"You're Thomas Lynn."

He didn't look like his portrait exactly, but it was a good enough likeness. This man was my ancestor, who should have died centuries ago.

He didn't deny my words, nor did he say anything more.

"You're dead," I went on.

"Not dead," he said. "Taken."

"You were captured by a faerie queen," I said, my voice

brittle. "It was her. Etaina. Not the Seelie *or* Unseelie Queens."

He inclined his head.

"How are you still alive?" I said. "It's been centuries. How the bloody hell does time even work here?"

"Time works according to the Lady's wishes," he said. "A year can pass here while a second passes in the faerie realm, if she wills it."

"Seriously?"

If that was the case, I still had a shot at making it back into the Summer Court in time to warn them of Etaina's upcoming attack—but I needed to get that talisman away from her first.

And where was Darrow? She must have brought him here along with me, unless she'd ordered him to kill the Seelie Queen and finish the job. None of that seemed to matter, though, not with a dead man standing in front of me with the answers to every question I'd ever had about the Gatekeeper's curse, my family's eternal enslavement, even the Erlking's role in it all. And I couldn't stick around to ask a single question without jeopardising the people I cared for.

Thomas was human. Long-lived, evidently, but still human. I, however, had trained to fight the Sidhe.

I met his eyes—so much like Mum's—and said, "I'm sorry about this, Thomas. I really am."

I brought my knee up into his crotch and slammed the heel of my palm into the crook of his elbow, forcing his hand to unclench on the knife. Grabbing it in my hand, I swept his legs out from underneath him. His hands snagged my ankle, and I kicked him hard in the face, feeling cartilage give way beneath my heel.

Thomas's gasps of pain pursued me to the door, which I kicked open and ran out into the corridor.

The winding tunnel was an unfamiliar one, and two more snaked in opposite directions. Closing the door behind me, I paced to the left. Dammit, none of this was familiar to me.

"Hummingbird," I whispered. The last ally I had, assuming Darrow was still under Etaina's thrall. His sprite could probably get me out of here—but that would mean giving up both Darrow *and* the Erlking's talisman.

Hummingbird appeared in a flash of light. "You should not be here!"

"Etaina locked me up," I said. "Please—show me how to get out."

He shook his head frantically. "You cannot get out under your own power. And my master is under her influence entirely."

"Please," I said. "Tell me which direction leads to the hall where Etaina is holding her congregation. I have to find Darrow."

He flitted down the left tunnel. "This way, but if she finds us, you're dead."

"Better stick together, then." I walked behind him on swift feet. "Does she have the talisman with her?"

"I do not know of any talismans. Darrow locked me in his room, out of harm's way."

Damn. "Okay, I'll check her office first."

Without the talisman, I'd be at a disadvantage, not that I'd be able to make a dent in any of the Aes Sidhe when they all carried protection against its power. All I had was my Gatekeeper's magic, which Etaina might well know more about than I did. And Thomas Lynn. *Dammit.*

Maybe I should have tried to talk him into taking my side rather than kicking him in the face.

The tunnel followed a looping spiral to familiar ground, where Etaina's office lay one corridor down from the main chamber in which I'd landed the last couple of times I'd been in here.

I rounded a corner and ran into an Aes Sidhe knight. His mouth opened, but I lunged forward and stabbed him in the neck. Blood gushed out onto the tunnel floor. For a glamour, he sure bled like a real person. But he *was* real, like any clone. Like all of them.

Etaina's office was locked, to no surprise, but Hummingbird floated over to the door's lock and it clicked open a moment later. With a nod of thanks, I entered.

The first thing that hit me was that the talisman wasn't here, and the office looked much the same as the last time I'd been here. Did that mean she'd claimed it? With that talisman, she could turn Faerie into a wasteland while doing no harm to her own people as long as they had the means of protecting themselves. *I have to stop her.*

Panic seized me as I opened one of the drawers in her claw-footed desk, finding nothing but a tangle of keys. The next drawer contained a collection of gleaming stones which resembled the one which protected the holder from the talisman's magic. *That's more like it.* Grabbing as many stones as I could hold, I stuffed them into my pockets. I might not be able to stop her from using the talisman, but I'd make damned sure I kept my loved ones safe from its magic in the meantime.

Backing out of the office, I headed for the main chamber. The murmur of voices grew louder as I ducked into the alcove and inched the wooden door open.

Etaina stood on the high platform at the front of the chamber, holding the Erlking's talisman in one hand. Towering tree trunks formed pillars connecting floor and ceiling, branches arching above the heads of several hundred soldiers dressed in the same brown and green uniform.

Darrow stood at Etaina's side below the high, arched ceiling, his expression as blank and emotionless as the rest.

"You will bring glory to me," she was saying to her congregation. "We will force the Courts into submission and kill the false queen before she can take what her husband tried to deny me."

The genuine passion in her voice disarmed me. It seemed Etaina truly wanted her people to love her. Yet she hadn't given them a choice in the matter, and she would never dare to set them free. After all, they might choose to betray her, as Darrow had.

Etaina lifted her gaze above the crowd. "You can come in, Hazel."

I pushed the doors fully open and walked into the hall. Darrow's gaze went to mine, and the stark horror in his expression tore at me. He wasn't under her glamour, but it didn't matter. She had him by the throat all the same.

Nobody else looked my way. All their attention was riveted on the woman at the centre of the stage. Not all of them were clones either. Maybe half the audience had the same identical features, but the others were as varied as any Sidhe nobles.

Shadows tingled beneath my skin. The talisman's

power was still mine. *Don't betray me. Don't serve her.* I clenched my fist, willing the shadows to rise, but every person in this room was armed with one of those stones, or worse, the marks. I hadn't seen which Etaina had, but it was safe to say *she* was safe from its magic as long as she held the talisman in her grip.

After all, the talisman was what she'd wanted all along. Everything else was just a distraction, nothing more. The talisman's magic existed to destroy, and Etaina was offering the Devourer everything I'd denied it.

"I wouldn't try to use my talisman against me, Hazel," she said. "You cannot harm me."

"Wanna bet?" I raised the knife, but a dozen cold hands grabbed at my arms, tugging the instrument from my hand.

"Let her come," she said sharply. "Don't harm her."

I found myself propelled towards the stage by a tide of Aes Sidhe until I halted beside her. Darrow tried to catch my eye, but I kept my attention on Etaina. Perhaps I could snatch the talisman from her, but if I fell under the spell of her glamour, it was all over. I had no weapons left, while a whole audience of Aes Sidhe soldiers held unsheathed blades, one order away from obliterating me.

The iron band pressed against my wrist. Thomas hadn't removed it. An accidental oversight or a deliberate one, I didn't know, but it was my last shot. If I could just get the iron to touch her, she'd be weakened. Maybe enough for the talisman's effects to break through and turn her to dust.

Etaina beckoned me onto the stage. I held my wrist steady, mentally calculating the distance I needed to move to press the iron to her bare skin.

Her gaze skimmed me from head to toe. The audience watched me without reacting, waiting for an order from their leader.

"Such a fuss over a simple human," she said softly.

Shadows coiled around my wrists, hiding the iron from view. "If I'm only a simple human and you're an all-powerful queen, why are you not the one who wields the magic of the Erlking's talisman? Why am I the one with freedom, while you have to resort to brainwashing an army you created with your own hands to avoid your allies stabbing you in the back?"

Rage frosted her sharp features. "You know nothing of your station, human."

"I know enough."

A lie. There was far too much of this whole setup I was clueless about. Why did she have Thomas Lynn held captive here? Why was he even still alive, for that matter? Did that mean I was bound to *her*, and not the Courts? Surely not—if she had control over my family, she'd have abused it by now—but if none of it mattered. Not with the Erlking's talisman a heartbeat away from turning its affections over to her. I willed the shadows to remain in my hands. *Stay with me. Etaina and her kind betrayed the gods and stole their magic. Wouldn't you rather serve me?*

No response came from the Devourer, but the shadows stirred around me as though I held the talisman in my own grip. Fury flickered in the depths of her eyes. She could glamour me, turn me into an unwilling servant for life—but she couldn't make the talisman obey her.

She held no power over the gods' magic.

I lifted my head high, turning up the volume on the circlet. Its glow bathed the cave walls in green, caused

Etaina's eyes to squint. I leaned in closer to her, my hand wrapping around the talisman's hilt, the other ready with the iron—

The army surged, weapons pointing at me, but Etaina raised an impatient hand, either oblivious to the iron close to her skin or uncaring of it.

"I think you misunderstand the situation here, Hazel," she said. "There's no doubt you have quite the repertoire of tricks, but you are nothing more than a mortal with no talent. Darrow, kindly remove Hazel's hands from my talisman."

With a curse, I grabbed her free arm, but Darrow moved blindingly fast, his hand seizing my upper arm. I didn't need to look at his face to know he'd had no control over his actions.

"I could command him to dispose of you," she added dispassionately. "But you may be useful yet. Release her, Darrow. I think it's time Hazel learned the truth of us."

Darrow's grip loosened, and he stepped to my side. I glimpsed his face, shadowed with remorse. She'd deliberately left him free enough to be aware of what he was doing.

"I know you're a jealous bitch who couldn't deal with the fact that the Erlking got the talisman and you didn't," I said. "I'm taking a wild guess that's why you split from Summer and pretended to be dead, too. I bet you're really pissed at your sister for giving the game away and forcing you to stop running like the coward you really are."

Darrow gave a faint head-shake, a warning not to provoke her, but I was too incensed to care. Etaina might scare the living hell out of me, but if she hypnotised

Darrow one more time, I'd ram my hand through her chest and rip out her heart.

"My sister will never get what she desires," she said, "but her hasty actions have paved the way for me to take back what is mine."

Shadows curled around the talisman. My gut tightened. *Don't choose her over me. Please don't.*

"So you want to take Summer's throne?" I went on. "You won't find it as easy to brainwash the other Sidhe as you would your glamoured army. They don't know you, and they sure as hell won't respect you. Nor do I."

"This army isn't my finest creation," she said, turning to Darrow. "He is."

The breath caught in my throat. "What?"

Darrow's expression froze, as stunned as I was.

"Oh, you must know I cannot tell an untruth," said Etaina. "Darrow is mine, and I would prefer not to harm him, but since you've taken a liking to him... I have no choice in the matter."

Metallic rage coated the back of my throat. "Don't you dare."

"Surrender your magic," she said, "or I will undo him."

19

Silence filled the cavern. The audience watched, without reacting, as Darrow and I stood frozen on the stage beside their triumphant leader.

"You're already holding the talisman," I forced the words out, addressing Etaina. "If the magic won't choose you, I can't force it to."

"You gave up its magic once already," she said. "I know you did."

"I didn't do it alone," I said. "The talisman chose me, twice, and I can't make it choose you instead."

"Very well." She raised her hand to point at Darrow. "I regret this."

A blinding flash of light engulfed the room. I glimpsed a small shape flit past. *Hummingbird.*

Then Darrow's hand closed around mine, and we vanished.

I staggered, disorientated. The army had vanished along with Etaina, to be replaced with the ambassadors' palace. Noise exploded all around the hall, filled with

Sidhe exclaiming and pointing up at the balcony. The body of Lord Talthain lay where it'd fallen on the stage, but Etaina was no longer anywhere in sight.

"This is the same instant we left," I murmured. "No time passed at all."

Everyone in this room had seen Etaina shoot Summer's future king dead. They'd seen his bizarre confession, too, and with nobody around to offer an explanation, the ensuing chaos would give one or both of the queens the perfect opportunity to strike.

I have to do something.

I scanned the room and caught sight of my sister. Ilsa was trying to cross the room to me, but the tide of panicking Sidhe barred her path. Cursing inwardly, I ran for the stage and jumped up beside the body of Lord Talthain.

"Hey!" I strode to the front of the stage. "Listen to me!"

The clamour continued, nobody giving me so much as a second glance.

Ilsa pushed her way through to the stage and shouted, *"Listen."*

The word rang out—in a language that wasn't English, but everyone in this room understood anyway—and half the crowd turned our way. Ilsa reached the stage and climbed up to join me, the aftermath of the Invocation rippling through the crowd.

"Listen to me," I repeated. "You know the woman you just saw? Her name is Etaina, ruler of the Aes Sidhe, who the Sidhe have believed to be extinct for centuries. The Seelie Queen angered the Aes Sidhe by attacking her domain, and their leader retaliated by killing the pawn the Seelie Queen sent to take the throne on her behalf."

The Sidhe stared at me, momentarily dazzled by the Invocation Ilsa had spoken, and I pressed on.

"Etaina's kingdom is smaller than Summer, but still formidable," I said. "If you look at those clones outside, they're what we're up against. She has a whole army of glamour creations, made to obey her."

"Like him?" spoke up one of the Sidhe. "The hybrid half-blood who was with you?"

Darrow. I scanned the room for him, but he was nowhere in sight. He hadn't gone back to Etaina, had he?

"No," Ilsa said, nudging me in the side.

"She tried to frame him because he turned against her," I added. "All her clones are created by glamour and look exactly alike. Oh, and she can glamour anyone into doing her bidding, as she does to her entire Court."

Noise filled the room, at least half of which seemed to be coming from Lord Niall's side of the room by the wine barrels. I'd thought Summer had been prepared for a war with the Seelie Queen, but most of them hadn't expected it, let alone the arrival of a new queen who'd split from the Court before most of the people in this room had been born. I looked for a supportive face and saw none aside from Ilsa and River. As for Lord Raivan and Lady Aiten, they'd been under Darrow's glamour the last time I'd checked.

"She killed our rightful king," shouted the fox-eared Sidhe who'd once been Lord Raivan's friend. "She brainwashed him and then shot him."

"He wasn't our rightful—" I broke off. What was the difference? There was no monarch, nor anyone waiting in line, however you looked at it. "The point is, there is nobody on the throne of Summer and two angry queens vying to take over. We need to assemble a defensive force, or else they'll take the Court to pieces."

More shouts of dismay rose, drowning out my voice and Ilsa's, too. She shook her head at me and climbed down from the stage.

I followed her, exhaustion settling on me like a heavy cloak. "How are we supposed to get them to cooperate? We might as well divide the Court between Etaina and the Seelie Queen here and now."

"You did great," said Ilsa. "Considering the Sidhe now have to adapt to the return of yet another enemy. I suppose our only consolation is that the two of them might decide to go to war with one another rather than with Summer."

"How'd you know how to make them listen like that?" I asked.

"The Gatekeeper's book showed me a bunch of words in the gods' language earlier," she said. "I figured that one would be the most effective."

"Even Etaina's hypnotism has nothing on the gods," I murmured. "Which is pretty much the only thing we have going for us now. I don't know when Etaina will strike. Her kingdom seems to obey different time laws than the rest of Faerie."

"That explains a lot," said Ilsa. "I saw you and Darrow vanish along with Etaina—she's exactly how I imagined her, by the way—and the next second, you two came back without her. I did wonder if some time slippage was involved."

"She was going to... kill Darrow." I looked around the room. "Where'd he go?"

"Outside," she said. "Maybe he went to find Lady Aiten and Lord Raivan."

Oh, crap. He'd glamoured them—and Mum had helped him do it.

River caught up to Ilsa. "I told my father the truth, but I was trying to prepare him to face the Seelie Queen, not the Aes Sidhe."

"You and me both," said Ilsa. "I don't know how many of them took in our message, but we have no leader, and with nobody to rally around, the odds of us pulling an army together are pretty low."

"We have the half-faeries," I reminded her. "They'll be ready. And the Sidhe you asked, River. How many?"

"Not enough," he said. "Have we tried sending an emissary to Winter?"

"Holly went to ask for their help," I said. "But she knows almost nothing about the Aes Sidhe. I didn't have time to explain everything, and I sure as hell didn't expect Etaina to show her face here in person. If it was Winter she was after, we might be able to count on the Unseelie Queen's cooperation, but…"

"I guess it depends if she wants to risk letting Summer be overrun," Ilsa said. "The Morrigan showed no interest in getting involved either. That just leaves the half-bloods, and there aren't all that many of them compared to two armies."

"You're telling me." Cedar still had Summer's crown, as far as I knew. It was probably safer in Half-Blood Territory, but the quest for strong leadership had gone up in smoke. There was no time to pull a miracle out of a hat now. "Etaina's clones aren't much tougher than any other faerie, but it's the ones with glamour skills you want to watch out for."

"You mean Etaina herself," said Ilsa. "I *felt* her magic take over me. It was like I wanted to worship her. If she does that to the whole Court, who can resist?"

Not even the dead, a voice whispered in the back of my mind, recalling how Darrow had scared off the Seelie Queen and her group of wraiths just by using his power for a few seconds. There was no doubt Etaina was the more dangerous of the two, but the Sidhe were prepared for neither.

"We don't know who will attack first," River said. "The Seelie Queen or Etaina."

"I suppose it's too much to hope that they'll destroy one another first," I added. "I'd lay bets on Etaina showing up first and the Seelie Queen trying to get the jump on her after the fact. Which won't go well."

But she hadn't been able to control or claim the talisman. It still answered to me. That meant, in all likelihood, she'd come to me first. To kill me or strip the magic from me—or both. Like most Sidhe, *she* could speak Invocations without consequences, so it'd be nothing to her to repeat the same spell Ilsa had used to take the talisman's magic away.

"There's Mum." Ilsa peered over my shoulder. "Hazel, can you—"

"On it," I said. "She tied up two of the Sidhe earlier after Darrow glamoured them to stop them arresting him."

Ilsa groaned. "Really, Hazel."

"Hey, it's not my fault." I made my way to the door. Outside, Mum stood on the stairs beside an irate-looking

Lady Aiten and Lord Raivan, while Darrow was visible near the fallen Aes Sidhe soldiers. *Good. Etaina didn't get to him.*

"Hey." I closed the doors behind me. "I don't know how much you saw of what went on in there—"

"I saw you disrupt the ceremony with your ridiculous antics," said Lady Aiten, white-lipped with rage. "And your friend has a death warrant on his head."

Movement stirred and I looked past her, but Darrow had disappeared again, leaving the bodies behind.

"Darrow isn't the enemy, Etaina is," I said. "If you saw or heard who shot Lord Talthain, it was her. Countless witnesses can back me up on this."

"The Gatekeeper is right." Lord Torin, River's father, exited the palace with River and Ilsa in tow. "We all saw the Queen of the Aes Sidhe appear in the ceremony and use a stolen talisman to shoot down our future king."

Crap. I'd forgotten she had the Sea Queen's talisman as well as mine. She hadn't been carrying it when she'd addressed her Court, and I hadn't seen it in her office, either. What had she done, locked it away, or given it to a fellow soldier? Surely not. She wouldn't have wanted anyone to use it against her.

Lady Aiten's mouth twisted with hate. "And what of his confession? She and her servant both forced our future king to confess to crimes he never committed."

"I'm afraid he did," said Lord Torin. "We did another examination of the bodies of Lord Walvein and Lady Horell, and found their wounds match those inflicted by Lord Taithain's own weapon. He was working against us from the start."

"With whom?" Lord Raivan demanded. "We have

spent the entirety of the trials prepared to face our former Queen, yet in the moment we should have seized victory, this... *other* queen comes back from the dead."

"Etaina was never dead," I told them. "She disappeared underground along with her Court when the Erlking gained power. After his death, she decided she wanted to steal his talisman for her own."

"And where is the talisman, pray tell?" said Lady Aiten.

Ah. "She took it," I admitted. "But she didn't claim it. It serves me, not her."

"Enough," Mum interrupted. "Whatever Hazel did, you face enemies on two fronts at once and if you waste time bickering, they'll tear the Court in two and divide up the remains."

Lord Raivan swore in the faerie tongue. "What manner of armies do this Aes Sidhe have?"

"You've seen them." I nodded to the bodies piled outside the palace, where Darrow had been standing. "Her elite assassins can change their faces to look however they like. Their most talented soldiers can also do what Etaina did and hypnotise others using glamour."

"Darrow did the same," said Lady Aiten. "He tricked us into inviting him into our Court. He's been manipulating us from the moment he arrived in Summer."

Uh... she's not wrong. "Etaina wants to destroy the Seelie Queen first," I told her. "Not Summer. Chances are, they'll declare war on one another before they attack you. But if they come here, you need to be ready."

Lord Torin stepped in. "My house and I are prepared to offer our help to defend the Courts. We have a force assembled to face whatever threats the enemies devise."

"The half-bloods have a contingent waiting, too," said Ilsa. "Led by Raine Whitefall and Cedar Hornbeam."

"And myself," River added.

"I don't have an army." The doors creaked open, revealing Morgan and the faerie dog. "But I do have a puppy who's trained to attack dead things."

The Sidhe didn't quite know what to make of that. Then, as Lord Raivan and Lord Torin began to argue and Lady Aiten stepped in to join them, I turned back to the bodies of the fallen Aes Sidhe and caught sight of Darrow hovering outside the gates.

He's not leaving, is he?

Without looking back, I descended the stairs and ducked between the large leafy plants outside the palace gates to meet him. "Don't run off without warning like that. I thought she'd taken you. Or… worse."

I will undo him, Etaina had said. One look at his bleak expression told me we weren't finished with the aftermath of Etaina's revelations, not by a long shot. She'd *created* him—used glamour to make him from nothing like all her clones. Yet he seemed as real as I was, and as Faerie had taught me a long time ago, reality was relative. Even the Sidhe looked and sounded different to each person they spoke to. The idea of Darrow not being 'real' didn't bother me nearly as much as the notion of Etaina snapping him out of existence.

I inched closer to him. "Darrow, do you think she's coming here? Etaina?"

"She will," he said, "but it's the Seelie Queen she wants revenge on. She doesn't care about Summer or Winter except in a superficial sense."

"She wants the Erlking's talisman."

"Yes, and so does the Seelie Queen," he said, still not looking at me. "Given their history, she'll try to take out the Seelie Queen first."

"Or the other way around," I added. "Don't forget Etaina killed the Seelie Queen's pawn in front of an audience. The Seelie Queen knows how to get into the realm of the Aes Sidhe. It'd save us a lot of trouble if they just destroyed one another's armies without us needing to get involved."

With Etaina's glamour skills set against the Seelie Queen's army of the dead, I wasn't sure who would be the victor. Doubtless Etaina was the stronger of the two, but the Seelie Queen's healing powers gave her an endurance unmatched by any other.

"They would not leave us unharmed, regardless," said Darrow. "My own command to kill the Seelie Queen remains intact."

"I thought she changed her mind when she told you to attack me," I said.

His mouth pressed together. "For all I know, I've been glamouring you as long as we've known one another. I wouldn't know, would I?"

"You think I'm brainwashed?" I gave an unconvincing laugh. "You think *you* could brainwash me? Get real."

He didn't smile. "I recall doing exactly that."

"Yeah, blasting me in the face with glamour," I said. "It wasn't *permanent*. It wore off pretty fast, actually."

I still hadn't told my family I'd met Thomas Lynn. Truth be told, our encounter felt like a faerie-induced fever dream, but even I wouldn't dream up something that bizarre.

"That doesn't change what I did," he said, "or make me any more real."

"Nothing here is real," I said. "If you think I'm real and you aren't, that implies humans are more real than fae. Imagine what Etaina would say to that."

My words didn't draw a smile out of him. "Hazel, I'm nothing more than some twisted manifestation of her desire for a pawn, or perhaps a child of her own. I suspect the two are interchangeable to her."

"She gave you free will," I argued. "She gave you the freedom to turn on her if you wanted. That's more than the Courts gave my family."

He winced. "I didn't mean to dismiss your situation, but I felt her... undoing me. Like a glamour. Willing me out of existence."

"If she undoes you, she knows I'll do the same to her," I said. "And if I have to stay at your side for the duration of the battle, then so be it."

Finally, the hint of a smile showed on his face. "And to think you once found it intolerable to spend time with me."

"Nah, I wouldn't say that." I leaned in, brushed a strand of hair from his face and held a strand of my own hair alongside it. "If I asked which of us was real and which wasn't, would you know the difference?"

His expression softened, but his gaze broke from mine. "There is no way to counter her glamour. If she wills me out of existence, there's no going back. All I can do is run, as I always did."

"I'd do the same," I said. "Hell, I'm an expert on running. Every single time I have the opportunity to get rid of this family curse, I end up turning my back on it. I even met Thomas fucking Lynn and instead of asking him questions, I beat him up and ran away. And it's my ancestor's fault all this is happening to us."

"It's not your duty to pay the price for his mistakes," said Darrow.

"Nor is it your duty to pay the price for Etaina's," I said, breathless, harsh. "Fuck her vows. Fuck her entire Court. And fuck her claims that you aren't real. You're real enough for me to love, and that's all I have to say to that."

Shock blanked his expression. "You don't know what you're saying."

"Like hell." A glint caught my eye. Hummingbird fluttered down to land on his shoulder. "And him? He thinks you're real."

"I created him myself," he said. "For companionship, after Reyna's death."

Tears stung my eyes. I couldn't make up his mind for him, and the last thing I wanted was to do the same as Etaina had. "The point still stands. Let me know when you come to your senses."

I turned away, spotting Ilsa gesturing frantically from beside the gate. Blinking hard, I walked to join her.

"I didn't mean to eavesdrop," she said.

"Thought that was Morgan's line." I sniffed.

"Who, me?" said Morgan. "I don't eavesdrop on people."

I scowled. "Look, if you're thinking of making derisive comments about Darrow—"

"That's not it," said Ilsa. "Did I hear you said you met *Thomas Lynn?*"

"Oh." I took in a breath. "Yeah. That. I was going to

mention it earlier, but I'm still trying to make sense of it all. Thomas said he was stuck in the kingdom of the Aes Sidhe for however long it's been since he got kidnapped by the faeries."

"He's… immortal?" Ilsa said uncertainly.

"Didn't ask," I said. "I think the realm of the Aes Sidhe is fixed in time. I was there for over an hour while you guys were here."

"Wait, you met our ancestor?" said Morgan.

"Yeah, I did," I said. "I also kicked him in the crotch and broke his nose."

Ilsa rolled her eyes. "Why am I not surprised?"

"In my defence, Etaina ordered him to keep me locked away while she showed off her shiny new talisman to her Court," I said. "We didn't have time to chat."

Ilsa's expression turned grim. "You left the talisman behind."

"I'm still the wielder. She hasn't claimed it." She might have the staff, but she wouldn't have its obedience. Not as long as the god decided it needed me more than it needed her. *Yeah, and that'll end well.*

"Yet." Ilsa shook her head. "Have you heard the Sidhe? They don't care that the two queens are at war for reasons that have nothing to do with taking over Summer. They think she's going to use that talisman to wipe this place off the map."

"Then why aren't they coming after me?" I said. "I'm the one who lost the damned thing."

"Because you aren't declaring war on them." Ilsa took in a breath. "I'm going to the Lynn house to get some weapons. Coming?"

"Yeah. I lost my knives." I didn't fancy hopping back

into Etaina's realm to retrieve them. Even if it might mean having another chat with my ancestor. At the thought of Thomas Lynn, curiosity burned like a furnace, tempered only with the knowledge that Etaina might undo Darrow's existence in one snap of her fingers. The thought unbalanced me, preyed on my thoughts. *I won't let her. Never.*

I'd had bloody enough of being a pawn to everyone, including Thomas Lynn. It was him who lay at the centre of everything, and here I was, running away again.

Fury strengthened my resolve. I was through with ignoring my family's curse in favour of acting as damage control for the Sidhe's temper tantrums.

I could still do both. I *would* do both. I'd free my family and save the Courts in the same instant. And Thomas Lynn would help me do it.

20

I returned from the Lynn house clad in my thickest armoured coat and armed with as many weapons as I could carry. The palace entrance hall had cleared when the Sidhe returned to their own abodes to prepare for war—as much as they could with such little knowledge of who they might face and where. There were too many variables. For all we knew, Etaina had already marched on the Vale, or the Seelie Queen had brought her wraiths to the realm of the Aes Sidhe.

Inside the palace grounds, the bodies of the Aes Sidhe assassins were gone. Mum stood talking to Morgan, looking up as Ilsa and I approached.

"Take these." I pulled the stones I'd taken from Etaina's office and handed them to my siblings and mother. "I can't guarantee she won't claim the talisman anyway, but these should at least stop you suffering the backlash."

"This makes us immune to the effects of the talisman, Morgan," Ilsa told him. "Don't lose it, that clear?"

"Yes, mother," he said. "Why are you giving us these now? This place is deserted. There's no war on yet."

Because I might not be here when it arrives. "Is River with his father? Give both of them one of these stones, too. And the half-faeries—" I broke off, spotting Darrow conversing with some of my former bodyguards on the steps leading into the palace. Coral was among them, and so was Willow. "Hang on a second."

I climbed the steps, and Coral's eyes brightened at the sight of me. "There you are. I've heard at least a dozen versions of a story where Etaina of the Aes Sidhe interrupted the coronation to declare war on the Seelie Queen, so I take it it's not a joke?"

"I wish," I said. "The two of them are at war over a talisman that still belongs to me. And the throne, too, I guess. It's an old grudge, let's put it that way."

Darrow wouldn't catch my eye. I didn't want to resume our conversation about our relationship with everyone watching, and besides, it was easier not to ignite that flame with a bigger wildfire on the horizon. I'd told him what I meant to. If the worst happened to either of us, at least I wouldn't have that regret hanging over me.

"Damn," said Coral. "Do you think they're more likely to declare war on one another before they come here?"

"Maybe, but they're as likely to turn Summer into a battleground as anywhere else," I said. "It helps that the two of them hate one another more than they hate the rest of us, but if that talisman switches sides…"

Even with the talisman still serving me, the knowledge that Etaina might end Darrow in a heartbeat made me feel cold inside. Darrow was valuable to her even after his betrayal, but that didn't mean I wanted him near her when the battle broke out.

"Yeah, I know how that feels," said Coral.

"I should have looked for your talisman, too," I said. "I'm sorry. I didn't see it, but…"

"It sounds like you were lucky to get out of there in one piece." She released a breath. "Besides, I'm glad to see the back of it. I just feel like I'm betraying my mother's memory by even saying that."

"Don't be," said Willow. "If my mother is anything to go by, she doesn't have the right to dictate your choices."

"Exactly," I said. "Here's to breaking tradition and kicking arse."

"Thanks, Hazel," Coral said. "Great speech back there, by the way."

"Exactly." Willow leaned closer to me and whispered, "The crown is safe. Cedar has it in hand."

I hope she's right.

I'd said my goodbyes, done all I could to prepare for the upcoming fight—and now it was time to find my ancestor.

As I moved to descend the steps, Darrow caught my arm. "Hazel, I know what you're going to do."

"I'm not going to Etaina *or* the Seelie Queen," I said. "I'm going after someone else instead."

Namely, Thomas Lynn. Assuming he forgave me for kicking the crap out of him, anyway. With Etaina ready to go to war, the last thing she'd expect was for me to sneak back into her home so soon after my narrow escape. I wouldn't have a better chance to find out how my family's curse tied us to the fates of the Sidhe who'd placed it on us—and how to use my Gatekeepers powers to bring the scheming queens' power play to a screeching halt.

"She's here!" came a shout from outside the gates.

"Which 'she'?" I hopped down the steps after Darrow, my heart lurching in my chest. "Where?"

Bells rang out, followed by the sound of hoofbeats, and the forest came to life with noise. Flashes of green light sprang up among the trees as Sidhe rode past the palace on horseback, led by Lord Raivan and Lady Aiten. Even Lord Niall sat astride a magnificent white steed, his silver-white hair glowing as bright as the ornate sword in his hand.

Behind them, the contingent of half-faeries followed Cedar and Raine into battle, and Coral and Willow ran to join them. I gave Darrow a nudge. "Go on. I'm right behind you."

Ilsa, Mum and Morgan ran out of the palace gates alongside us, following the army into the forest. A riot of noise surrounded us, as Sidhe on horseback trampled undergrowth, rearranged paths or made trees and other obstacles move out of their way.

"Vale beasts!" Ilsa called over her shoulder, pulling out her talisman.

It's the Seelie Queen.

A blast of coldness rushed overhead, bringing a cloud of wraiths descending on the armies of Summer. Armoured Sidhe fought back with magic, flashes of bright Summer energy clashing with the wraiths' shadowy forms and blades of bone and branch dealing deadly wounds to the trolls and other Vale beasts that fought on the ground.

Raine stood back to back with Cedar, fighting off a swarm of wraiths. Her sceptre seemed to terrify them, its bright blue glow standing out among the Summer Sidhe. Cedar fought equally hard, his bow firing a volley of arrows into the midst of the enemy's forces.

"Hey," I said, cutting down a sluagh as I made my way to his side. "Do you still have the crown?"

"It's safe, don't worry," he said. "Will the Seelie Queen come after it?"

"Last time, she made her own crown, so probably not." The sluagh writhed beneath my blade, its translucent skin peeling away as the iron bit into the part of it that was still solid. "I think the crown's beyond our reach now."

Cedar swore, firing off an arrow at another oncoming sluagh. The arrow passed through the sluagh, but Cedar's hands glowed, the light mingling with the flow of Winter magic radiating from Raine's talisman to turn the sluagh into nothing more than dust.

The other half-faeries put up a fierce fight, Summer and Winter both. I'd lost sight of my family, so I dropped back to search for them. The glow of River's talisman caught my eye as he dealt a killing blow to a troll. Close by, Mum sank her knife into a sluagh's head, which popped like a balloon, raining semi-transparent gore onto the path.

Ilsa's glowing talisman drew the wraiths like a magnet, but none of them could touch her through our family's shield. The Sidhe were a different story. Wraith after wraith cast chilling shadows over their glowing forms, and their magic, for all its power, couldn't destroy the dead. One warrior fell from his horse into the brush, and the wraith descended on him. Clouds of icy magic billowed outwards, pinning the Sidhe to the earth.

As the wraith closed in on its living prey, the cu sidhe

leapt at it, sinking his teeth into the wraith's transparent form. It flailed and writhed, unable to reach its target.

"Told you he can deal with ghosts," said Morgan, firing a blast of necromantic power that knocked the wraith away from his captive, allowing the Sidhe to free himself.

Despite my siblings' best efforts, the wraiths refused to relinquish their grip on whatever tenuous grasp of life they had left. Ilsa might have her Gatekeeper's book, but the gates of Death weren't accessible from here in Faerie, and without them, she couldn't banish the wraiths permanently. For each one she destroyed, another took its place. The Seelie Queen must have called every Sidhe who'd ever died in the Vale to her side.

Dammit, I need my talisman back.

A tremendous blast of cold energy shot overhead, stripping the leaves off trees and rocking even the Sidhe's powerful steeds. I gripped the nearest tree, my nails digging into the bark as the storm tore through the battlefield.

Then the forest folded outwards, revealing a path that hadn't been there before. At the end, the Erlking's territory lay wide open, and in front of the gates stood the Seelie Queen.

All around her, wraiths floated like living shadows. Trolls and ogres wearing chains accompanied the ghostly sluagh and tentacled death stealers, skin-eating beasts and all manner of other monstrosities.

"I have had enough of being defied," she said. "I will take these lands for my own. They are mine by right, after all."

"Like hell." I stepped forward onto the path leading up

to the open gate to the Erlking's territory. "You don't have a right to a single inch of this realm."

She regarded me with a cool expression. "What did you do with my late husband's talisman?"

"Lost it."

Her eyes narrowed. "You... *lost* it?"

"Yep," I said, in cheery tones. "Shit happens. Tell you what, we can go back to the Vale and talk about it."

She drew a blade. "You will pay for your insolence, Gatekeeper."

"I don't think so." I bared my teeth in a smile. "My family curse is still active. In fact, I saw my ancestor himself earlier today, and I was on my way to speak to him when you so rudely interrupted me. This is your last chance to go into the Vale and take what you can get. Otherwise, you might end up losing your last remaining territory to another monarch."

"The Vale is not my territory," she said. "And the Queen of the Aes Sidhe is nothing compared to me."

"I beg to differ," said a cool, melodic voice.

Shit.

Etaina strode through the forest, the staff in her hand. Silence fell over the treetops as the two faerie queens looked at one another for a few long moments.

"I confess, I hoped never to set eyes on you again, sister," the Seelie Queen finally said.

"Likewise," Etaina responded. "In answer to your query about who took Hazel's talisman, it was I."

"But you still haven't claimed it, have you?" said the Seelie Queen. "No... I thought not. As before, you are nothing more than a plain imitation, like those glamours you adore so much. Allow me to take it off your hands."

She reached for the talisman, and the world slowed to a standstill. I grabbed my knife—too slow—and felt the chill of a wraith at my back. Shadows whirled around my wrists, as though aware they held the fate of the realms in their hands. Or rather, *my* hands. Yet the shadows didn't leave, didn't flow to the enemy's side.

The Seelie Queen gave a smile. "There you have it. The talisman claims neither of us. Even in the centuries you've had to devise a revenge scheme, you had to wait for me to act before you dared to strike."

All eyes turned to Etaina's face, which glowed as though lit from within, bringing the overwhelming conviction that she was all-powerful, beautiful, and that I wanted nothing more than to declare myself her worshipper.

Then the sensation passed, leaving me reeling on the spot. "That was a mere taste of my power. Who would you rather serve, me or her?"

"You can't use everyone as puppets, Etaina," I called to her. "Yes, including the gods. Or whatever was left of them after people like the two of you ripped out their magic and drove them out of their own lands."

"You understand nothing of the nature of the gods," said Etaina. "You are not worthy to wield this talisman."

"Apparently, you two aren't either." I strode behind Etaina, revelling in the shadows unfurling around my hands. "Perhaps it doesn't like power-hungry despots who are weaker than they'd like to pretend."

The other Sidhe remained silent, perhaps still stunned by the aftermath of her magic.

"You think the Erlking stole the talisman from you?" I

went on. "You're wrong. It chose him, the same way it chose me."

Etaina's mouth twisted. "If that's the case, you will be my wielder. Your hands will hold the talisman on my behalf, or my soldier's life will be forfeit."

She raised a hand, and a gasp tore from Darrow's mouth as his body flew backwards against a tree, pinned by the impact of her magic. From her pitiless expression, she was prepared to make good on her promise to erase him. Yes, she'd mourn him if she did, but she didn't value his life higher than the talisman. Nothing mattered more to her than her revenge on the Erlking.

I crossed to her side, my pulse racing, my steps as slow as I dared. I had *one* idea, but I didn't know the full extent of Etaina's power over Darrow, and if I guessed wrong, he'd pay the price for my mistake.

His eyes locked with mine, and he mouthed three words. *I trust you.*

I stopped beside Etaina. Her breath whispered on my cheek, and I felt the chill of unfamiliar magic. Something more than the stones protected her from the talisman's touch. Something dark, ancient. An Invocation. She'd marked herself, too.

"Has Thomas Lynn ever tried to escape?" I asked. "He seemed lonely in there. Couldn't you have used your glamour to create him a friend to play with? Or were you scared he'd use them as a decoy to help him escape?"

Darrow caught my eye. I willed him to understand what I needed him to do—win me time. Five seconds would be enough. After all, in the kingdom of the Aes Sidhe, time was relative.

"I don't think you're taking your situation seriously,

Hazel," she said. "Perhaps if I unravel your lover inch by inch, it will be enough."

She raised her head, and Darrow vanished. Several Darrows appeared where he'd stood, all of them fanning out to surround the two queens. All identical down to the last feature. Etaina's eyes narrowed.

"Hummingbird," I whispered. "Take me to—"

A flash of light ignited, and the world vanished, to be replaced by the realm of the Aes Sidhe. Two guards appeared on either side of me, weapons out. I punched one of them and kicked the other's kneecap, sending him sprawling into the dirt.

"Who are you?" the guard demanded, as I grabbed his collar and clenched my fist.

"I'm Hazel Lynn," I told him. "And I'm here to see Thomas Lynn, my ancestor and royal pain in the arse."

I gave him a swift punch, knocking him out cold, and stepped over his body.

Thomas. I'm coming for you.

21

When I neared the room of my captivity, the plucking of harp strings reached my ears, forming an eerie melody that made the hairs stand up on my arms. Only the lack of any magical side effects distinguished it from faerie music.

Inside the room, Thomas Lynn sat on a tree stump, playing a harp. His face still bore the impact of the kick I'd delivered to his face, and blood streaked his face on either side of his nose. While it didn't look broken after all, I'd probably given him a serious headache.

"Hey," I said. "Sorry for kicking you. Etaina didn't punish you for my escape, did she?"

"You shouldn't have come back," he said.

"I need answers," I told him. "My Gatekeeper's position is making me into a pawn between Etaina and the Seelie Queen and frankly, it's annoying the crap out of me. It all started with you, so I'd really appreciate it if you told me how to use my magic to stop those two queens in their tracks."

He shook his head. "It's not that simple."

"No," said Etaina. "It isn't."

Shit. I'd assumed Darrow's clones would keep her busy for a while, but she must have abandoned her armies to come after me. Time would hold still as long as we were here, after all.

"Really?" I said to her. "Were you that desperate to avoid the humiliation of failing to claim the talisman you've spent centuries looking for in front of an audience that you left your armies behind?"

Anger tightened her expression. "If I had known the advantages you had in that curse of yours, I would have taken you out of the picture sooner, Hazel Lynn."

"What advantages?" I said. "Waking up to piskies in my underwear drawer every morning? Being threatened at knifepoint on my first day as Gatekeeper? Please elaborate."

"I find it difficult to believe your time in the Summer Court didn't teach you better manners."

"Ah, see, I've only had people like you to learn from, and you don't set a good example." I glanced at Thomas Lynn, who stared slack-jawed at both of us. "I thought you seduced or kidnapped him, but he's been here an awfully long time, hasn't he?"

"This man is the reason for your family's predicament," she said. "He was a diversion, once, a passing fancy. Mortals are only good for a short while, then they wither. As you will, Hazel."

The talisman's magic coiled around my hands, and I looked her in the eyes. "You once tried to get me to give you my talisman for information on my past. Now you have it, right from my hands. Won't you do me the honour of telling me the truth? If it's your fault my family is cursed, you owe us."

"Your family is cursed because Thomas begged me to spare his life," she said. "He offered to serve me for seven years, and I accepted because he amused me. And then he conspired with Oberon against me. He stole both the talisman *and* the Gatekeepers from my clutches."

The world tilted under my feet. "Thomas helped the Erlking?"

"Oberon desired my talisman and my power," she said. "He asked Thomas to steal the talisman from me, and in return, he would see to it that he escaped Faerie alive. Little did Thomas know that Faerie still owned his soul, even in his escape. I should have taken better care when I advised him. You see, he swore to my Court, not to me. When my Court left Summer, the curse was left behind."

Then it passed onto us. If Thomas had bound himself... there was no way the Erlking didn't know the consequences of that binding.

"He escaped, and procreated," she went on. "Meanwhile, the Erlking expelled us from Summer, and with that, the Aes Sidhe were no longer welcome in the faerie lands."

"I thought you said you left Summer on purpose." It sounded like she'd been chased off instead, and the Aes Sidhe had gone into hiding. Then again, this was Etaina's version of the story, in which the Erlking was the villain who'd stolen her talisman in order to gain power. But it seemed clear from my interactions with him and from what I'd seen Etaina do with the talisman that the Erlking had known she would abuse its power. Just like his wife.

Perhaps he'd felt Thomas Lynn's soul was a worthy

trade to keep her from claiming it. After all, what was one family's future compared to the fate of the Courts?

"Leaving the Courts was the only course of action," she said. "If you had not allowed the talisman to claim you, you would have been safe."

"Don't look at me," I said. "It's the Seelie Queen who killed the Erlking and started this. I'm surprised you're not the one who got him, but I guess you're not really that powerful without using your glamour."

She'd been waiting for him to drop dead for centuries, hiding underground and making those stones to repel the Erlking's power in the hope of one day getting the upper hand.

"I really wouldn't test me, Hazel," she said. "I am more than the talisman's equal. It sees you as a pawn, nothing more."

"Why are you so obsessed with it?" I said. "I'd have thought you'd be flaunting that second talisman you stole, the weapon that actually did murder the Erlking. Unless you're afraid that talisman will reject you, too."

"The bow?" Her lip curled. "I had my people destroy it."

"You're—" No. She couldn't lie. "Talismans can't be destroyed."

"Anything can be destroyed, mortal. Even him, though it amuses me to see him suffer for his sins." I followed her gaze to Thomas, who hadn't said a word in my defence. "Many times have I wanted to destroy him, but he is immortal, a consequence of his own meddling. Thomas stole what was not his and gained curses and gifts in equal measure."

He can't be immortal. Not like the Sidhe, anyway, surely.

Their immortality source had been wiped out, and its origin, the blood of the Ancients, was all but impossible to obtain. The closest thing to a god inside this room was the talisman.

"If he didn't die, shouldn't the curse have stayed here with him?" I said. "With him still alive, he should be bound to the Courts, not us."

"Thomas was freed from his binding after seven years," she said. "Yes, he also promised to come when his assistance was needed, but the curse released him after those seven years had passed, and his daughters were bound instead."

"And you took him back." My head spun. "But—you said the curse was left behind. Who did it bind them to?"

"Not who," she said. "That was never the question, Hazel Lynn. Not who, but what…"

"The Courts." *Impossible.* "You can't bind someone to a place. Not without a person to carry the anchor."

"Really?" Her voice was soft, her eyes glittering. "Have you never questioned why your house is formed of pure Summer magic, and why our power answers to your call and runs in your blood? You are tied to the heart of Faerie, and I intend to purge the rot from it while you still have breath in your lungs."

Shock punched me in the chest. *Faerie?* Had the Erlking known? Perhaps he'd gambled on it, so Etaina would be left with Thomas and the Courts would gain the Gatekeepers for their own use.

I'd always thought my family were bound because of one man's mistake. Not a conspiracy between rival Sidhe which had ended with a human family gaining power over the very realm itself.

"The curse can't be broken, Hazel," she added. "But it will come undone when Faerie is destroyed. Perhaps you will thank me for it, in the end."

The impact of her revelations rippled through my mind like the sea after a storm, tearing through everything I thought I knew. No wonder the Gatekeeper's magic was strong enough to resist the power of the Erlking's talisman. The whole of Faerie was bound up in it.

And if the Courts fell, we'd be free. The ultimate price for our freedom would be the end of Faerie itself.

"I'll take *him*—" She held up Hummingbird by his wing. "Thomas, kindly see to it that she does not escape this time. It will be exceedingly painful for you if she does."

And in a flash of light, she was gone, leaving me alone with my traitorous bastard of an ancestor, who stood at a distance from me as though he expected me to kick him again. Which I might, if it would do any bloody good whatsoever.

"How can no time pass in this realm at all?" I said instead. "It must do, if she expects to come back."

"It's part of the glamour of this place," he said. "Time passes only when Etaina wills it to. We will remain frozen in time until she returns."

"Damn." I paced to the door, then halted. *We're frozen in time. You can get answers without missing the battle.* "You were there when I was chosen as Gatekeeper. I heard your voice."

He laid the harp down. "Etaina's last piece of revenge on the Courts... I was ordered to pick the sibling who was least likely to be a threat, or most likely to make trouble. Your sister, studious and loyal, would have been easier for the Sidhe to control. Your brother was already showing signs of another talent which would've been troublesome to the Sidhe if he'd become Gatekeeper. That left you."

"Oh, thanks," I said. "You picked me because I was the last resort?"

Granted, Morgan's psychic talents would have terrified the Sidhe, while Ilsa's non-confrontational tendencies would have made her less likely to piss them off. So Thomas had picked me as a middle finger to the Courts. Even my own ancestor had used me for his own ends.

"Yes, and you still enabled Etaina to get her hands on the talisman again," he said. "Now she will use it as she always intended to."

"Blame the Seelie Queen for shooting the Erlking if you must," I snapped. "The instant he died, Etaina started plotting to get it back. And I bet you knew it, yet you were too much of a coward to reveal yourself to me. You know, I'm not sorry I kicked you in the face at all. In fact, I might just do it again."

The anger melted from his expression. "It isn't like she said," he said, his voice quiet. "When she took me, it was for more than her own amusement. She called upon a god, one of the Ancients, for favours, and every seven years, she offered the soul of a mortal man as a tribute. I would have been that sacrifice if I hadn't bound myself."

"And bound the rest of us," I said heatedly. "Was it worth screwing over your descendants to save your own neck? Generations of us have had to bow before the Courts, obeying their every whim while knowing they might dispose of us in the blink of an eye. I hope your long life was worth it, Thomas Lynn, because if I can deliver you to hell myself, I'd gladly do it."

He said nothing to argue with me. Everything I'd said was true, after all. He knew nothing of the suffering his decision had caused my family, let alone the effects on Faerie itself.

"If I were capable of leaving this place and moving to the world beyond, I would take your hand and let you lead me there in a second," he finally said. "But that fate is not for me."

"You know, the stories paint you as kind of noble," I said. "Or at least less of an arsehole."

"What is the story they tell of me?" he said.

I thought back. "There's a lot of versions of the same tale. Even the regular humans know some of them. They say you were saved from Faerie by your mortal lover…"

"Correct," he said. "On Samhain seven years after I bound myself, I was forced to ride alongside the Sidhe in the mortal realm. My true love rescued me that night, pulling me from the horse I rode. In doing so, she prevented me from becoming the sacrifice, but I was unaware that Faerie still owned my soul. And I was unaware that the binding existed in my bloodline. When my daughters were grown and taken into Faerie, the Lady of Light brought me here. And so I remain."

"Your daughters were taken to Summer and Winter," I said. "As were their descendants. I've been at the mercy of the Seelie Court's nobles since before I could walk."

Pain flickered in his eyes. "I didn't know. I thought my own soul would be enough, and that my death would bring the end of the curse. But I cannot die. The impact of the binding is such that I am an immortal, like them, and I can no more lie than the Sidhe can. I suppose I will know when she wins, because the curse will disappear when the Courts fall."

And so would I. The curse would dissolve along with the Courts, allowing me to walk away free with my family while leaving the Sidhe to reap what they'd sown.

I'd spent my life resenting Faerie for what the Sidhe had done to me, yet a not-insignificant part of me had always believed I had to serve the Court because nobody else would. Knowing so many people had had a hand in my fate had shaken away any last shreds of loyalty to Summer I'd possessed, but the warring queens wouldn't stop with the Courts. Earth would be next, and the humans would suffer a far worse fate than any Lynn had.

"What will she make you do to me if I try to escape?" I asked. "How far under her influence are you?"

"Too far," he said. "There is no safe way for you to leave this place. When this realm was disconnected from Summer, all doors were closed."

"The only way out is to borrow someone's sprite or use a spell?" No wonder I'd never seen any doors here, nor been able to find the entrance in the real world.

"I know only what I have been told," he said. "I have walked these corridors for countless years and never found a way out."

A chill raced through my blood. "Then I guess I'll have to rope one of her soldiers into helping me. I take it you don't have any of her skills with glamour?"

"No," he murmured.

"Well, either she'll show up in a second or not at all," I muttered. "Unless she changes her mind and decides she needs me to wield the talisman for her."

His eyes widened. "You are still the wielder? Yet she carries it?"

"She's immune to its magic, even if she can't use it." My mouth tightened. "We're at a stalemate. She and the Seelie Queen are, too, but I doubt they care much for collateral damage. Humans and faeries alike will die in their war. I'd rather keep the curse and have my family walk away alive than gain my freedom and lose everything else. As for the talisman, I bet there's a reason it picked me, and it has to do with the centuries of curses and treachery you've brought on my whole family."

Thomas remained silent for a moment. "If you are still the wielder, there may yet be hope. You retain a link to the gods, through its magic."

"Not much use here." I called the shadows, experimentally, but no chill of familiar magic came to my hands. "I'm too far away from her to use its power."

"It matters not," he insisted. "You still have other advantages, do you not?"

"What, the ability to cross between realms?" I frowned. "I take it I can't just use that power to step into Faerie from here?"

"No, but you can speak to the gods," he said. "As long as you're bound to that talisman, you're free to use their language without consequence, as the Sidhe are."

"Speak to the gods?" I said. "They're dead. The Devourer is gone, and even if he wasn't, Etaina is impervious to the talisman's power. She and the Seelie Queen both."

"Not forever," he said. "The Sidhe's one weakness is the power of their predecessors, however much they tried to fight it by exiling their gods and stealing their magic.

Etaina may have marked her army, but those bindings will last a day at most. She means to win today."

"Those marks." My heart jolted. "Those are Invocations, too. They aren't permanent?"

"They aren't." His mouth tightened. "The Sidhe did terrible things when they spilt the lifeblood of the gods and used its remains to fuel their immortality, Etaina most of all. After I thwarted her sacrifice, she stopped contacting the gods altogether. She feared they would turn on her."

"That's why she wanted the talisman." I understood that much, but it wouldn't help me get out. "I'm guessing she and her sister got into an argument over it, too."

"Because the Erlking used the gods' magic to cut this realm off from Faerie," he said. "There is a chance, however, that the same magic can set you free."

"You mean I can use an Invocation to break out?" I said. "I told you, I can't read the language if it isn't in front of me."

The runes on my talisman—and inside Ilsa's book—had been understandable to me, but none came to mind off the top of my head which would allow me to break out of this place.

Off the top of my... A shiver ran through the symbol on my forehead. An Invocation that meant 'Gatekeeper'.

The power of the Gatekeepers had won out when faced with the staff. If my family's curse was fuelled by Faerie itself, it was no wonder even the Seelie Queen feared the backlash. Etaina had known all along what we were capable of, but she hadn't wanted to make an open challenge against the Gatekeepers... until now.

Because we were stronger than her.

"What does it mean?" I said. "Gatekeeper? Last time I spoke the word aloud, it took me to the Erlking, but he's dead."

Perhaps because he'd once been at the heart of Faerie. But nothing remained there any longer except rot and decay.

"I will take you to the border where our realm was once linked to the rest of Faerie," said Thomas. "Perhaps you can find a way to open it."

He strode out of the room with surprising speed, and I had to half-run to keep up. Winding corridors led us along a route I didn't know, until he came to a halt in an empty chamber. On the wall, symbols had been etched into the packed earth, their edges shimmering with light.

"Who...?" *The Erlking.* I recognised his hand in the scrawled symbols, and their meanings filtered through my mind. A binding spell, sealing this tunnel and cutting off the Aes Sidhe from Faerie at large. "This is where the Courts used to be connected? And you think I can get us out where nobody else has succeeded?"

"You have done many impossible things already, Hazel Lynn."

He wasn't wrong, but I suspected nobody had succeeded because Etaina had ensured she was the only person here in the Court who could read the symbols at all. Perhaps there was another reason she'd denied her soldiers a chance to learn how to read. Because if they learned the language of the Ancients, they might use them against her.

Thomas reached for the wall, rubbing his palm against the surface. Below, more text became visible. "The Erlking himself wrote these words."

I read the words carefully. *One gate became two*
One key became two
One lies below the earth
One lies above the surface
Two must belong to one
To make two become one.

"He carved a riddle into the wall?" I read the words over again, but unlike the ancient symbols, the plain words were written in the usual faerie language with no embellishment. "Why would the Erlking leave a way out? Did he know the Gatekeeper might end up trapped here one day?"

He'd known Etaina, so perhaps he'd seen her power grab coming. In the event of his death, he would have expected her to go after both the talisman and the Gatekeepers. The guy was devious, that was for damned sure.

"We have to find two keys," I said. "No idea what gates it's talking about, though. This is a wall, not a gate, and faerie riddles tend to be literal."

"Two keys," Thomas repeated. "One lies below the earth, one above the surface. That means one of them is here in the realm of the Aes Sidhe."

"Did Etaina know about any of this?" I said. "Because she had a lot of keys in her office. I saw them when I was looking for the talisman."

"It makes sense that Etaina would keep one of these keys for her own," said Thomas.

"Guess it's time to stir up some more trouble." I backed up from the wall. "You don't seem worried that the guards will come after us."

"Most of them will be with Etaina, fighting for her

Court. She trains every one of her people as warriors, if she can."

Figures. I let Thomas take the lead, taking the two of us to Etaina's office. Two guards stood outside the doors, wearing the same uniform as the rest.

"You." A guard with foxy features looked me over. "You should not be here."

"The Lady of Light told me to watch her," said Thomas, his face bland. "You are needed elsewhere."

As the guard opened his mouth to speak, Thomas struck him over the head. The second guard lunged at me, and I hit him hard in the jaw, knocking him backwards into the wall. Thomas pulled a key from the guard's pocket and inserted it into the door, while I blinked at him. "You just… no, that wasn't a lie, was it?"

"I am accomplished at evading untruths by now," he said, in calm tones. Like he hadn't just knocked a guy out. Thomas had learned the Sidhe's games well. If he'd been here for centuries, it was no wonder.

We entered the office and I made for the desk drawer where I'd found Etaina's keys. "How am I supposed to know which is the right one? Does she have somewhere she keeps hidden?"

Thomas crouched and pressed a hand to the floor, unearthing a hidden trapdoor the same colour as the earth. "It has been a while since I last saw this place, but I believe she keeps some of her valuable possessions underneath the floor."

I crouched at his side and recoiled. A pool of stagnant water lay inside a shallow hole in the floor, its surface dull and grey. Despite that, an odd sheen glittered atop its rippling currents. Around it lay tools—pens, carved knives, all glittering with the same colour. Even the stones did, but the water itself looked faded, sickly, as though she'd leached the very life from it.

Thomas was silent for an instant. "I've seen her using those pens to mark her soldiers."

"With Invocations." I clapped a hand to my mouth. "*This* is the blood of the gods?"

Not only was the blood capable of bestowing immortality, it carried the gods' own power. When Etaina marked her Sidhe with the right symbols, they became immune to the talisman's destructive magic. But she'd overdone it, and now the pool of enchanted blood was reduced to almost nothing.

"Did she mark all her guards recently?" I asked Thomas. "She did, didn't she? She put markings on everyone in her Court to ensure the talisman wouldn't harm them, and she used up most of her supply of blood in the process."

If I destroyed her blood supply, it wouldn't put an end to her, but maybe she'd think twice about wielding the talisman if the marks wore off. And they would do. No magic lasted forever.

Faint shadows stirred in my fingertips, and the instant I touched the surface, the blood gave way to dark mist, revealing a key lying on the bottom.

There it is.

"One key down." My hand closed around the cool metal shape. "The second one lies above the earth. Does that mean it's in the Courts?"

"I'm afraid I do not know, but I suspect you're right," Thomas said. "What are you going to do with those?"

I picked up the pen he'd indicated, then tossed it aside. "It's out of ink."

Not all of them were, though, and an idea sparked in my head. The Erlking must have used one of them to write the words of the binding onto the cave wall and disconnect the two realms. Perhaps I might use the same method to make the two realms become one once again.

Two become one. Might that be what it means? Maybe, maybe not, but getting the pens away from Etaina could only be a good thing.

After grabbing the few pens with ink left in them and stuffing them into my pockets, I left Etaina's office behind. Thomas and I retraced our steps through the winding tunnels to the chamber with the writing carved into the wall. The lack of any challengers unnerved me, if just because I knew Etaina's army would be fighting on the battlefield right this instant.

I walked up to the writing on the wall. The image of the symbol on my forehead appeared in my mind's eye. I'd seen it in the mirror enough times to be able to recall every detail. Fixing my attention on that image, I let my mind skim the surface in search of meaning.

Then I wrote the word. *Gatekeeper.*

A breeze kicked up from nowhere, sweeping through the tunnels. Earthen layers peeled back from the cave wall, revealing a hollow opening. A spark of sunlight beckoned at the end of a long path winding between trees.

"Is this the way out?" I breathed.

"Yes," Thomas murmured. "I recognise this place. But to traverse it, we must take a steed with us. If he's still here, that is."

He gave a whistle, and a giant white horse cantered into view. A tremendous beast with a horn the length of my arm galloped down the path, halting in front of Thomas.

Not a horse. A unicorn.

"You've got to be fucking kidding me."

22

A unicorn. Had the stories ever mentioned Thomas riding on a unicorn? I supposed it was close enough to a horse for humans without the Sight to confuse the two of them. The beast lowered its head, and I tentatively raised a hand to stroke its ivory-white horn. The unicorn snorted, gave its head a shake. It wanted me to climb onto its back.

Here goes nothing. Taking a deep breath, I swung my leg over the unicorn's neck and settled behind its shoulders.

"Aren't you coming?" I said to Thomas. "I could use someone to steer me in the right direction."

He hesitated, then swung up to join me. It took one light tap of my foot for the unicorn to spring into motion, just as several guards appeared behind us. "Stop right there!"

"Gangway!" I yelled, urging the beast into a gallop.

The guards leapt aside, avoiding the unicorn's spear-sharp horn, and we rode on through the tunnel towards the light. I didn't know what I expected to find on the other side. The Vale, perhaps. Instead, I found a blank stretch of road, flanked with briars and thorny plants. The gleam of water nearby indicated a river, but when I drew closer, I saw the waters were crimson.

"That's the Blood River," Thomas said. "They say every Sidhe who dies in battle is washed away in its flow. The Huntsman takes their souls and the River takes their blood. The River travels through both Courts, and if you follow this path, you will end up in the part of Summer beyond reach of the Erlking's lands."

"Hold up." I twisted to face him. "You mean we're back in Faerie."

Which meant Etaina and the Seelie Queen were doing battle right now, and I was stuck on a unicorn in the rear end of nowhere.

"We are in the forgotten part of the faerie realm." He urged the unicorn forwards, and I held on tight as our steed broke into a gallop. *What was the deal with the keys, then?* They hadn't got us out, but surely the Erlking wouldn't have left that riddle for me if he hadn't intended me to do something with it. Something that involved stopping Etaina.

"Someone's up ahead!" Thomas warned. "Stop!"

A woman carrying a sword walked onto the path, clad in jeans and a leather jacket. Her features were starkly human, her dark hair tied back and her sword glimmering with blue light.

The woman turned, eyes widening, and the unicorn skidded to a halt, its horn inches from impaling her.

"Hey!" said the woman. "Watch where you're putting that horn… is that a *unicorn?*"

"Yes, it is," I said. "I know you from somewhere. I'm Hazel Lynn, Summer Gatekeeper."

"I'm Ivy Lane," she said. "I'm also your distant relation and a friend of your sister's."

Of course. Ivy was employed by Faerie, though I'd ever seen her in the Court during my tenure as Gatekeeper. The *distant relation* part had slipped my mind, though. "How distant are we talking about?"

"Very." Thomas's voice was quiet. "Etaina took great delight in telling me that after my twin daughters were taken by Summer and Winter, my wife left the Lynn house behind and set up a base somewhere else. She remarried, and her descendants scattered. As the bloodline became diluted, the effects of the Lynn curse faded."

"Yeah, I had zero magic until I found this." Ivy waved her sword, which gleamed up to its hilt. *A talisman. Another human with a talisman.* Ivy had tricked a Sidhe into giving her their magic, the rumours said. Perhaps it ran in the family.

"Meet Thomas Lynn," I said to her. "The originator of the Lynn curse. Also, I don't know if you heard, but there's a war on in Summer."

"That's where I was going," said Ivy. "Faerie thought it was funny to get me lost instead. Do you know the way out?"

"No, but I'm trying to find it." I patted the unicorn's back. "You'll have to follow us on foot, and I can't promise I know where I'm going."

But if Ivy was here, surely the Courts couldn't be too far off.

Ivy fell into step with us on the path. "Can you explain who I'm supposed to be fighting? I know the Seelie Queen murdered the Erlking and tried to take over Summer. I also heard you had his talisman, but I don't see it."

"Long story short, the Courts are in a deadlock between two angry queens, and one of them stole my talisman," I said. "She also happens to be able to glamour anyone into obedience. I don't know if she wants to take over Summer, but the Seelie Queen does."

"How do I always manage to miss these things?" said Ivy. "I've been dealing with an argument between the Unseelie Queen and the borderlands for the last few weeks, and I assumed Summer would sort itself out. How *did* you end up with a talisman, anyway? No offence, but they don't tend to go for humans."

"No clue," I said. "But both queens want to stick it to the Erlking. They're also sisters."

"Family disputes," said Ivy, with an eye-roll. "With the Sidhe, it's always about blood, or family, or both."

Yeah. And I'm not linked to any of them by blood, just by an accident that enslaved my whole family.

"Or riddles," I added. "The Erlking left one for me in the realm of the Aes Sidhe. I'm supposed to look for a key. What it has to do with winning the war, though, I wouldn't know."

"I don't know anything about keys," said Ivy. "But I did get the impression someone wanted me to find you. Or Faerie itself did."

My heart lurched. "You joke, but my family is literally bound to the heart of Faerie itself. When the Aes Sidhe split from Summer and Winter, they left the curse behind in the realm itself. Which means breaking the curse is pretty much impossible without destroying Faerie... and as luck would have it, the talisman might do exactly that."

Ivy's eyes widened. "Seriously? You know, I always thought this place was conscious, but I figured I was just imagining things."

Damn. She's right. The number of times I'd walked through Faerie and been convinced some invisible force was moving the paths around, and had the sense that even the Sidhe didn't truly know the depths of it.

"The gods created it," I murmured. "They must have. I mean, they were the Sidhe's predecessors, so it's not that far out of reach."

But does that mean one of them *lies at the heart of Faerie?* That might explain how the Gatekeeper's magic could stand up to the gods, but that didn't change the fact that the Erlking's destructive power was one mistake away from devouring the whole realm.

A rustling noise came from the trees and my body tensed. Then a dark cloud of ravens and crows swooped overhead, forcing me to flatten myself against the unicorn's back to avoid them.

"What's got the Morrigan all fired up?" Ivy said.

"Oh, good, she did decide to help out." I watched the crows and ravens fly towards the sounds of fighting, the clash of blades, shouts and snarls and other inhuman noises. "The Seelie Queen recruited wraiths from all over the Vale to join her team. Guess the Morrigan finally decided she was encroaching on her territory."

The unicorn made a sharp turn, and at once, I recognised our surroundings. The path of the dead wove into the distance, utterly flat as though hammered by the impact of countless footsteps. It extended in either direction in a straight line, but instead of following the path, the unicorn veered away.

"There's the gate," said Thomas, indicating an expanse of ice-covered hawthorn points looming in front of us.

"That's not our gate." I swore. "We're still in Winter."

"I know that gate," Thomas insisted. "I entered Faerie this way."

"You haven't been here for a while," I said. "There are two gates. One in Summer, one in Winter."

"The gate must have split when you were cursed," he said. "To allow both sides of the family to enter Faerie."

There was one gate. One gate, now two. Two keys. Like the riddle. I looked down at the key in my hand, then at the gate. What *did* the Erlking want me to do with this?

Ivy cleared her throat. "I'm going to join the battle."

"Go ahead." I hopped off the unicorn's back and walked to the gate, key in hand. "I'll catch you up."

"Sure." Ivy hefted her sword. "Good luck."

A nagging voice in the back of my head told me the battle wouldn't wait for me, but the symbol on the Winter gate gleamed arrestingly. *To make two become one*, the riddle had said. Our curse was tied to the heart of Faerie, and if two became one again, maybe we'd be able to harness that strength to defeat the two queens.

Perhaps it took a god to defeat a god, after all.

The key fit snugly into the lock and turned, once. The clicking sound it made brought a chill to my skin. *It worked.*

Which meant there was an identical key for *our* gate, somewhere on the surface. But where in Faerie was the equivalent of the realm of the Aes Sidhe? Summer, perhaps. The Erlking himself had hidden the keys, so the second one must be hidden on his own territory. Somewhere only the Gatekeeper could find it.

"Swift," I said, aloud. "Swift, where are you?"

No reply came. The sprite must be hiding from the battle. *Think, Hazel.* The first key had been hidden inside a pool...

The gate flew open, revealing an expanse of pristine snow, and Holly recoiled from the unicorn's horn. "What the hell?"

"Sorry, but we have to use your gate." I hopped onto the unicorn's back again. "C'mon. We're going to Summer's gate."

The unicorn had other ideas. It bounded through the gate and across the Winter Gatekeeper's lawn, kicking up snow-covered grass as it careened towards the woods.

"Hey!" Holly shouted. "What the hell are you doing to my garden? Is that a *unicorn?*"

"I don't think he's a fan of snow," I said over my shoulder. "Sorry, I can't stop—"

I held on tighter, and the unicorn snorted in a combination of discomfort and terror. Thomas yelled in alarm as the unicorn flew full-tilt at the forest—

The trees vanished, moving aside to reveal the Summer Lynn house behind Holly's. The gate was still there, but the hedges of the Inner Garden had peeled back, exposing the pool of shimmering water, bright as starlight.

The polar opposite of that stagnant pool inside the realm of the Aes Sidhe.

"I think," I said, "I just found the source of our binding to Faerie."

Thomas exhaled softly. "It's beautiful. I remember seeing such a pool when I first entered the realm of the Lady of Light."

"I bet you did," I murmured. "That's how she got you."

The Inner Garden was our biggest secret. I'd always thought it odd that the Sidhe would give us access to something so powerful, as the waters could heal any injury no matter how serious. They'd even managed to counter the magic of my talisman, for a time. Yet I'd never seen such a place elsewhere in Faerie.

Its magic came from the gods. Of course it did. It's the lifeblood of one of the Ancients.

I rode on towards the pool. I didn't really have a plan —the unicorn was still whinnying and kicking bits of snow off its hooves—but if one pool contained one key, the other must be inside this one.

And then what? Breaking the curse wouldn't save Faerie from the warring queens, and it wouldn't protect humanity from their wrath. I couldn't even sense the talisman's shadowy power at my fingertips any longer. But I'd come too far to go back. I had to see this through.

I jumped off the unicorn's back, my feet sinking into soft grass. As I reached for the water's surface, sharp cold bit into my hand, causing me to recoil. Shimmering with silver light the same colour as the mark on my forehead, the waters rose into the air to form a barrier before me.

"Who is this?" boomed a voice. *"Someone called on my magic. I felt it."*

Holly swore from behind me. "What the hell did you do?"

"It's not me!" I said. "This is our family's curse... the source of it all."

Holly's garden didn't contain an equivalent to our Inner Garden pool. I'd never really thought about it before, but with the forest gone and the world stripped bare, it couldn't be more obvious that the Inner Garden was ours alone. Perhaps because the Erlking was the one who'd transferred the curse to Summer and Winter in the first place, and he always had a bias for his own Court.

"What the bloody hell are you talking about?" said Holly. "Why were you on the other side of my gate?"

"I will explain, my lady." Thomas moved back to speak to her, while I faced the shimmering barrier of water.

"You are the one who carries the Devourer's power in your blood. I will not allow you to lay a hand on me, Gatekeeper. I felt part of me die, deep underground. Were you responsible?"

"No," I said. "That was Etaina. You... you were in the other pool, too?"

The gods might be dead, but if pieces their consciousness lived on inside any sources of their magic, it stood to reason the pool would have its own innate consciousness, too.

"Can someone please tell me what's going on?" Holly cut through Thomas's attempted explanation. "What does this have to do with our family's curse?"

"The curse bound us to Faerie, not to a person," I explained. "But the gods *created* Faerie, and this pool—it's the lifeblood of one of the Ancients. I think."

The shimmering barrier darkened. *"I was once free. I know nothing of how I came to be in this state, but many have held fragments of my power in their grip. I sense them, while I remain trapped here."*

A shiver travelled through my skin. "You aren't the only one. We're trapped, too."

I was starting to guess what had happened. The Sidhe had slaughtered the Ancient and taken its blood for their own use, as they had with so many others. When the

Erlking had cut off the realm of the Aes Sidhe, he'd seen to it that the Gatekeeper's curse would transfer to the Court, and he'd given us access to the pool to ensure our survival.

But before he'd done so, he'd left instructions to the Gatekeeper behind so they would be able to find the keys he'd hidden. In the event of his death and the talisman's loss, our only hope would be to find the two keys and unlock the gates, awakening the gods' magic in the process.

"You, trapped? You walk free, while I do not."

"I can help you," I told the shimmering barrier. "But I need your help. If one of the two queens who are currently fighting over that talisman wins, you and Faerie will both be destroyed."

"Why should I aid you, Gatekeeper? You act on the word of a king who would see my people cast into the void."

"The Erlking is the only one of the Sidhe who regretted what happened to the Ancients," I said. "He gave his life to keep this realm safe from the Devourer's power. I don't agree with what he and the others did, but if you help me win this, I can find a way to set you free."

"I will make no more bargains with you."

"It's not a bargain, it's a promise." I took in a breath. "The Sidhe hurt me and my family, too. I won't forget that, and I won't let them punish either of us again."

The Sidhe had caused this. Too long had they made humans into scapegoats for their crimes, forced us to take the fall for their mistakes, tortured their gods into supporting their quest for glory. Not anymore.

"Please," I went on. "Just let me take the key. I won't

harm you. And I won't use the Devourer's magic against you."

The waters pulled back, revealing the key lying on the bank. I knelt to pick it up, feeling its cool, slight weight. The world seemed to hold its breath as I walked to the gate, pushed the key into the lock, and turned it.

A rushing noise sounded behind me. As I turned around, the waters flew from the pool, evaporating into fine mist. The symbol on my forehead throbbed, and Holly exclaimed, clutching her forehead, too. Magic swirled in my hands, the Gatekeeper's power yearning to escape.

The Gatekeeper wants to take our magic. "Please," I gasped out. "Help us stop Etaina. Then I'll let you go. I promise. I swear—"

The waters flung themselves at me, covering me from head to toe. Holly shouted in alarm, while my mouth flew wide, speaking words I barely grasped the meaning of. A heavy weight settled on my shoulders, and I knew I'd voiced my promise aloud in an unbinding spell that wouldn't break.

Now all I had to do was honour it. No pressure.

23

The mist pursued me as I walked up to Summer's gate, covering me in a fine layer. Weirdly, it didn't feel wet or cold, but I didn't know what advantages it might give me in a fight.

Behind me, Holly bombarded Thomas with questions, reacting with about as much shock as I'd expected to the notion that our ancestor was alive to see his descendants reap the benefits of the chaos he'd unleashed on our lives.

She caught me up at the gate. Her gaze flickered over the semi-transparent layer of magic cloaking me like thin mist. "So this is the Erlking's fault? He saw to it that we were enslaved so he'd have someone to set up against Etaina after he died, knowing she'd go after his talisman again? And our power is really from this... god?"

"Yes, from the god whose magic lies at the heart of Faerie." I rested my hands on the gate. "What's the situation on the other side?"

"Winter's forces were on their way to join Summer's, last I checked," said Holly. "I came here—to be honest, I was looking for you, Hazel. I worried when Etaina came back and you didn't, but I hadn't a clue how to find those Aes Sidhe."

"Anyone will be able to find them now I've blown a hole in the wall of their realm." I pulled open the gate. "Thomas, lead the way."

Still on the unicorn, Thomas rode through the gates, while Holly and I followed on foot.

A number of Sidhe on horseback rode along the path from the direction of the Winter Court, bearing the banners of the Unseelie Queen. *Good. They did come.*

Holly drew a blade and ran to fight alongside Winter's forces, her iron sword cutting into a sluagh bearing down on the oncoming Sidhe. Ahead, wraiths drifted in clouds of magic, freezing trees and dodging any attempts the Sidhe made to pin them down. A troll rampaged through the carnage, chains swinging, and knocked one of Etaina's soldiers off his feet.

I'd never seen a battle like it. Without two clear sides, the Vale beasts ripped into anyone they could—Summer, Winter, Aes Sidhe, even their own people. The Aes Sidhe themselves looked so much like regular Summer faeries, aside from their darker clothing, that they managed to evade notice, sneaking up on their targets with deadly stealth. The half-Sidhe fought, too, and relief swept through me at the sight of Darrow. Etaina had spared him, no doubt so she could finish him in front of me. Perhaps she'd known I'd find a way to escape. After all, she couldn't use the talisman alone. She needed me.

The misty cloak shivered against my skin as the shadows woke in my blood. *She's close. Etaina is close.*

"Hazel!" Darrow withdrew his blade from a troll's

neck, letting its heavy body thump to the ground. His clothes were streaked with gore, but he appeared to be unhurt.

"I'm glad you're okay," I said. "That is—if it's the real you and not a clone."

I knew it was, though, as surely as I knew my own name. I couldn't guarantee both of us would survive, but I'd do my damned best to try.

"I'm real," he said softly. "I always was."

Clapping rang out, and the fighting around us ceased as Etaina strode into view, unleashing her glamour on all the surrounding Sidhe. At once, everyone stilled, watching her. Worshipping her.

"So you came back," said Etaina. "I wondered if you'd run away, given the chance, but I knew your ties to others would always bring you back to die upon my sword."

"There's a lot of things you don't know about the Gatekeepers," I said. "After all, you and the Erlking both conspired to keep us in ignorance about the true identity of the one we were bound to. Thanks for the key, by the way."

Her eyes widened. "Key?"

She hadn't known. The Erlking—and Thomas—had hidden the text until the Gatekeeper arrived. Sneaky bastard.

The cloak moved around me, a living force, pressing the shadows into my skin. A frown sprang to my mouth. With the cloak in my way, I couldn't use the talisman's magic... but neither could anyone else.

I wouldn't be Etaina's puppet. Never again.

I faced her with a smile. "I have the gods on my side. Turns out they aren't too pleased with you."

The Seelie Queen strode into view, her armoured clothes stained with blood. Someone had dealt her a deadly blow, but she'd healed from the injury as she always did. "What is the meaning of this? You dare to flee from me in the middle of a battle? Have you realised that without the talisman's cooperation, you cannot win this?"

Etaina raised the staff. "Let's try this again. Gatekeeper, you will be my hands and wield the talisman at my command."

Her eyes glowed with power, but the shimmering mist deepened around me, and I felt nothing.

She can't control me.

My smile widened. "Like I said, I have a new team behind me."

Her mouth twisted. *"Thomas Lynn.* You are responsible for this."

"You are correct." Thomas rode into view on the unicorn's back. Its horn was encrusted with gore. "The blame is mine, not Hazel or her family's. My daughters were trying to correct my mistake when they came to Faerie to fix the damage, but it is I alone who defied the gods, and it is your people who slaughtered them and claimed their magic."

Etaina raised a hand. "I can still undo you, Hazel Lynn. *I summon you.*"

She said a name, a single syllable that rang with darkness. Thomas exclaimed in alarm as the unicorn reeled backwards, sending him flying into the air—where he hovered as though propped up on invisible strings.

My body trembled. Etaina had *summoned* something. Using an Invocation. I didn't need to be fluent in the gods' language to know it wasn't good news.

"This is the life I was promised," echoed a booming voice. *"The life I was denied."*

Thomas didn't struggle. He didn't even seem to be awake.

"This human tricked you out of claiming his soul," said Etaina. "Now I offer you what he denied you once before. Take him."

"One soul is not enough."

Raw fear clawed at my chest from the inside. The speaker was the god she'd enslaved to do her bidding, and as a price, she'd offered the soul of a mortal every seven years. Except Thomas had thwarted her and worked behind the Erlking's back to prevent anyone else from being sacrificed.

A *lot* of seven-year cycles had passed since then. And she still thought the god would serve her without question?

Etaina faced the spot where the voice had come from. "He is not a mortal anymore. His soul is worth more than one, more than the years you missed."

"He is immortal because he has bathed in the blood of my kin."

The cloak shivered around me. Of course that was how Thomas had become immortal. That pool in Etaina's office had more than one use. He'd used the blood of the gods to be reborn, like the Sidhe once had. Under duress or not, it hardly mattered to the being whose voice spoke.

The air split in two, a wide slash as though a blade had seared the forest down the middle. Around us, the whole forest trembled as though caught in a storm. Leaves tore free, wraiths drifted past, and even Etaina and the Seelie

Queen cringed away from the gaping slash in mid-air, and the void waiting on the other side.

The talisman was still in Etaina's hands, but her eyes were on the void instead. If I were closer, I might snatch it back, for all the good it did. In the end, undoing the vow hadn't brought about the end of Faerie, yet Etaina might well have seen to it anyway.

"Please," I whispered to the cloak on my shoulders. "If there's anything you can do to stop it—"

Close the rift. Could I? I might be able to find the words in the Ancients' tongue, but the beast would not yet be satisfied now Etaina had drawn his attention. If someone didn't act, it would consume everything around us.

"Stop!" shouted Ilsa's voice. *"Stop."*

The Invocation ripped through the air, but the gap in the air continued to grow larger. I heard Ivy shouting, too.

"All of you!" I called to the Sidhe, who'd begun to back away, no longer caught in Etaina's spell now her attention was elsewhere. "Add your voices. We can close the rift, but only if we all speak at once."

A Sidhe stepped forward, a dark-skinned male with armour dappled with feathers and bloodstains. Lord Anther, the disgraced lord who'd been disqualified from the contenders to the throne thanks to the Seelie Queen's machinations. He must have returned to join the Courts in battle regardless of the lies she'd spread. He spoke first, and his deep melodic voice rang out with the words of the gods.

One by one, the other Sidhe added their voices to the chorus. I heard Raine and Cedar speak, too, as did Ivy and Ilsa. Gradually, the rift slid closed and Thomas floated to earth.

His eyes opened. "It won't hold," he rasped. "Not now Etaina has awoken him."

I turned to Etaina. "Did you think the god would be happy to see you? You owe him several centuries of sacrifices."

"Quiet, mortal," she snapped. "If you had cooperated with me, I would not have had to take drastic measures."

"Nobody made you try to force the gods to obey you," I retaliated. "Nobody made you steal their lifeblood for your own use. Did you tell your soldiers those marks are temporary, and you used up your entire supply of blood? When those marks wear off, the Erlking's talisman will be able to destroy any of them. She's not protecting you—any of you."

Gasps came from the Aes Sidhe soldiers, many of whom wore expressions of shock and horror. They hadn't known their leader had slaughtered the gods and used the blood to make them stronger. And they certainly hadn't known her protection would have a time limit.

A breeze tugged at the trees. Thomas exclaimed, bracing his feet on the leaf-strewn earth. "It's opening again."

I dropped my voice to speak to Thomas. "Can the Devourer's magic destroy that god?"

"Only in its original form, and that is long gone," said Thomas. "But he is weakened after so long without any souls to consume."

"If that's him at his weakest, I wouldn't want to meet him at full power."

"Enough of this!" Etaina marched over to Thomas and me, her eyes blazing. "I will tear the Devourer's power out of you by force and claim it as my own."

Her mouth opened to speak an Invocation, but Darrow appeared behind her, swinging a blade at her neck. She blocked the strike, her mouth opening in a snarl, but before she could retaliate, Thomas tackled her. The two of them went flying backwards, crashing into the earth. While surprised at his violence, I didn't blame him. Thomas had centuries of fury to unleash on her, after all.

But the rift was still opening, growing bigger by the second. The Sidhe shouted Invocations of closing, as did Ilsa and Ivy, but this time, their words had little effect. Cold air buffeted the trees, and oblivion beckoned on the other side.

Thomas's nose was bleeding, but he continued to pummel Etaina's body, the two immortals clashing in a bitter struggle. They hardly seemed to notice the slither of the void opening behind Thomas, preparing to claim him again. The Seelie Queen had, though, and she shouted Invocations along with the rest.

"What *is* that?" Holly stood behind me, her feet braced on the ground.

"Trouble." I looked up at Darrow, who'd grabbed the talisman when it'd fallen from Etaina's hands and extended it for me to take. "Thank you."

The instant my fingers closed around the staff, the misty cloak around my shoulders brightened and a hiss of displeasure sounded in my ear. The god was less than enthused about me carrying the Devourer's magic in my hands again.

In a sudden rush of finality, I knew what I had to do.

I caught Ilsa's eye and mouthed, *"Unbind me."*

Ilsa spoke the words, quietly at first, then louder, reciting from memory. The same words she'd spoken when she'd removed the talisman's magic from me the first time around.

At once, magic tore from my skin, from my bones and blood. The staff fought back, shadows pressing against me, only to collide with the rippling cloak surrounding me on the outside. Magic fought against magic, but the cloak was stronger, the god's rage far from sated.

In a wrenching tug, the Devourer's magic poured out of me, shadows flooding into the air from the staff's edge. Forcing my legs to move, I ran, hurling the talisman towards the widening gap in mid-air and the dark shape of the god waiting below.

"No!" The Seelie Queen ran towards the rift, arms outstretched. Her hands snagged the staff's edge, but when she tried to tug it out of the gap, something on the other side tugged back.

Etaina released Thomas, diving at her sister. Together, they scrambled for the talisman in wild desperation, and neither saw Thomas approach them from behind. Nor did they see the grim smile on his face.

I didn't hear the words he spoke, but I did hear the Seelie Queen's scream of rage and terror, mingling with her sister's, as the talisman hurtled over the edge of the rift, carrying both queens along with it. The Devourer's shadowy magic swirled around them as the rift drew them into its embrace.

The ground trembled as though an earthquake shook the very foundations of the world. My body swayed on the spot, reeling with the shock of losing the talisman's magic, and only the traces of the misty cloak on my shoulders kept me from collapsing altogether.

"Gatekeeper…" I whispered. "I let you go. As I promised."

Holly swayed beside me. The symbol on her forehead glowed as bright as the sun, as did mine, and I screwed up my eyes against the glare. Through my lidded eyes, I saw Thomas's form etched against the rift, blocking it from sight.

Thomas had held the original kernel that had started the Lynn curse. The moment he crossed the border into the rift, it would bring an end to the cycle, and transfer the magic back into the faerie realm where it belonged.

The cloak lifted from my shoulders, surging over to Thomas. The image of a gate flashed before my eyes—two gates, merging into one. I saw Holly sink to the ground, and a sharp, terrible pain burned my forehead, a deafening shattering noise piercing my eardrums. My head hit the earth, landing in a soft bed of leaves and fragments of the broken circlet.

I lifted my head, seeing the void wink out of existence along with Thomas Lynn—then the light turned to darkness, and all was gone.

24

I opened my eyes. I lay in a room that almost looked like my bedroom, but not quite. For one thing, there were two beds, and Holly lay in the other. Weird.

I got out of bed and walked to the window. Outside the panes of dusty glass, rolling hills extended into the distance. I recognised the dirt track leading to the village of Foxwood on the right-hand side, but I'd thought there weren't any houses this far away from the village.

Footsteps on wooden floorboards sounded, and the door opened to reveal my sister.

"Good, one of you is awake," Ilsa said. "I'm having to sleep on the floor because there aren't enough rooms in this house."

"Why are we in this house?" I looked between the rolling hills and the wooden frame of the bed, uncomprehending. "Whose house is it?"

"It's ours," said Ilsa. "Well, in theory it is. This is what our home used to look like before the curse turned it into the Lynn house."

Holly groaned and yanked the pillow over her head. "Shut up, can't you? I'm trying to sleep."

"You might want to take a look around," Ilsa said. "There were… changes, when Hazel broke the curse."

Holly sat up. "What am I doing here? *Where* am I? This bed is like sleeping on a rock."

"The two Lynn houses merged along with the gates," said Ilsa, an apologetic expression on her face. "They didn't really do comfy beds in Thomas Lynn's era."

Holly blinked a couple of times, comprehension dawning. "My house is gone? And everything I own?"

"Everything the faeries owned," Ilsa corrected. "Or everything created from their magic, anyway. Mum found all our weapons in the garden, and we've been finding things scattered all over the place since we got back from Faerie."

Holly shoved the blankets aside and pushed to her feet. "That is bullshit. They can't steal my things."

"What do you expect from the faeries?" I looked between her and the window, half numb with shock. "They weren't going to let us keep their magic now we aren't bound to their realm."

Holly raised her hand to her head as though feeling for the circlet. The symbol was gone from her forehead, same as mine. We looked at one another for an instant. Her eyes were brown, not blue, and I'd bet mine were the same. Our magic had gone. We were free.

Holly broke her gaze from mine. "I'm going to find my possessions. Try not to wreck anything else while I'm gone."

"Bloody cheek," I said, when the door closed behind her. "As though we didn't just *fix* the mess that Thomas

Lynn started. Anyway, where's she going to live? I'm not rooming with her, and Mum won't either."

I didn't have to stay. I could walk away from the Ley Line without fearing the backlash of a curse. I wasn't Faerie's servant, not anymore.

"Don't ask me," Ilsa said. "Not to deflate your bubble, Hazel, but you and Mum have no money. The Sidhe took it all when they left the house. Or it turned into leaves. I'm not entirely sure which."

"Of course they did." I glanced after Holly. "I'm guessing there aren't a ton of jobs open to an ex-Gatekeeper?"

Ilsa rolled her eyes. "I'll make sure she doesn't get lost. Also, Darrow is looking for you."

"Oh." I didn't know what else to say. Nor how to take it all in. But before I could get a grip on myself, Ilsa had left and Darrow entered in her place.

"Hazel." Darrow folded his arms around me. "I feared you'd expired along with the curse."

"Like I'd go quietly into the afterlife without bargaining with my sister to bring me back." I squeezed him back. "I'm kind of in shock right now, just so you know."

"I thought so," he said. "Would it calm you if I told you the Courts suffered no damage from the rift opening?"

"Thanks to the Gatekeeper," I said. "The real Gatekeeper. I think she was some kind of guardian who kept the other gods in check. Did you see what happened to her magic? I mean, my magic, and Holly's?"

"You mean when your circlet broke?" he said. "I saw a great deal of magic disperse throughout the faerie realm.

But I would very much like an explanation of your side of things."

"Well." I fiddled with the woollen blanket on the bed. "Which part? I suppose you guessed I went back to Thomas for answers…"

I told him about the Erlking's scheming and the riddle he'd left behind, Thomas Lynn's revelations and the gods' arrival. He listened with great patience, though I sensed he must have heard at least some of it already from Ilsa, or perhaps Ivy. Thomas, though… he'd be at peace now, no longer Etaina's plaything. When I'd finished, Darrow watched me in awe, shaking his head. "You never cease to amaze me."

"I had my doubts back then," I said. "A lot of them. The Gatekeeper's god might have turned on me as well as the Sidhe. I'm lucky she didn't."

"You got rid of the talisman," he said. "The bow, though—"

"Etaina destroyed it." I looked around the room, at the deceptively normal view from the window. "Like I destroyed my circlet. I can't… I can't use magic anymore."

Did that mean I no longer had the Sight? Was there a faerie revel taking place outside my door without my awareness? *Crap. The protection in my family's bloodline won't work anymore either.*

I'd better hope the Sidhe didn't come after me, then.

"We'll handle it." Darrow took my hands in his, and my heart lifted. Screw the Sidhe. I'd survived.

"I'm free, by the way," I added. "Just in case you were wondering. No lifetime obligations to serve Faerie and pass on the Gatekeeper's title to my offspring. So if you want to file that away for future reference—"

He leaned in and kissed me, cutting me off mid-sentence. I grinned and kissed him back, pulling him onto the bed next to me, and we stopped talking for a long while.

Sometime later, we lay side by side on the bed. I shifted closer to put an arm around him. "Ow. This blanket is not made for comfort."

"It's odd, seeing your house like this," he said. "It feels more…"

"Please don't say real," I said. "It's like I stepped several centuries into the past and into someone else's life. This was probably Thomas's twin daughters' room."

"That wasn't what I was going to say," he said.

"Uh-huh," I said. "You aren't going to start on that *I'm not real* crap, are you? Because you're real enough that you didn't die when Etaina did."

He winced at her name, but he shook his head. "No, I didn't. None of us did."

"The other Aes Sidhe," I said. "Wait—did the path between there and Faerie stay open? What happened to the survivors?"

"The Summer armies cleared out their tunnels and brought anyone they found to stand trial," he said. "Those willing to plead for forgiveness will be offered the chance to re-join the Summer Court."

"They wouldn't, would they?" I said. "Not after everything they did for Etaina?"

"Many of them will accept any Court who will take them," he said. "They are no threat to anyone. They feel they have lost themselves without Etaina. And I would be lying if I said I didn't relate."

"You and me both," I said. "I don't know that I want to

stay here in Thomas's house, but now I'm human, I can't even move to Half-Blood Territory."

"Their doors are open to both us," said Darrow. "I've been back into Faerie, to explain myself to the Sidhe and to do my best to help those who acted in Etaina's interests out of desperation rather than malice."

"If the Aes Sidhe need a leader, there's someone they might follow," I said. "Hint, hint."

He shook his head. "What little loyalty they have for me is born of the fact that we were all creations of Etaina's magic, nothing more."

"Darrow, the whole of Faerie is a glamour, including everything in it," I said.

He waved a hand. "It doesn't matter. I was wrong beforehand, but I know I am as real as I will ever be."

I tilted my head. "What made you change your mind, then?"

"Because I'm in love with you, Hazel," he said. "And if that isn't real, I don't know what is."

———

It was some time before we went downstairs to join the others. The murmur of voices came from the kitchen, and I opened the door to find Morgan sitting at the table beside a man who looked a lot like he did, tall and thin with dark hair. Someone I hadn't seen in years.

Dad?

"What are you doing here?" Disbelief rooted me to the spot. Dad was human. How in the world had he got here?

"I heard," he said, in his strong Irish accent. "I heard you broke the curse, and that you are permitted to leave the Ley Line. This faerie told me you were in trouble, and that I was needed."

The Erlking's sprite fluttered down and landed on the table. "I was told to find this man and bring him here."

"Lady Aiten." Was that supposed to be her way of apologising? "Sorry, Dad. I know things are weird at the moment even by our standards."

The faeries. I should know by now never to underestimate their capacity for the impossible.

Mum entered the room and cleared her throat. "I apologise for the disruption. I didn't know the Sidhe planned to bring you here."

"Hazel was injured," he said. "A father should visit his children. I should have done so more when you were younger."

"Don't blame yourself, blame the Sidhe," I said. "That's what we do. It's usually their fault."

"You aren't the only one of us who's pulled a disappearing act once or twice," added Morgan.

Swift flew to my shoulder. "It is good to see you awake, Gatekeeper."

"I'm not Gatekeeper." I startled as the faerie dog's wet nose brushed my bare hand. "Morgan, do you still have the Sight?"

"Why wouldn't I?" He gave the puppy a stroke. "Our family's special."

We still have the Sight. Did that mean I had any magic left, or had it all dried up with my Gatekeeper's powers? Any faerie could make humans able to see them, but the ability to see through their glamour was rare indeed. It came as more of a relief than I'd expected to find I hadn't lost all the skills Faerie had given me.

Ilsa came into the room behind Mum. "Holly's gone to Foxwood. I reckon she wants to be alone for a while."

I didn't blame her, but Holly would adjust in time. Mum and I would, too, and I'd be lying if I said I wasn't thrilled that for once in my life, I'd be sorting out my own problems, not the faeries'.

I looked at the sprite. "What's happening in Summer? Will there be a repeat of the Erlking's tests, or will someone else be chosen?"

"The Sidhe elected to choose a leader from the remaining contestants. Erlking Anther will serve us well."

Lord Anther? "He was put back in the running again?" I asked. "The Sidhe found him innocent of trying to poison the others?"

"Yes, of course," said Swift. "As the Sidhe who ranked highest in the trials, he was a clear choice. Now the crown is back in the Sidhe's hands, they will crown him in one week's time."

I was more relieved than annoyed at being left out of the decision. Finally, the faeries had taken matters into their own hands. It didn't hurt that the one Sidhe who'd helped Darrow and me during the second trial would be sitting on the throne, either.

"We're invited to the coronation," said Mum. "As spectators. I rather think the Sidhe will resent our presence."

I grinned. "Then it'd be my honour to remind them of my existence."

Some things never changed, yet others changed beyond measure.

On the day of the coronation of the next monarch of Summer, I went looking for the gate into Faerie again.

The Ley Line might still be where it'd always been, but it took several minutes of tramping around the hills before Darrow spotted a hawthorn gate hidden in a patch of trees. Humans who stumbled across it might find a gate that led nowhere an odd sight, but they wouldn't be able to reach the realm on the other side.

"At least we can still see through glamour," I remarked. "I wonder why that is?"

"I've often assumed that once you see the truth of something, it can't be unseen," said Mum.

"Like a Sidhe orgy," said Morgan. "Hey, Hazel."

Ilsa and River walked behind my older brother, dressed in their finest clothing. The finest any of us could achieve without glamour, anyway. I suspected River had tried to glamour Ilsa anyway, and she'd refused on the grounds that neither Morgan nor I had the same advantages. We'd all be going in as human—and proud of it.

"Hey, Hazel," said Ilsa.

"How's the guild?" I asked.

"Not too bad," said Ilsa. "Quiet, for a wonder. It helps that there aren't wraiths attacking Edinburgh every other day anymore. I've been coming back to find all the books that were in our family's library."

"Of course you did." I rolled my eyes at her. "Dad isn't here, by the way. He's visiting Foxwood."

There was no animosity between him and Mum, as she'd said, but it wasn't really safe for any of us to be in Faerie. Without my Gatekeeper's magic, I was stripped of my advantages, and while my Sight had remained, all I had left were the same advantages as a regular human—

namely, iron, luck, and the ability to annoy the shit out of any faerie I ran into.

Didn't stop me feeling vulnerable as hell when we entered the gate and found ourselves facing the bright meadow of the Summer Court. The colours seemed brighter than before, the smells more overwhelming. All the joys of being human. I wore my nicest outfit, but it didn't hold a candle to the clothes I'd once been able to conjure up using glamour. *Hope the Sidhe don't throw me out.*

"I thought we'd end up in the Aes Sidhe's place," I said to Darrow. "Probably for the best that we didn't."

Lord Raivan stepped onto the path in front of us, dressed in an antlered hat and a gold-trimmed coat. "This way, humans."

As we entered, Ivy Lane strode up to join us. Like us, she wore ordinary human clothes. "Mind if I tag along? It'll be nice to have some humans to hang out with for once."

"Sure." I let her fall into step with me, joining our group of humans invited to Faerie. Without my Gatekeeper's magic, the sights and smells of Faerie might be more intense, but it was still survivable. Even with my tolerance for elf wine as low as a regular human's—or Darrow's.

The ambassadors' palace was as magnificent as ever, decorated in the green and gold splendour of the Summer Court. The Sidhe filled the hall, dressed in their finery, their attention on the stage. Lady Aiten greeted me with a nod, but she didn't walk over to make conversation.

I scanned the assembled crowd and spotted Coral and some of the other half-bloods standing in a group near the back. When she saw me, Coral ran over and hugged me.

"You're okay!" she said. "I didn't know if I'd ever see you again."

"Now I'm human?" I said. "Nah, I'm as good at being human as a fish out of water."

"Or selkie," she said. "Actually, believe it or not, I'm actually enjoying staying out the water."

Given the band on her wrist and Willow's matching one, I figured I could guess why.

"You're staying in Half-Blood Territory?" I said. "The talisman—"

"I know Etaina destroyed it. Between you and me, I'm glad of it." She smiled. "The merpeople are welcome to the Sea Court. Besides, I think they'll find a crown is harder to hang onto than they think. I'm done with politics."

"You and me both."

I settled back to stand with the half-bloods and humans and watch the ceremony, soon finding my attention wandering. The Sidhe didn't seem to care, which made a welcome change from being expected to stand on the stage and make speeches. Halfway through, I caught sight of Holly lurking near the back as though she wasn't sure whether she was welcome. I slipped my hand out of Darrow's and whispered, "Back in a second."

Holly watched me walk over. It was still odd seeing her with brown eyes, not blue, and without her circlet. For a moment, she and I looked at one another. "How are you doing?"

Holly shrugged. "Better now the shock's worn off. I'm still staying in Agnes's attic until I can find an employer who'll hire an associate of the Unseelie. Maybe I'm better off going somewhere nobody knows who I am."

I understood what she meant. Blending back into the human realm would take some adjustment. To be honest, I didn't know how to be human, not like someone who'd grown up as one of them. "You never know. You might find an employer looking for someone just like you."

She made a sceptical noise. "It feels like I've been dropped off on an alien planet. Isn't it ridiculous that I was *relieved* to get an invitation to the coronation, as though it was the only proof that anything in my life happened at all?"

"Not really," I said. "It's to be expected. We had a major upheaval, but we'll survive."

She exhaled. "I guess so."

"I know so."

I turned back to my family, more than ready to leave the Sidhe to their revelry. Perhaps Darrow and I would go for a walk in the Courts, so I could see them with my newly human eyes. Or maybe we'd go and see more of the mortal realm. The choice was ours.

And if the faeries made trouble, I'd be more than happy to teach them a lesson.

ABOUT THE AUTHOR

Emma is the New York Times and USA Today Bestselling author of the Changeling Chronicles urban fantasy series.

Emma spent her childhood creating imaginary worlds to compensate for a disappointingly average reality, so it was probably inevitable that she ended up writing fantasy novels. When she's not immersed in her own fictional universes, Emma can be found with her head in a book or wandering around the world in search of adventure.

Find out more about Emma's books at
www.emmaladams.com.

www.ingramcontent.com/pod-product-compliance
Lightning Source LLC
La Vergne TN
LVHW041622060526
838200LV00040B/1396